Anna Whitwham was born in 1981 in London, where she still lives. *Boxer Handsome* is her first novel. It is a world she knows well: her grandfather, John Poppy, left behind a life of poverty and street violence by joining Crown & Manor Boys Club in Hoxton and becoming a young featherweight boxer. He is the inspiration behind this book.

BOXER HANDSOME

Boxing runs in Bobby's blood. His Irish dad was a boxer, and so was his Jewish grandfather — yanked up by their collars at Clapton Bow Boys Club, taught how to box and stay out of trouble. So Bobby knows he shouldn't be messing in street brawls a week before his big fight with Connor 'the Gypsy Boy', an Irish traveller from around the way. They're fighting over Theresa, a traveller girl with Connor's name on her. But Bobby is handsome, like his dad. Boxer handsome. For Bobby, the ring is everywhere, and he can't afford to lose . . .

ANNA WHITWHAM

BOXER HANDSOME

Complete and Unabridged

CHARNWOOD
Leicester

First published in Great Britain in 2014 by
Chatto & Windus
The Random House Group Limited
London

First Charnwood Edition
published 2015
by arrangement with
The Random House Group Limited
London

A catalogue record for this book is available
from the British Library.

ISBN 978–1–4448–2316–5

Published by
F. A. Thorpe (Publishing)
Anstey, Leicestershire
Set by Words & Graphics Ltd.
Anstey, Leicestershire
Printed and bound in Great Britain by
T. J. International Ltd., Padstow, Cornwall

This book is printed on acid-free paper

To my granddad, John Frederick Poppy;
featherweight, Crown & Manor Boy,
and my champion.

1

Bobby knew he would win.

He was shirtless, his head low, neck naked and stiff with fight. He smacked Connor hard.

Bobby the Yid and the Gypsy Boy. Same weight, same height. Dragged into the same boxing club as boys. They'd skipped and sparred together for thirteen years. Won and lost the same. Trained on the same bags, on the same pads, at the same club, at the same time. They'd shared a childhood. Their bodies growing, battered and beaten and better again. Two faces of the club. The tale of the tape read the same for both fighters. Both brick-jawed, strong-legged boxers, built for the fight under white lights. Nothing between them but the places they came from. And her.

Connor's shot came back hard with a groan that came from his gut, cutting the corner of Bobby's eye. Bobby first felt the sting and then the blood. Connor gave him two more, below the chin and another to the eye. Bobby rocked on his legs, willing his head to keep him up. Connor's punches were wild and hard. Bobby could feel the sharp pain from each gold ring stacked on his brawler's fingers, and breathed in against the blows. They picked off skin. He heard shouts in the dark. Heard his own voice, choking through blood.

'Connor, how long we known each other you

1

cunt, she's just some fucking girl.'

Rain began to fall on the canal. He saw Theresa's thin shape under the moon, leaning on the damp, cool archway he'd nearly finished fucking her in. Just for a moment, she moved like smoke before Connor pushed Bobby's face down in the bank so he could taste the blood and mud, could smell the ground against his nose, the belt buckle digging into his groin. Bobby tried to get up and couldn't.

He started to count as Connor's knees dug into the back of his neck. Counted away the night sounds, one by one, until it was quiet again. Then it happened fast.

Bobby whipped himself round, grabbing Connor firm by the throat. Both hands round the back of the neck to pull himself up, meeting face to face, their lips so close they could kiss, and then cracked the bridge of his nose wide open. Skin split. Blood spat. Connor stumbled about, headless.

Bobby was on his feet again. Tired, but he found his legs. Panting, his head down and his curly hair wet with sweat, plastered to his forehead.

Connor's punch back was big. Bobby felt his jaw begin to swell straight away, from his right temple down his cheek, and his knees buckled. He almost went down a second time, but didn't. Bobby knew he was going to win.

Those thick gold rings on Connor's fingers burned his jaw. Hot and nasty punches. A bottle lay on the ground between them. A large Grolsch, within reach of them both. It was wrong but it was there, and Bobby was bleeding and desperate. Each caught the look in the other's eye, each saw a red fire deeper than skin and tissue.

It was Bobby who limped to it quicker, licking his lips clean, and as Connor lifted his head up and came for him again, Bobby smashed it over the side of his face. It broke, leaving half a bottle in Bobby's hand.

Connor fell to his knees. He held his cheek, the cry stuck in his throat, as if he'd swallowed the broken glass.

'Stop now, Bobby. You fucking won this. Enough.'

Bobby couldn't stop.

He knelt over him and cupped the back of Connor's head in his hands. Connor stared up at him. A face Bobby knew well. He had laughed with him. Learned to fight with him.

Connor mouthed something but Bobby looked away. He didn't want to see what he was saying. He picked up a shard of broken glass to his right. Connor's legs thrashed the air and his body twisted in pain. Bobby held the glass to Connor's throat, so tightly that the palm of his own hand began to bleed. Then he looked up at the stars and breathed out. This was for the gold rings that had chewed up the skin around his eyes. He took the glass and cut Connor from cheekbone to lip. Deep enough to leave a scar. The bright blood rolled down Connor's face.

Bobby rolled away to rest on all fours, his chest rising and falling. Trying to breathe again as his body slowed down. It was an ugly end to

3

an ugly fight. A fight about nothing but her. He turned, coughing up phlegm and the sickness he felt from his stomach.

Theresa came running. Half-cut and scared, almost naked in a skirt and bra. Her hair extensions twisting around her neck. Her beautiful long back bending over Connor's body.

'Bobby — what you done?'

Bobby looked up at her. They'd been at the pub. She was walking about in heels too high, and Bobby was drunk. They were kissing and cuddling by the bar like old sweethearts.

Halfway through their short cut home they'd kissed again, moving under the bridge where the homeless went to sleep. He didn't know he'd been followed and didn't even know Connor cared enough to fight for her. He thought everyone had been somewhere on Theresa. She was fair game.

The pain was better than no pain at all. Bobby needed to be hit back too. It haunted him if a fight only went one way. In the ring there was an art to it: you hit and tried not to get hit back. You used your space; you used your body and your head. You mapped out your punches. But here in the dark, without the bright lights, you lashed out hard and kept going until it was finished. As quick as possible. Except Bobby hadn't just hit harder, he'd broken codes. He'd won ugly and it would not end here, by the canal. He'd left a scar between them. Bobby walked. He could not find the air he needed.

'Bobby, what am I going to do now?'

4

Bobby sniffed and spat more blood on the ground.

This was a cheat fight. A brawl for street scrappers.

The one Connor and Bobby would have when they met in the ring was real. They would face each other in the first stage of the North East Divisions.

The fight. The fight. The fight. The drum and the bang and the war. Bobby picked up his top and wore it like a veil. He walked away the way he should have done from the start. He knew it hadn't ended there. This would follow him.

2

He woke to pain, damp and hangover, and brilliant white walls, kept bare to make his room look bigger. His jaw howled in agony. He took two painkillers from the packet on his bedside table.

The black and silver clock ticked towards noon. One poster. A shot of Tyson cast in shadow, his Everlast gloves raised high and just below his shark eyes. Baby-face grinning. Bobby had a mirror opposite his bed so he could see every part of his body. Full-length and silver-framed, it picked out the metal of the clock and the glint in Tyson's tooth. When he got out of bed he took a good look at himself.

Maggie was walking up and down the landing in her dressing gown, holding a can of air freshener in one hand and a cup of tea in the other. She held down the nozzle as she sipped.

'Morning, love.'

Bobby walked through the mist with an arm over his nose, covering his face so she didn't see the evidence of last night's fight. He scratched his bare belly, right hand dipping into the waistline of his boxers for comfort. He waved the fumes of her freshener away. She was too close. She leaned in and lowered her voice.

'You got someone in there?' She was used to him bringing girls home.

Bobby shook his head. It was sore to move it.

6

'Get us a cup of tea, Mum.'

He went into the bathroom, shutting the door on the acid-peach smells. She went down the stairs to put the kettle on.

At the mirror, Bobby saw his nose was still fat and the bruising under his eyes bright and black like grease. His jaw a little fatter on the right side. His knuckles were puffed up and sore, his ribs hurt.

He was angry with himself. Weeks of training for a big fight he couldn't walk away from. North East Division's finest thrown together in a final. Two from the same club, going head to head. The stars had crossed to make them meet. Connor and Bobby. The Gypo and the Jew. It was bad for Bobby to fight on a feud. Faces to save, neither would step down. The club had said it was a shame to have them against each other, but it was better to have one of them through.

'A show fight. Can only make us look good, can't it?'

And he'd only had a week to go. All he had to do was keep his head down. Bobby's body was ready to do brilliant things. He'd been off the drink, working and running hard. Kept his weight down, eaten right, stopped smoking. His mum had cooked him up the porridge, the fish. Everything he knew he had to do and be, he had done and become. He was lean and spare; hard and ready, winding down to save something for his fight.

And now he'd have to spend the next few days mending. Now he would fade. To rest is to rust.

He needed a shave. His dark hair grew quickly.

7

The hair on his head was thick, long at the top and curly. Oily with last night's sweat.

Outside his bedroom door, waiting for him, was a mug of tea. Maggie had put a plate of toast beside it. She had done this since he was a little boy and had started at the club. He never had time to sit down at the table, so she left it outside his room, setting her alarm with his to get up at dawn and put the kettle on. Now when she heard him get up, she got up too. She shadowed him.

Bobby downed the tea, holding it with both hands. It hurt to bend his fingers. He looked through the crisp line of ironed-flat clothes in his wardrobe. There was a pile of the same white T-shirts, folded high on his shelf. Gently he pulled the one at the top off the others, keeping the rest in their pile, and threw it on with the jeans hanging over his chair.

He stood in the kitchen doorway with his head down.

'Seen my jacket?' His voice was bunged up.

Maggie knew every angle of her son. She knew if there was something wrong.

'Come here, what's happened to your face?'

Bobby smiled. It hurt. He looked away.

'It was nothing, Mum.'

She got closer. She'd seen her son hurt many times before. She never got used to it.

'Nothing doesn't look like that. You got one cheek coming out there like a pillow and a mouth that looks like you kissed a snake. What happened?'

'They fight with gold. Makes it look worse than what it is.'

'They? That lot, was it?' Maggie made a face. 'Looks like they went and hit you with hammers.'

Bobby kissed his mum on her forehead. 'Don't be silly, Mum. It's a fucking bruise, that's all.'

'It is not a fucking bruise and you got your fight coming up. How can you fight like that? Let me put the kettle on.'

'No, I'm going down the cafe.'

His mum looked hurt.

'Sit down. I'll do you something right now. What do you fancy?'

'Just fancy a walk.'

Maggie moved to the kitchen and tightened her gown. Bobby's face was a reminder of a long history. Bruises and scars she'd seen before.

'You shouldn't be eating food from the cafe. I'll do you a porridge. Save your money. Go on, sit down.'

Bobby had his jacket on.

'I need to walk.'

Maggie raised her hands, shaking them at her son. 'You had your body ready and now look at you.'

Bobby sniffed and opened the door. He gave her a painful wink and stepped out.

Down the lift, twelve floors, out of the flat and into the open. Fresh damp air after spring rain. Nappy smells and lamb curry, chicken heart stews and boiled bacon. No huddled mountain bikes this afternoon; no fights near the swings. Across the rows of green doors and silver letterboxes, he heard the tick of a beat in a room somewhere. Young boys with nowhere to go and

9

nothing to do. The party falling asleep on sofas, the night on its sloppy last legs. The large metal bins were full and boxes of fried chicken scattered wherever they fell, the bones picked clean by foxes. Old men shuffled back home with their papers and waved to Bobby. Heading back up the lift to their small flats in a leaning grey block, squashed in, keeping quiet. No bother or trouble to no one. Bobby smiled back.

Two peeling plastic-seated chairs had their backs up against the wall of a flat opposite, a few yards away. A door opened and Theresa came out into the light with a cough.

There, under the sunlight, was mad, fit Theresa. No extensions now. Just a short, blonde bob and long legs in little shorts. She told Bobby she kept her hair short to stand out from the rest of the traveller girls. She faked it when she needed with clip-on extensions. That way she was always her own person. Except she wasn't: she was theirs. Bobby kept his eyes on her when she turned around to pull out her chair.

Denny's grown-up little girl. Denny's dangerous and beautiful little girl.

'How's your face?' Her voice curled its way over to him. Silky and soft. A different girl to the night before.

Bobby clocked her in the chair, making her legs look leaner by turning them to the side, propping them up on the wall.

'S'alright.'

'You scarred him, you know.'

Bobby didn't want to look at her. She'd led

10

him there, the kind of girl who liked men fighting over her.

Bobby shrugged. 'He'd have done it to me.'

Theresa pulled at her top.

'Would he?'

She looked at Bobby. She studied him, from the top of his head to the white trainers on his feet.

Bobby felt the sharp ache in his jaw again, and he felt the pull of Theresa. Her racehorse legs and skinny hips. Her fleshy lips puffing on a cigarette. Freckles on her shoulder blades, a mix of gold and silver chains dangling at her cleavage. She set him on fire.

'It went too far. It got stupid.'

'Because of you.'

'Me and Connor aren't even together.'

Bobby looked around him, already watching his back.

'You know what you're doing, Theresa.'

'What you talking about?'

'Connor and me have our fight coming up.'

The fight that would bring everyone together for one night, mixing up myths and blood from these streets. Theresa had not wanted Bobby to get hurt. But she wanted his attention and she got it.

'Next time walk away then.'

Bobby laughed, but she was right. He went to say something nasty but couldn't. Bobby walked on and left Theresa sitting and smoking. She would stay there until there was no daylight, moving the burning tip around her empty day.

Apart from a few dog walkers, the road was

11

clear. Bobby liked walking. Walking was real. He walked until home was far behind him. He put his knuckles into fists at his sides, letting his arms get heavy, letting them hang, relaxed, as he walked the long way around the Marshes. His jacket was snug. The clouds were close. He gently put a hand in his pocket to see how much money he had, holding a few pound coins in his palm. He'd nicked his life line where he'd held the glass.

Most days in the week he helped out at Clapton Bow Boys Club to train the youngster boys. He couldn't get a job anywhere else that paid enough to help his mum out and buy clothes. But it was more about the free boxing time and days spent away from his bedroom than how much he got paid. It was his home away from home. He even had his own set of keys to come and go as he wanted. They were his family and a fight like that with Connor broke all the rules.

'Some boys just want to fight,' his granddad used to tell him. 'Those are the boys that aren't worth fighting; the ones looking for it.'

Boxing ran in the blood on both sides. His dad was already a long-serving Clapton boy when he took Bobby by the hand on his seventh birthday and paid their dues. They were happy to have him: his granddad on his mum's side had been one of the club's early fighters in the Fifties, dragged there by their dads to toughen up when they first moved to the area. Some little Jewish kid always getting his nose broken, until one day he hit back harder.

Bobby was proud of his granddad. A man who'd come to the East End as a boy, got over diphtheria and learned how to fight. Bobby had a picture that he'd taken from his mum's room of him mucking about with his pals on a beach in Clacton-on-Sea, his face too kind for a fighter.

Bobby had been proud of his dad too. Proud that he didn't back down, even though he was thin and pretty-looking. His dad's face was fresh out of Hollywood, not Hoxton. Even after his face changed from fighting, he was still a looker. He needed those few knocks to look tough. Bobby took after his dad; both needed their good looks beaten up a little.

New arrivals learned of Bobby's background at the club and looked up to him. He was good-looking and angry. They liked that he'd had real fights. They loved his broken nose and bruises. Bobby's first real fight came after a group of Millwall boys had started to follow him when he was leaving a rave in Battersea. He'd tried walking on. They followed him. Trying to shake him up. Make him frightened. Over nothing but drink and the way Bobby looked.

Always be the one to get the first punch in. Don't wait to get hit, his granddad had warned, in his curling mix of Belfast-Jewish boxer tongue. 'If you are going to fight, hit first. Otherwise you've lost.'

Feet shuffled around in a scrappy circle. A drunk dance, with Bobby in the middle. Knuckles that couldn't get a clean shot and stabbed around. He didn't know how it stopped, but it did. Those early fights always stopped.

They had to. Two minutes of misfired clumps. And then enough. No energy for more. He was on the floor when they left him. The boom of his heart beating in all the places that hurt. Each muscle begging him to lie back down as he moved to his knees. And then the thrill of standing up again. They hadn't knocked him out.

He'd gone to bed that night unwashed, sleeping with his sour fighting sweat and the scabbing on his knuckles that had showed he'd given back. Sleeping with a smile. Knowing he'd wake up tougher and harder.

There were others. Some where he'd really hurt people and some where he'd been really hurt. He found himself on streets in Luton and Romford, visiting friends and getting stuck into everyone, from BNP thugs to gangs of Bengali boys. They were all fighting a corner; all fighting for space. All up for a fight.

Bobby walked down the road, and with the sun on the back of his neck, he put a finger and thumb to his nose, going over the bit where the bridge didn't meet and could click under the skin. He never got round to getting it fixed. All the hiding from his Mum made it too late for a hospital appointment. By the time she'd seen it and had her cry, Bobby had become attached to it.

He looked at his reflection in a car he was passing and smiled. Dark hair, curly and thick, shaved at the back but falling into his eyes at the front. In fights he had to gel it back to get the head guard on right. He was tall, just off six foot

14

two, with a good stride and honey-coloured skin that Maggie said came from her side of the family. He had a big heart and big hands and a battered nose that twisted up his good looks. Gave him a good stare, but just stopped him being as handsome as his Dad had been.

He could see the cafe straight up ahead. Inside, he looked over the tables. Workmen let out their cackling laughter and the dull greasy eyeballs of the waitress took him in as he opened the door. And there, no surprise, was his old man, back bent over a mug of tea.

'Alright, son.'

His dad wore a white T-shirt too, and had his hair scraped and gelled. It receded a little, and had thinned to look wet against his skull.

Blood was blood. His dad was his dad. Bobby made the effort.

'Want another tea, Dad?'

The day when his dad could treat him to breakfast had long gone. Bobby could see that his dad hadn't touched the tea; he was just holding it, hands on either side of the mug, filth under his nails. Trying to keep his hands steady in front of his son.

'Nah, I'm still working on this one.'

Bobby nodded. 'Alright, Dad.'

He bowled over to the counter and ordered himself a full English. The woman looked up at the board with drooping eyes, the mascara on her lower lashes thick and black. She wrote it down, took his money, and told him to sit.

'I'll bring it over to you.'

He went back to the table. The gel slicking his

dad's hair back made him look like he'd had a wash. But when Bobby sat down opposite him, he could smell that he hadn't. The waft of old man lifted in the air. Even with the cafe's fug of frying meat, his mixture of must and drink was strong. The same air that sat around his flat, moving only when Bobby's dad walked in and out of rooms. His nails were long on fingers that were slender. His upper arms were sticks. They didn't look like they could carry the mug to his mouth.

The years had been unkind to Joe. He looked up with yellow eyes, one of them sinking into a well-worn scar, revealing yellow teeth as he went to say something and couldn't. His gaping mouth yammered and said nothing.

They sat there, listening to the chatter of other men getting stuck into plates of meat and yolk and baked beans.

'What's happening, Dad?'

'Much the same as ever. How's your mum, alright?'

'Yeah she's good.'

Maggie had got rid him for the drink a year ago but he still thought well of her. She said she'd had enough of sleeping next to a sack soaked in brandy. He'd chosen the bitch in the bottle over his wife. Couldn't help himself, his body needed the drink more than it needed Maggie. He regretted it now. Now, he was stuck with it.

'Who'd you piss off this time?' Joe made a nod to Bobby's face.

'That lot. Nothing serious.'

16

Bobby's dad rubbed his quivering right hand over his face like he was waking himself up.

'Anyone to worry about?'

Bobby looked at his dad, and took the sugar from the middle of the table. He poured it into a small mound in front of him and began to push it around with his finger, making a circle. Bobby remembered the time his best friend Mikey had come round after he'd cracked his leg in a car accident and was in a wheelchair for a bit. Bobby had helped Mikey to the sofa, so he could put his leg up when watching the TV. His dad had wheeled himself to the doorway, banging into walls, laughing into his right-hand turns, before it tilted and fell. A laughing lump on the floor, with the wheel spinning next to him.

Bobby wished he'd kept his hands off Theresa.

Everyone had girlfriends now. He didn't see his mates anymore. And he didn't want to anyway. They'd chosen their beds and their boredom. Sitting next to their men like a bunch of ducks. All of them wearing the same, tight V-necks and saying nothing. All of them fat and dumb.

Theresa was thin and smart. She'd done him over.

'Just Connor.'

Joe winced.

'What you do that for?'

Bobby's dad bent low to take a sip of his tea, his mug still on the table. His mouth didn't make it, and he put his head up again.

'Must be cold by now, Dad. Sure you don't want another?'

'No, no. You're alright.'

Bobby's food came. A plate of bacon, eggs, sausages, toast, tomatoes and a thick wedge of black pudding. It all slid around the plate when it hit the table. He looked down at it and let his hunger take over. Cutting up the meat quickly. Getting it down as fast as he could. Looking at his dad made it harder to swallow, the sickly sight of Joe's face tested Bobby's hunger. His dad stared at his son's plate, taking in all the food, imagining the pleasure of tasting it. If he could still taste.

'What did Connor do to you?'

'He came for me.'

Joe moved his mouth around his gums.

'Well, did you win? Don't fucking look like it.'

Joe's voice was raspy, his throat stripped away through the years.

'I was still standing. He wasn't.'

Joe smiled. 'When you fighting again?'

Bobby laughed. 'You winding me up?'

Joe grinned and showed the gaps where his teeth should be. 'I mean in the ring. Proper.'

Bobby nodded and chewed on a bit of sausage, picking up his toast and sponging up the yolk and tomato with it. He spoke with his mouth full. He was ashamed to tell his dad he had a fight coming up. Drunk or not, Joe knew you didn't start messing about in street brawls a week before.

'I'd love to see you fighting again.'

Bobby swallowed.

'Got one coming up, actually.'

Joe moved his body forward. 'When's that then?'

18

'In a week. Me and Connor meet at York Hall. All them London clubs and us two from Clapton end up fighting each other.'

Joe shook his head. He still worried about Bobby.

'You can't fucking fight like that.'

Bobby shrugged. 'Have to.'

'Well you played that one fucking stupid then, didn't you?'

'Can't *not* do it.'

Joe breathed out of his mouth. A gummy, petrol-smelling sigh. 'Denny's lot will make a load of noise. You know that, don't you?'

Bobby had tried not to think too much about it. Denny struck a chord with Joe. They'd had their run-ins.

'There'll be too many there for noise. Can't start too much trouble in public.'

Joe smoothed back the slick hair on his head. 'You're stupid for heating things up like this. You look a mess.'

Bobby looked up at his dad. He changed the subject.

'You still handy, Dad?'

'Not half. Sharp and strong. Look at these paws.'

His dad held out his filthy, quivering fingers. Shaking and spluttering and laughing. Then coughing, wheezing, holding on to the table for support against the breakdown of his body.

Bobby put his knife and fork on the plate and pushed it to one side. He swallowed more bread and looked away embarrassed, his eyes to the window, on the road. Back to that Saturday sun,

19

much softer now behind the clouds. He could see the faint fuzz of his bruised reflection sitting up, and the crippled, bent back of his dad.

Maybe he'd go back home and walk through the afternoon's sweet laundry air. Get a paper and lie in bed.

Joe put his hands on the table for support and stood up. Up and standing he shook Bobby's hand like he'd always done. He wiped his mouth, cleaning it of the spittle.

'Next Saturday, is it?'

'My fight? Yeah.'

Joe smiled. 'I'll be there.'

They looked at each other for a moment.

'Good to see you, Bobby.'

Bobby watched the door of the cafe open and his dad shuffle out, taking his time to do up his coat, his fingers fiddling with the zipper before giving up. He spotted the end of a cigarette on the pavement and went to bend down. Joe's legs shook so hard he left it alone and shuffled away, patting his pockets.

Blood was blood but it had thinned, and even though they were made of the same stuff Bobby felt his dad disappearing. He'd looked for the sharp blue in his dad's stare that had eyed up other fighters and left them cold. It was gone. There was nothing between Bobby and Joe except their past.

Bobby had seen his dad knock back beer after beer in the pub and walk home calm as a monk. Being in the pub with his dad was like being with a king. Joe would be stood by the bar, dapper and dandy. His neat torso sinewy and hard in a

20

collared shirt, tucked into jeans that stopped a little off the ankle to show shining, black loafer shoes. A black porkpie hat at a tilt. No one dressed like Joe. He was rock and roll, and that bothered people. It bothered them when they sloped into the pub in parkas and fading Lees and bad shoes and trainers they tried hard to keep white and clean. Trainers that had to survive winters. Or in their work gear, straight off the site, their faces dry from dust. Their lungs too. But after a while, they stopped being bothered. When they saw Joe's fights and heard what he was about, Joe's wardrobes started making sense. He'd earned those shiny shoes. The tough little pretty boy with the mean right hook. Joe's hair was Elvis-black and he creamed it to the sides. Kept it the same through each decade, up until the Nineties. Always out of fashion, he'd made his look his own. He had an all-year tan from years of working on building sites with his top off and was freckled at the nose. Joe was the best-looking man in this manor.

Men used to move out of the way for his dad. Bobby remembered his twelfth birthday, when his dad had taken him down to the pub with real men. It was the day he'd tasted his first drink, and that sip of a brown, bitter pint had been the best present Bobby had ever got. Joe had walked slowly to the table, looking about him, left to right. How the crowd of men in the pub had parted to let them through. He was a rover. A rogue. A black-haired, dark-eyed darling. And Maggie, his beautiful blonde bombshell wife, sat away at another table with the girls. They had met when she was eighteen. She was young and pretty. He was ten years older and scarred. Maggie and Joe looked good together.

'Hello, Joe. Good to see ya. Sit down, sit down.'

'Your boy stopping by, is he?'

Bobby was always big and brave when he was with his dad. Joe had sat him between his two friends, Little Freddy and Big Frank. They were all smiles and patted him on the head. Freddy pushed forward his pint.

'Go on, boy. Have a bit.'

Bobby had looked at the drink in its thick glass, sitting still like treacle. Joe looking on. He remembered hating the sickly, bitter taste, but kept drinking to make his dad proud. Maggie looking over every so often to make sure Bobby was behaving.

'Alright, steady. Your hands a bit tight round the neck, son.'

Always laughter when he was sat between these two men. Bobby had always joined in.

Frank and Freddy. Their rolled-up sleeves on muscled, hairy arms and hands that built, carried and lifted; folded betting slips neatly into shirt pocket with nimble fingers and brains that had sized up the odds.

Frank was always tired. 'Been up four in the morning for a month running now. Back after dark. Knackered. I'll need shooting down like a carthorse by Christmas.'

They knew working hard got you nowhere. Eventually they stopped clocking in and gave it

22

up. Started drinking, like Joe. They became old quickly. They wanted Bobby to get rich and take care of them.

'You gonna make a bit of money like your dad, Bobby boy?'

Bobby had blinked and folded his arms. 'Like fighting?'

'Yeah, like fighting.' Bobby tasted Frank's cigarette smoke in the air when he spoke.

'Yeah, I'm gonna fight like my dad.'

The door of the pub had swung open then and a hulk of a man, ducking under the frame, walked in. Followed by two other men of about the same size and a small red-headed boy. The pub grew a little darker. Like at the Millwall and West Ham games Bobby had been taken to, he felt the grit in the air. His mum had shifted in her seat, her double gin gripped tight, staring over at Joe by the bar. Bobby had kept smiling to make her smile too. He didn't like her looking worried. Both Freddy and Frank muttered something about letting the dogs in.

'I wouldn't say I was from the same Emerald Isle as them.' Frank had put his fag out and grinned at Bobby, winking.

'There's Irish and then there's them, Bobby. Remember that. This is an Irish pub. For grafters, not a fucking tinkers' inn.'

'I'm not just Irish.'

A silence. Both men working out what to say.

'There's green blood in you.'

'I'm Jewish too.'

Freddy had glanced at Frank and winked, and Bobby had laughed, thinking they would too.

23

'On your mum's side.'

'Don't knock a Four-by-Two, Freddy. They're clever cunts. Know how to fight too; they've been at it since the start.'

'I'm a bit Irish on my mum's side too.'

The men had soothed him.

'Yes you are, boy. You're a tough little mongrel.'

Joe had clocked the door and watched the big man come over to the bar and stand beside him. Denny was bigger than Joe, untidy and sprawling. His sideburns were bushy, his shirt wrinkled and unbuttoned to the chest, his wiry hair brushed through with fingers and water, not combs and cream. His eyes were black, wild and watching, twitching beneath the thick brows.

Bobby hadn't liked seeing his dad look so tiny.

'You alright, Dad?'

Joe had pulled his son towards him and ruffled his hair, messing up the curls with his fingers. Bobby had smelt the mix of spices from his aftershave. Joe always used to smell good. Used to smell like he had money.

'This your lad?' A thick Irish accent that had more of a song and swing to it than Little Freddy's.

Joe squeezed Bobby's shoulder and nodded. 'This is my boy, yeah. My birthday boy. Bobby, this is Denny. He's from around the way.'

He'd been watching his dad's lip twitch when Denny asked.

He had looked over to his mum. She had beckoned him over with her lovely long fingers

24

that wore her grandmother's stones. Bobby had wanted to put his hand in his dad's but remembered not to. Instead he had looked Denny up and down, from his wide feet in thin, leather shoes, to the scowling hot-faced, red-headed boy — Connor — who stood behind him. The other two men were thick-necked and lifted the boy on to the bar stool. Connor sat with his arms folded. None of them smiled.

From around the way. Years later, Bobby learned what that meant. It meant someone was local. Meant he was about, behind your back, round the corner.

Bobby left the cafe, the smell of grease and fried fat clinging to his clothes. The usual deep pain whenever he saw his dad. Today Joe was tinier than he'd ever been.

Bobby walked with his fists at his sides and let the pain sink and become silent. Walking was real.

3

Bobby walked back through the Marshes on his way home.

When Bobby was smaller, Joe had taken him to Hackney Marshes for kickabouts. Bobby remembered him swaggering across this grass, smoking as hard as he fought, dribbling the football before lobbing it high for Bobby to trap with his new Umbro trainers.

'All this for free.'

Joe had swept his battered hand across the big green garden.

Bobby could hear games of football far away and walked towards them; he liked watching a game on the sidelines. But he stopped when he saw his dad again, his back to his son for the second time that morning.

He was sat with Daphne on a picnic bench. Bobby often saw Daphne around in parks and pubs. She wore a blue cardigan, her hair up in a dark ponytail and had large crystal stars clipped on to her ears. She called them her crown jewels. The old, weak clasps often fell from her lobes.

'Pick them up for me, Joe.'

Joe did as he was told. Bending with shaking knees. Taking too long to straighten up again.

It still upset Bobby to see his dad with another woman and for a moment he thought about turning back or walking on, but he couldn't move, staring at Joe as he handed her the earrings. He heard his dad laugh.

She was not as beautiful as his mum had been, but nice enough. Stained like paper soused in tea, but still more upright and smarter than Joe. Daphne saw in Joe the man he wished he still was. The young boxer in his Lonsdale vest, his shirt tucked into the right back pocket, wallet shoved into the left. But above all, Daphne saw someone who would stop her feeling lonely.

Daphne lifted her bag to her lap and pulled out a can of cider. She handed one to Joe.

Daphne had been Maggie's best friend. She had stepped out once with a nice man. Jim. Kind, loyal Jim. Liver packed up early and he died fat and yellow. Daphne found herself in pubs by herself. And then Denny had found her. He holed up with her for a while and hid things in her wardrobe. Daphne told the police they were hers and before anyone knew it, Daphne was in prison. She was lucky to have kept her flat. Months later and she and Theresa were together in her one-bedroom.

She had tried to be a good mother, but she had a bad daughter. Theresa took her mum's flat calmly and coldly. Everyone knew Daphne had no backbone, no fight, and was kicked out easily. She moved in with her old, unmarried brother, who hardly left his bed. She had her room and she did his dinners. And that was her life. And now she had Joe. Drunks had a way of finding each other.

Bobby looked away. He could feel it. That grit in the air. Two local drunks were being circled by a couple of lanky teenage boys on dark blue bikes. They had the close-shaved sides and combed forward cuts of the Kildare boys, but Bobby couldn't be sure from where he was sitting. From Denny's crowd, from his side of the site. They were bothering Big Frank and Little Freddy.

The boys screeched their bikes to a stop, slouching on the saddle. Both no more than fifteen years old.

'Oi! You smack him and I'll give you a fiver.'

Big Frank looked stunned. 'Me, smack *him*? But I'm bigger than him. I'll kill him.'

The boy looked. 'Depends where you hit him.'

'Why does he get to smack me? Why can't I smack him?' Little Freddy was getting upset.

Big Frank walked up close to the boy. 'I've not hit a man for years. I'll do it. But you get me the beers first.' He must have slobbered when he spoke because Bobby saw Frank wipe his mouth with his sleeve.

The boy on the bike wheeled backwards from Frank and made a face.

'Keep back from me when you're talking.'

Big Frank stepped back. 'Sorry,' he mumbled. A child.

There was a time when these men were proud. There was a time Joe would have stepped forward and knocked a sorry out of these young boys. Back when Joe was somebody.

Little Freddy's Irish voice was singing now, singing and begging that Frank not hurt him. He trilled for mercy. He danced for it.

'Smack him now, proper right hook, and you get your money.'

28

Little Freddy began to look frightened.

Bobby looked again at his dad. In his day, Bobby would have seen Joe take care of this. Now, in his baggy suit trousers, he watched and said nothing.

'You really want me to hit him?'

'Yeah.'

Big Frank and Little Freddy looked at each other, scared to rupture a friendship that had lasted over thirty years.

'Can we have the money now?'

They had become beggars. The boys sneered.

'Please?'

'If I don't like the look of the punch then you get nothing.'

They were caught up in it now, and didn't have the balls to walk away.

'Get on with it. I'll count down.'

Joe and Daphne were slumped on their bench, staring in a dream.

Bobby started to feel hot. Big Frank looked at his friend and there were tears in his eyes as he made a fist. He mouthed the word sorry before he took a swing.

It was a soft touch. A jab on the jaw. A nothing punch.

The boy laughed. His friend laughed too. Little Freddy touched his jaw and grinned like an idiot.

'Can we have our money, please?'

The boy laughed again.

'Smack him properly, and you'll get your money.'

Joe watched on in a daze. He could not get up.

29

Joe and Daphne. Two lumps on a bench.

Bobby felt the fury rise up in him. All those years his dad had told him to stand up for the underdog, stepping in to sort out trouble. Joe stopped as many fights as he started them. He liked being the local hero.

He knew those days were over, but Bobby still waited. He looked at his dad's bent back and longed for the days they would walk into this park together and play football. Joe took another can from Daphne and brought it to his thin, dry lips and Frank raised his arm again.

Bobby leapt up and ran over. He was there before Frank could take his second punch.

'Put your fucking arm down. And you two cunts,' he said, pointing to the boys on bikes, 'fuck off.'

The boys were not just boys. They stood their ground as Bobby loomed over them. His face dark, his eyes fixed into a fight.

'What the fuck has it got to do with you?'

They could see the shape of Bobby's broken nose and the bruising from his fight with Connor. But they'd seen a lot of broken noses in their time.

'We know bigger men than you.'

Bobby stepped up to them.

'I don't give a fuck who you two know. I'll knock the pair of you out.'

The boys knew they could do nothing. Not at that moment anyway. They shifted slowly back on to their saddles and flipped their hoods up over their shorn heads. But as they turned on their bikes, and before they vanished behind glossy green trees, they yelled out: 'We'll see you soon.'

Bobby sighed. Tired, his heart beating quickly. He turned to look at the two drunks, pulled out a tenner and handed it over.

'You can fuck off too.'

They bleated and gabbled.

'You're a good man, Bobby. You're a good boy. Like your dad.'

Bobby turned to where his dad was sitting. Joe tried to hop out of his seat, tried to croak his son's name out. Bobby could feel the blood between them alive, pumping and red.

But Bobby ignored it.

Fuck his fight. Fuck his dad. Fuck these drunks.

4

The ashtray needed changing. A day's worth of cigarettes. The flat was a mess. She'd spent the morning watching and waiting at her window, expecting him to turn up, her belly in knots when she heard the buzzers above and below her go off and doors slam shut in flats, waiting for her own door.

Theresa had known Bobby all her life. She had waited for him to notice her. And soon enough, he did. Going down to the canal with him had been something she'd wanted to do. She wanted to be with someone who wasn't anything to do with her dad.

But, he had a lot to do with her dad.

It felt good. Fucking Bobby made her feel good. The thought of Connor's pale, freckled, muscled body beside hers made her ill. But fucking Bobby had got her in trouble. She sat at her kitchen table waiting for it.

Theresa added another cigarette to the pile in the ashtray and put the kettle on. She never used to smoke, up until she was fifteen. Then she couldn't stop. She got addicted to things quickly and when she sat alone in her flat, expecting one of them to come knocking, she smoked even more.

Theresa was still in her pyjamas and dressing gown when the door went. It was no shock to see her dad there, his back turned as he finished a phone call. She felt naked and strange, in shorts and a T-shirt. She pulled her T-shirt down and waited for Denny to finish talking. He took his time to keep her waiting, to remind her that he was her dad. Gobby and rude to anybody else, Theresa was shy and obedient for him. She waited her turn.

When he did turn around she felt tiny.

'You want to come in, Denny?'

She had never called him Dad. It wasn't how it was done between them. He wore a blue pair of jeans and a black shirt done up to just below the collar. His loafers creaky-new, cheap and polished; his wrists evenly weighed down in solid, market gold. It was Sunday. He'd been to church. She could smell the incense and blood of Christ coming off him. He walked in and pulled her to him, his hands on her upper back, and tried to hug her. His aftershave, the smell of his hair grease, the stuffy sweat in every shirt he owned, the hard bristle on his face when he kissed her on the cheek.

'We need to talk.'

She shut the door behind them and felt the knots in her tummy grow harder and tighter than before. The sweat of fear on the back of her neck. Once inside, his face flushed with blood, his eyes wider and whiter and his breathing short and sore. Undoing the top button of his shirt he grumbled about the heat in the flat. 'Too fucking hot in here.'

'I'll open a window.'

Theresa opened the window by the sink and

let the breeze cool the room. She walked back to him.

'Tea?'

Denny shook his head.

'Only stopping by.'

'Got the kettle on.'

Denny tried to smile at his daughter. She was being mindful of her manners.

'There's a good man out there carrying a nasty-looking scar.'

He kept his hand firm on her little bony shoulder, his palm burning right through her body. Her father's right hand holding her still. She tried not to look frightened. Looking frightened never got Theresa anywhere.

'You seem to be in the middle of all this, gal.'

Denny's voice wasn't Irish. But it wasn't English. Wasn't East End London and wasn't a rambling brogue. It was Denny. Lilting and low and stripped of all those ways you were taught to speak. He barked and scratched his sounds out.

'Nearly ruined Connor's chance of meeting that braggart in the ring.'

He took his hand away.

Theresa desperately wanted another cigarette. She knew the two of them met up to fight. Everyone came to watch them. They were the best local boys in the area. She moved back out of Denny's hold and walked to the kitchen.

'He was minding his own before Connor went for him.'

Denny opened and shut his dry mouth and ran his tongue around his lips. His heavy, droning voice got quieter. The kitchen filled with menace.

'Now listen.'

Theresa held herself still.

'I didn't come here to care too much about your story and I won't be mincing my words. He was minding Connor's business. Ripping your clothes off by the canal and you let him, like you haven't been brought up to know better. You're lucky there are people here looking out for you.'

She looked back at Denny, her eyes hard. She lit a cigarette.

'You *never* fuck someone for the world to see. Next to where I live.'

Theresa blew out her smoke.

Denny cocked his head. 'You behave like a fucking daughter and you stick to the side that feeds you.'

Denny sneered at his daughter. 'I wish there were still laundries to send girls like you to.'

He came towards her, rolling up his sleeve over his elbow. His fat, hairy arm rising up above her. Theresa didn't move. She'd seen how Denny worked on fear. He loved it. She'd seen him do it to her mum. How Daphne's fear of him only made him bigger. Instead Theresa stood and waited, smoking as if the cigarette smoke curling around her kept her safe. She let the ash fall onto the kitchen floor and looked up at her dad as he stepped close to her, trying not to blink in front of him. So frightened that she needed to shit. She could smell him again. The stuffiness, the hair, his hot skin from this temper.

He placed his hand on the back of her head

and felt the ropey, raised skin from the base of her neck to the ear. A scar growing with her. Covered by hair extensions.

Then he put his arm down on her shoulder again and with his left hand drew a handful of notes from his pocket. He put them in the pocket of her dressing gown and pulled her in for a hug. Her face squashed into his chest, damp and warm. She turned her face to the side and let him hold her as long as he wanted. He spoke calmly.

'Theresa, don't you ever be caught with that Jew boy again. Don't ever let me hear about you fucking him by the canal or by anywhere or fucking him at all. He's trash, a flash piece of trash like his old man.'

He kissed her on the forehead.

'Was the other half of you that done it. Her half. The bad blood. But you do it again and I'll chop you up and throw you in the canal myself.'

Denny's breath was foul. Theresa felt his kiss on her forehead. A burn that blistered her skin long after he pulled away. With nothing to say that could save her, Theresa nodded and let him threaten her. She let him be her dad.

'And stick a fucking cross up somewhere, you could do with the fucking help of it.'

He coughed as he opened her door and let himself out, reaching into his pocket to make another phone call. Theresa stubbed out the butt in the ashtray and felt inside her dressing gown for the money. Seventy quid, to keep quiet and do as she was told.

5

Clapton Bow Boys Club had survived the Second World War and been around way before the First. In a corner of East London, it stood proud between two old, Blitz-dodged workhouses. The building was grand, good and solid, made up of red brick, art deco windows and champions. It had been the sanctuary for any poor boy from Dalston and beyond, giving him fresh soap, warm water and a pair of boxing gloves.

The sign was white and Thatcher-blue. Local boy after local boy had been yanked by the collar through the gym, pitches and nearby parks to keep the lads clean and away from trouble. Dabbing at the cuts on their knees and tying up their laces, playing pool and kicking a ball out the back. But it was a boxing club. More than anything else, boys came to learn how to fight. In the middle of stabbings and warfare the club had a mix of kids boxing happily together learning about respect and manners; love and hate.

It limped along thanks to the time-on-their-hands help of a few recovering heroin and crack addicts, who helped keep the young ones busy while the experienced and older trainers found the talent and nurtured it. There were a few always smoking outside, a pick-and-mix of men who'd done a U-turn on a bad life. That, and charity handouts and donations from a few high-profile, old-school boxers, kept the club coughing along. It was the one with the most care and history. It was in the club's blood to win.

Inside the old, blue-tiled walls and dark ceilings, Chloe felt like she was walking back in time. An old bathing house, still full of damp and echo. She could smell the dripping pipes, the years chipping off. But the floors were glossy and new. Trainers squeaked across the disinfected corridors and the bang-bang of kid-fists on the chocolate and crisps dispensers gave a heartbeat pulse to the mad chatter of children spilling into corners and tables in the large room. And it was hot. It was baking in there.

Chloe pushed Devlin forward. Into the noise, the world of boys and girls laughing and shouting, scraping back plastic chairs.

'They aren't arguing. They're just having fun.'

Chloe let go of Devlin's hand. For his own sake. But he held on again. Chloe knelt down and looked at him.

'Devvy, I'm going to let go of your hand, because if people see an eleven-year-old boy, from big school, holding onto a girl, they're going to rip the piss out of you. You understand? I'm not going anywhere, but you need to let go of me.'

Devlin's face, whiter than it'd been all day, crumpled as if he was going to cry.

'Don't leave,' he whispered. 'Please.'

'No, Devlin. No. No tears here.'

He pulled it back, and let go of Chloe's hand. He put both hands in his tracksuit pockets as fists, biting his lower lip.

Chloe laid a light touch on the broad shoulder in a white Apex T-shirt, bent over a red plastic table lined with children eating crisps and drinking Capri Sun. His big back was warm under the cotton; she took her hand away.

'Excuse me, are you Derek?'

The tall, black man straightened and turned around. His body wide and his T-shirt snug over arms that Chloe suspected had been built for boxing once upon a time. Now, he was half fat, half muscle. His head was shaved, and his hairline receded away from a slightly sweating forehead. Chloe thought he must have been in his late forties.

Derek put his hand out, and she felt hers lost in his shake.

'Hello, yeah I'm Derek. How can I help?'

'He wants to start training — we spoke on the phone.'

Derek smiled at Devlin, sizing him up and down. Derek's eyes were slightly slit, hidden in the largeness of his face and he squinted when he gave Devlin the once-over. Chloe felt him size her up too.

'We got ourselves a sharp little featherweight here, eh boy?'

Devlin hung his head.

'You fast?'

Devlin looked at Chloe.

'Answer him, Devlin.'

'You run quick, yeah? If you were getting chased, you run quick, yeah? You're a runner, a little night fox.' Derek put on a special, spooky voice. Showing fast, scuttling legs by making his fingers dance.

'I don't know.' Devlin shrugged.

Derek frowned and folded his arms. An old tattoo of a deck of cards was splayed open like a fan on his forearm, hidden on his skin. Another on his other arm, a fading, twisting mermaid buried and barely there.

'You don't run? You never run?'

Devlin shrugged again.

'We don't do shrugging in here. That's for boys who don't know a yes from a no. This place is for men. Men can answer straight. Tell me. You run, or not?'

'No. I don't run.'

Derek winked at Chloe.

'All men run.'

Chloe held back from holding Devlin's hand. She heard Devlin's breathing get heavier, but she stepped away from him. He looked up at her and saw her move away, leaving him to stand alone.

'Yeah, I would run fast.' His voice quivering.

Derek laughed loudly and shook him by the shoulders.

'Good boy. Okay then. That's where we start. We take you to the park and see how fast you go. We'll get you moving about.'

Chloe rubbed the back of Devlin's head. 'See?'

'We got ourselves a little greyhound for the ring.'

Devlin let out a small smile.

Derek looked up at Chloe. Girls didn't come into the club often and when they did it was to try and get a look at the older boys. This girl

40

looked far too young to have a child this old.

'He yours?'

Chloe shook her head. He wasn't. He belonged to her neighbour, Fiona. He kept getting bullied; boys turning up at his house, waiting on his doorstep. Chloe didn't know how twelve-year-olds could be so tough. Devlin didn't either; he was just another kid that needed toughening up. 'Clump one of them. That'll stop the rest piping up,' Chloe's dad had said. But Devlin wasn't a fighter.

'He got a dad?'

Chloe shook her head again.

'Okay. Well, you can drop him and leave him, or have a look around. Best thing I reckon is to drop him off and go. Longer you stay, longer he'll cry. I'll get him coached up by some of the other boys and get him in the mix.'

'Can we walk around first? Then I'll go. Just so he knows where he is.'

''Course. Gym's around the corner. Walk straight in. We got the young boys in today.'

Chloe placed Devlin in front of her and told him to walk. She looked around for Derek, who had gone back to his table of rowdy children, telling them to pick up the crisps packets off the floor, getting a boy to sit back down in his chair. He was smiling when he did it though. Chloe liked Derek; she got a good feeling from him. He made the place feel safe. As she walked away she heard him belly-laugh. It was followed by the sweeter, squealing laughter of smaller children, the ones too little to box properly.

Walking towards the gym itself, Chloe could

41

feel it getting warmer. Hot air steamed from the punched bags and skin, building up a fog of hot bodies. They walked past a cream-coloured wall, decorated with thin, black frames filled with old photographs of boxers.

She stopped to look at the wall of photographs. It started at the beginning: wartime fighters with tight white vests, black shorts and staunch, broad shoulders. Hair, waxed down, short back and sides. Their noses all snapped and fluffed out again in the same way. In time, and as London got more mixed up, the photos hit colour, and so did the boys. Tall, lean boys with neatly combed side-parting Afros and Irish, black-haired gazers, holding up their fists. Old pictures showed gloves against jaws of fighters turned to jelly mid-fight, spraying sweat and spit. Some boys wore head guards, some didn't. Spanish and Italian. Tanned boys. Faces that could have come from everywhere were at home here. The same white vests, the same bare chests, the same honed, toned, curving shoulders and the same precise muscle sloping from neck to arm. Their eyes starting to look like they were rolling closer together as they got older, drinking in more punches; their noses puffed up around the twists of another break. Twinkling eyes full of dark red mist, snazzy grins and scowls. Born to blood and effort and growing pains.

The spirit had got hold of Devlin too. He was in a new world, a man's world. He took his marks and set off down the corridor.

'Chloe I am fast, look. Watch how fast I can run.'

Devlin ran his long, wiry legs across the shiny floor, before skidding and falling to his knees.

For a moment, Chloe thought he was going to cry, but the pale, blond-haired boy picked himself up off the floor, turned to her and shrugged. Two older boys turned a corner and he moved against the wall to let them by. He kept his head down and walked slowly back to Chloe. She could feel him try to lean against her and she moved him gently away.

To her left she heard the slapping of twenty young boys' fists punching bags. It was a sauna in there. Her back started to sweat up under her top. The army of boys ferocious and focused, everyone hitting hard like an off-the-beat soldier's march. Five big-bellied, pit-bull-faced trainers in their sixties held up pads, barked orders and patrolled the ring and floor. A couple of younger ones sniffed and skulked about, overweight and sleepy, trying to look tough. The older boys looked like boxers. Chloe watched the white-haired trainer nearest to her, leaning on the side of the ring shouting. The skin on his face splattered with veins and his nose smashed almost flat on his face. He was handsome still, with the kind face of a father. He frowned and yelled at the ring.

'Kill your distance and put your fucking feet in.' His eyes never left the two sparring boys for a second. His hands had lived. Tattooed crosses on the knuckles done roughly. Now blurred ink spots. *Mum* on his arm. Gold rings on his left fingers.

A mix of kindness and menace, of love and

toughness, in the air. The boys wrapped their arms around each other when their rounds were done, gasping for air through their gum shields. They ducked under the ropes and waited to get their gloves taken off. The white-haired trainer took their head guards off and patted their damp hair. As one was praised the other waited his turn and scratched at his squashed face with his gloves like a dog.

A young black boy, smaller than Devlin, skipped past them jabbing at the air, spitting and hissing, his eyes fixed on an imaginary opponent. Another boy, sweating so hard he kept blinking, sat with his head between his legs on a chair in the corner, holding a towel round his neck and breathing heavily. He glanced up and looked Chloe up and down before hanging his head again. A chubby, white skinhead was getting a telling-off from a trainer, his gloves at his sides and his head hanging.

'What are you, a fucking puppy?'

The boy straightened his back and frowned, ready to go again. The trainer held up the pads and the boy knocked them cleaner and harder. He coaxed him. 'Good lad.'

Music poured out of the speakers and inside the ring, in the middle of the room, two new boys were up.

The trainer laughed. 'Come on then, let's bash each other up.'

They danced around before laying into each other's faces with stiff punches. Three rounds. Three minutes each. The trainer at the ring turned on them with the same focus, the same intense attention he'd given the last two boys.

'That's a good shot; throw them when he comes.'

No one was more in favour than anyone else and he took turns in telling them what to do.

'Work him, that's it.'

Devlin would find a dad here. Everyone here meant it, and meant well.

One trainer was skirting round a bag, flicking and grazing it with light jabs as it swayed, hard and heavy. A couple of young teenagers watched him, wide-eyed and in love. She saw his back first. Thick muscle. Lean, but big. Then he went to hit the bag hard, trying to smack it dead. The punch echoed through the gym. The boys around him laughed in awe. The big trainer caught sight and laughed.

'Bobby, careful of your hand, son.'

He turned, out of breath. He had his knuckles bound up in tape.

She stood in the doorway watching him. He let his fists fall at his sides, before taking a forearm and wiping the sweat from his face.

They checked each other out in the bright white lights and damp, heavy air of the gym.

Bobby felt hot. He took his right hand up and pushed back his hair, wet from sweat and workout, and ruffled the head of each boy who'd been watching him. He didn't see girls like her come in here.

She watched him walk. He wore a black vest, with the gym's name on the back in red letters, black tracksuit bottoms and running trainers. Chloe could see he had the same army cut that

45

all those other boys had in the photographs. Shaved up the back, short at the sides and a naked neck. All razor and no scissors, like a soldier boy from Iraq. Except his was much longer on top. A curling quiff in spirals, almost. When he turned, he looked like a Teddy boy. A greaser from way back when. All wrong for now. As dated as those photos in the hallway.

His body was longer than his legs, just a little, overworked. His shoulders rolling in muscle and shape, his torso tapering in to his waist, etched out and showing in the thinning, worn-out vest. Thin enough to have a ribcage. He had no problem meeting her stare as he walked up to her.

His face looked like it had been in a fight, Chloe could see that. There were shades of yellow bruising across his jaw line and flicks of red blood in his eye. His nose had been broken more than once.

'You looking for someone?'

His voice was deeper than Chloe thought it might be. A smoker's voice. Still, he stared at her. Right in the eyes. His face was tanned, his eyes such a light brown they were almost gold. Hair falling over his eyes. He took a bandaged hand and swept it back off his face to see her.

Chloe did not speak. Instead she swallowed and put Devlin in front of her. The chatter and noise and heat still swarming around her.

'I took him to see the gym. Derek thinks he'll be quick.'

A tattoo, more visible than Derek's, carved out on his left biceps said *To Rest is to Rust*.

Chloe carried on talking.

'He said to look around. At the gym.'

He looked back at Chloe.

'Yeah? Well, this is the gym, this is it.'

He smiled.

Chloe looked at his hands held at his crotch. Grazes on his fists.

He saw Devlin and turned to him and smiled. 'You like a fight then, yeah?'

Devlin shuffled and stepped a little bit apart from Chloe. 'Never had one.'

'Nah? Come on then.'

Bobby bent low and started play-jabbing the air around Devlin. Chloe worried that Devlin's blood would drain from his face and the tears would come, but instead his cheeks filled with colour and he blushed, excited by what Bobby was doing. Devlin giggled and hid behind Chloe.

'I can run really fast.'

Bobby folded his arms and pretended to look impressed.

'That's a start.'

He looked at Chloe as Derek turned into the doorway. Chloe could feel and hear his presence before he even spoke.

'You met our best boxer, then? He's training up for his fight. Aren't you, Bobby?'

Derek walked slowly, with steady rolling steps, into the gymnasium. Slow as he liked. With all the time and weight in the world. He put his right hand on Chloe's shoulder and gave her a small pat.

'Boys love him. Devlin, you gonna learn from this man, y'hear? He's gonna put you proper

47

right. Boy's gonna turn into a man. Trust me.'

Devlin looked up at Derek, and his shoulders rolled back and he started to stand up straight. He looked to his teacher and blinked, putting his hand out to Bobby's tattoo.

'What's that?'

'It's a saying.'

'What does it mean?'

'It means keep punching.'

'Why?'

Bobby gestured to the boxing ring behind him.

''Cos if you stop, in there, you'll get your face bashed in.'

'Why would they bash my face in?'

''Cos that's what happens.'

Derek smiled.

'Let him learn a few jabs first.'

He put a heavy arm around Chloe. 'Big tournament coming up and we got two of our boys finishing each other off. It'll be proper. You should come. Bring Devlin.'

Bobby looked away, embarrassed.

Derek squeezed Chloe tighter. 'You'll have to come. See this one fight. Won't she, Bobby? She'll have to come to your fight.'

Chloe didn't know anything about fights. Derek let go and put his arm on her shoulder. He was affectionate without being intrusive. Chloe didn't mind his hand there. There was something reassuring about Derek.

'When you want to bring him here? Tomorrow?' He bent low to speak to Devlin.

'You and me are gonna get tough. You're

48

gonna stand your ground.'

Devlin smiled.

Bobby's hand was held out to Chloe. She took it. No shake, just a faint grip as she looked smack into his eyes, where she could see herself reflected.

'Bobby. What's your name?'

Chloe looked down as she said her name.

Bobby took his hand away and put his arm around Derek. He squeezed gently. Derek gave him a bear hug back and messed up his quiff.

'Was in the best shape of his life, this one. Then he decided to walk into trouble.'

Bobby flung the words away with his hand. 'I need a shower.'

Derek made to kick him up the arse as he walked away and Bobby laughed.

He turned at the doorway, lowered his head and bowed. His arm tensed and strong, holding onto the door frame.

'Chloe, it was nice to meet you. Maybe see you tomorrow?'

He winked at Devlin. 'See you in the ring, Champ. Watch your nose.'

Then he was gone, and it was quiet.

Derek had his hands on his waist and watched him go.

'We've all tried to knock that out of him, that rawness, but I can't. It's why he'll never go professional. Loses his vision.'

Derek kept his stare on the doorway long after Bobby had gone and Chloe didn't think he was really talking to her. Watching the space he'd left, looking to the light Bobby had walked out into, listening for his steps on that greasy-clean floor.

And then he must have seen Chloe, her eyes still on the doorway, at the space he'd left behind. She was holding on to Devlin, who, after Bobby's performance, was trying to break free and monkey-jump a punchbag.

Derek winked.

'Handsome too, ain't he? For a boxer. He's our stud. Gets groupies and everything.'

Chloe went red.

'He needs a nice girl.'

He laughed loudly, his tiny eyes vanishing almost completely in his huge face.

6

The old East End sun shone on her face as Chloe left the gym with Devlin. A glinting, happy light that made her feel as if her mum was around. She walked home down Newington Green, listening to Devlin talk about Derek and Bobby. She bought some flowers on the way too. White peonies to sit at the kitchen table, next to the shelf with her mum's dancing porcelain figurines.

Chloe's mum had died two weeks ago. It had been sudden. A heart attack that had knocked her tiny body like thunder.

They'd only just had the funeral. A cold, Catholic service on a rainy day that got her heels stuck into the soil around her mum's plot as they threw flowers on the coffin. Grim and lonely. People who'd done a duty and turned up stood around talking as the priest said his few, toneless words, and got pissed afterwards in a pub that played no music. The small gathering sat in four corners of the room sipping gin and beer until they were drunk enough to hold Chloe's hand and tell her they were sorry. She'd thought of her mum in the box, on her own. She didn't want her to be on her own in there.

She remembered sitting in the kitchen with her mum, watching soaps on the TV and second-hand-smoking her cigarettes. The noise from the rest of the house seemed to happen around the two of them, sat there in the warm kitchen together. There had not been time to miss her mum. Because it didn't feel like she'd really gone. Except for today. Today she wanted to go home and tell her mum about a boy.

This had been the first real time she'd been out and about since it happened. Chloe worked as a nursery assistant in a primary school. She'd gone back only two days after the funeral and it was two days too soon. Had started crying when helping one of the children with their alphabet. The child had cried too and the school had sent Chloe home. Her agency were keeping her on hold until she felt ready to return to work again.

Polly was in when Chloe walked to the kitchen. In her joggers and a topknot bun, her mouth full of pasta, she looked up and yelled hello. Chloe had always been the quieter of the two sisters. They were both pretty girls, but Polly's look was more obvious. More confident, more skin on show. Chloe was thinner, smokier. Her skin and eyes were darker and her hair, thick, straight and black, looked better piled up on her head to show off her thin neck. Chloe was born just after her mum had had a late miscarriage, and everyone thought she was going to be the strong one.

'She's a bit small, isn't she? And so dark. Where'd she get her hair from when you and Jeff are so fair?'

They shrugged. Her dad laughed.

'You want to watch them Dalston Turks, Jeff. Sneaking in when you're on the night shift.'

And her mum would blush, even though it was untrue.

The kitchen was the only room in the house her mum had bothered to keep tidy. The rest of the house was clean, but stuffed full of old family furniture that Chloe's dad wouldn't take to the tip because it had belonged to his parents. The rooms were still decorated as they'd been the past forty years. Browns, greens and oranges on the wallpaper, mucky and loud together. Old Liberty-print curtains, once a luxury to show off to the rest of the street, were now ugly and tired.

But the kitchen was new. Chosen fresh out of a catalogue, and hers. White and clean. The room she sat and read the paper in, smoking and drinking tea. Three pots in the morning; two pots in the afternoon. There were still bits and pieces of her everywhere. Duty-free Rothmans, photos on the fridge from their holiday to Tenerife two summers ago, with her tanned, happy face showing no signs of the end. There were bottles of rosé wine in the fridge that she hadn't had the time to drink and bars of Cadbury's in cupboards. Chloe had just got round to throwing away the last bunch of the flowers that kept coming, sent from friends, family and neighbours. The water had started to rot and smell.

The atmosphere about the house was still heavy. They moved around slowly. Instead of putting the kettle on in silence, today Chloe smiled and put the flowers on the table. She took down the Tupperware box of biscuits her mum dipped into her tea.

'Those are nice flowers. What are they for?'

'For Mum.'

Polly turned towards her little sister. Her cleavage spilling, pale and pink, out of her too-small vest.

'Everyone sends flowers for us. So I bought these for Mum.'

Chloe got her mug out of the cupboard.

'Think the flowers are for all of us. Mum too. But they're pretty.'

Chloe reached for a tea bag and kept her back turned to Polly. She thought about the way he'd smiled at her as he left for a shower and the way his back was damp through the vest he was wearing.

Bobby. A sweet name for a tough boy.

'What about work?'

'The school?'

'Yes, when are you going back?'

Chloe missed the children. She liked helping them understand the sun and the park and the seasons and the alphabet, holding their hands across roads, sorting out their pens and pencils. She loved listening to their broken sentences telling her what they'd just drawn, made and written. She would go back soon, as soon as she could.

'They didn't think it was good for me or the children, because I kept crying.'

Polly nodded. Polly had stopped her crying in public and gone back to business. Chloe, at eighteen, found it harder to be as brave.

They heard the cab pull up to their house. A house their dad had managed to keep in the

54

family with a little luck. The house had made him. He could stand tall because of it. After Lynn died, he left it rarely, only to take the black cab out for an odd job, which surprised both daughters because when his wife was alive he hardly spent time in it with her. Guilt or grief, he was lost and alone.

He came back with a box of chocolates in his hands. He patted each girl on her head with his spare hand and placed the box on the table.

'I got you some chocolate, girls.'

Then he coughed, with nothing more to say, and walked back to the front room, to his chair and shut the door. They heard the racing pour out of the television.

Chloe looked at her sister. 'You want any of this?'

Polly shook her head.

Chloe put the box of chocolates in the cupboard, finished making her tea and left the kitchen. She went up to her mum and dad's bedroom, a room her dad wouldn't go in since it happened. He slept on the sofa with the television on. Chloe could understand. The sheets hadn't been changed. Lynn always did them and Chloe didn't want to change them yet.

Sipping the tea in her parents' bed, Chloe sat up with the duvet around her. Then she lay on her mum's side and could smell some of her body cream on the bedding. There were books still piled high on the side table. Sunday afternoons her mum would lie down, read a few pages, and fall asleep after lunch. She had a library card and the books on the table needed returning.

When the tea was finished, she put her mug on the bedside table, curled up, her head turned to the open window. The curtains, sheer and simple, were something her mum had added. Something that made the home lighter.

She remembered.

Chloe had found her first. Her body twisted on the floor where her heart had snapped and her mouth hung open, as if she was about to call to them. Chloe stood for a few shell-shocked seconds, before crouching down and resting the back of her hand on her mum's tiny face that had aged a hundred years when her heart stopped.

The death happened so quickly. Life after had been sinking slowly, like mud.

Chloe cried, the April breeze cool on her face. When she wasn't so tired she'd go back to the classroom. She didn't want to spend too long in this house.

She walked to her mum's wardrobe. All the dresses hung up as they had always been, on identical wooden hangers, with her perfume faint on the collars. Chloe was as small boned and narrow hipped as her mum. Polly was busty, too wide in the back and fat in the belly. She undressed. In her knickers and bra, she slid each dress along the rail until she saw the one she wanted. Black silk and green flowers, the colour of mint leaves. Buttons down the front and big shoulders. Chloe slipped it on. The silk was heavy and soft on her thighs. It moved with her.

7

By Monday morning, Bobby was starting to feel better. Although his body would not be what he wanted it for the fight, he didn't ache as much and was back on the rounds. Slowing down a bit now, saving his energy for the day itself. Building up his time at the gym bit by bit to let the bruises cool. Arnica oil in hot baths and cool, early nights with the window open.

Bobby wanted to light up now as he left the gym, but he didn't. He walked into the evening air and let his lungs fill with it. He thought about her. The girl with hair blacker than his, knotted up so he could see the nervous vein in her neck like a whip. She wore one chain, a cross, and he could smell her perfume. Two beauty dots on her chin. Darker than a freckle, lighter than dirt. She had a stare on her and wasn't afraid to look someone in the eye and keep them there. She'd kept Bobby there. He had kept his eyes on her until she had smiled at him. Then he had to look away.

He crossed the road, jogging the last bit and was smiling as he walked into the park. Walking tall, a little bit cold, smelling of pine from the shower. He rolled back his shoulder blades, heard the click, felt the muscle and rolled his neck, gently as he turned into the park.

And there he saw Mikey, sitting with his head in his hands on a bench, his back shaking, crying without shame in broad daylight. Bare arms in a white vest and a jumper round his neck. Mikey worked as a sometime roofer. Sometimes he ran with the travellers who got him the work. Mikey was one of those shape shifters, moving in different circles easily. The joker in any group. A harmless, fat fool. But loyal to Bobby. Bobby had known him long enough to love him.

Mikey was the closest thing Bobby was going to get to a brother. Nothing in common but their background and roots, they were as good as blood. And even though he knew, like an omen, that talking to his friend was going to bring Bobby problems that weren't his own, he couldn't turn away.

'Alright, mate?'

Mikey lifted his head. Red around the eyes, no sleep in his strained face. His vest ripped, his jumper hanging off his shoulders. His hairline receded so much he might as well have shaved it, and drink had given him a chin and made him soft around the arms. His gut pushed out where he sat down.

'Nah. Been having murders with her.'

Bobby put his bag down.

'She fucked your vest up like that?'

'She says I try and *control* her.'

Mikey had froth and spit around his lips. Where he'd been crying to himself, and shouting at his Vanessa. Bobby was not good at telling people what to do with their love life. He had never been in love.

'She's fucking someone else. I know, I fucking know it.' There was no point trying to talk his kind of sense. He was wired and mad, pouring drink into a body that needed to lie down and sleep. Even so, Bobby tried. He was in a good mood.

'You aren't thinking right. You need to go home and sleep this off and deal with her tomorrow.'

Bobby sighed as Mikey nodded.

'You need to go home and sleep, Mikey. Home's that way.' Bobby pointed behind him.

'Don't want to go home. What do I have to go home for? She isn't there and when she does come home, if she does come home, it's just gonna be murders all over again. Might as well just stay out.'

Bobby picked up his bag. 'Not here though. Let's get home.'

Mikey shook his head. 'I know who it is though. That fucking fat cunt who started managing the pub.'

Mikey wiped his bare arm across his face and trailed pale snot on the hairs of his forearm.

'I'm going to sort it. Going down there right now.'

Bobby put his arm on Mikey's shoulder. 'Walk with me. You're in no state to fight.'

Mikey shook his head and blinked back tears, cracking his fingers and forming small fists. 'I can get a touch on him. Watch.'

'No, you can't, not like this.'

'I saw her phone. She's been working shifts there, too many shifts there. I said I'd pay for everything. Why she want to keep going there to work for? Then I see her phone.'

Bobby felt for his friend. Hopeless, flabby, Mikey was sitting on a bench around the corner from the pub his girlfriend was cheating on him in. Mikey who could pay for nothing.

'I said I want to marry her.'

'You what?'

'I want to do right by her.'

Mikey, the boy trying to be a man. Bobby laughed and put an arm round him. Mikey frowned and wiped a face with his sleeve.

'We're twenty years old. How many people do you know that have got married?'

Mikey thought about it.

'My mum and dad. Your mum and dad.'

'No. Our lot, I mean.'

Bobby lifted Mikey's vest to show his grey-white gut.

'Look at you, fat as fuck. Who's marrying you?'

Mikey laughed a painful laugh, pushing Bobby's hands away. He sat trying to get his breath back.

Mikey nodded. 'You make me feel stupid now.'

'Why do you want to?'

Maggie and Joe were still married and it had meant something to them both. Bands of gold and the white dress and those photographs in albums. Maggie kept them all, everything she'd ever had with Joe. But Bobby had watched his dad get sick and his mum grow lonely, awake at night washing tablecloths and wiping down lampshades at three in the morning. Sitting in the sounds of the washing machine, reading her book.

'She's the only girl who liked me. How else do I keep her?' Tired, he squinted when he was talking. His tongue large and hot in his mouth. He spoke with a rasp.

'You got choices, Bobby. The way you look lets you pick. You can keep dipping your cock all day long.'

Dipping his cock into the same girls he had pushed over in the playground. The same girls and their friends, over and over. When Bobby wasn't at the club he was watching the four walls of his room with nothing on them apart from the odd flyer for a rave and his picture of Tyson. Thinking about some of the girls he had fucked and wondering about the ones he hadn't.

'You're only with Vanessa because she's here.'

'So what?'

'So, Vanessa and you will always fight. And she'll always cheat. And you'll always drink and you'll take it from each other because it's better than being here and alone.'

Bobby could see Mikey's eyes fill with tears and he turned away.

'You can have better. You've always had your boxing. You can always get out.'

'Maybe.'

Bobby felt heavy between these nowhere and somewhere corners of his life. The tower block had looked after him just as much as it wore him out. He knew the faces behind the curtains, and as a kid Bobby would always be fed if Maggie was working late. You knew your neighbour. But the blocks were too high, too dark and too small

61

and there were too many windows and too many doors. There were too many homes and not enough space. 'Right, where's your missus?'

'Working there now. She just left. Scratched the shit out of my shirt and left. Fucking mad bitch.'

Bobby sniffed his last clean, fresh bit of early evening air.

'I need to sort this, Bobby. She's making me look like a prick.'

Mikey used to bring Bobby's mum a bottle of wine or some chocolates when he came round. Just after she'd got rid of Joe. Had paid for her to get taxis to Asda and back for her shopping. He said he remembered Maggie looking after him when his mum was at work. And Mikey's mum had watched Bobby the same way.

Mikey's softness was beginning to irritate. The spineless sulking, the sad way he looked up to Bobby. Mikey needed to fight back.

But you helped out family. And Mikey was family.

'Take me there, then.'

They turned a corner, and it was like walking into winter. The late spring in the air was gone, and the houses went from old to new; from old red brick to the concrete of an ugly tower block ahead, one of the bad ones, and a sleepy garage on a cul-de-sac. The pub stood next to a blank whitewashed wall, and even this was stained, as if the cigarette smoke from inside had crawled its way through the stone and brick and paint. One man, wearing a knitted jumper over a hardened ale-belly, stood outside puffing. Two wooden tables and a rubbish tip down an alley. A crispy-looking St George's flag hung from a top bedroom window, waving weakly like a dirty rag. It looked like it had been hung there since the Eighties, a bloody cross over a door.

This England was shit, Bobby thought. Who could live in this?

Mikey sat at one of the wooden tables outside and put his head in his hands.

'Which one is he?' Bobby asked.

'He's the bald one.'

'The bald one?'

'You'll know him. He's the one who runs the place.'

Bobby pulled open the wooden door and took in the dank smells: the grime, the Scotch and shitty plumbing.

Vanessa, with her hair up and her eyes swollen from crying, stopped what she was doing. She knew.

'Alright.' Bobby nodded.

She went to move from behind the bar, her eyes widening and her hands shaking on the pint glass she was putting back.

'Did he send you here?'

Bobby held his hand up.

'Clear your glasses, love. You're alright.'

Bobby could hear her calling him from the bar, begging him not to do whatever it was he was about to do. He pulled himself together. He pretended that nothing meant anything and let the creeping little violent buzz in his

63

head get louder and his fists get harder. He was not Bobby. He was a walking punch, and there'd be no thought behind it. No honour either. Bobby knew even before he knocked this man out that it was not a fair, decent fight.

He went first to the Gents. It was a lucky first look.

He was a tall, broad man, and Bobby, for one small moment, wondered if he had it in him to knock him down. He was bigger than Bobby. Taller and staunch.

The bald man turned from the dryer and didn't even see it coming. Bobby didn't wait. He got on with it. Didn't put the fear in and didn't prowl jungle-style beforehand. Bobby wanted to be here no more than minutes. It was just a quick three-punch-and-out against the dryer of the men's toilets.

He didn't have time to ask Bobby who he was.

Bobby walloped him once around the face: cheekbone, once in the stomach and a last clean crack on the jaw to send him spinning and into a short, slumpy sleep.

The man's shirt gathered around his neck, burying his cracked chin and catching the dribble from his mouth.

'Keep your hands off Vanessa, you understand?'

The world came back for a second and he could hear his name being called out.

'BOBBY! LEAVE IT BOBBY. LEAVE HIM ALONE BOBBY. *BOBBY*!'

The world calling his name. Blood pumping,

heart moving up and down through his throat, to his gut, to his balls. He felt big.

Heart pumping and face hot, he drew his arm back. Smash. Crack. The man's face soft against his hard fist.

8

They were not touching when Bobby woke up. Though he had fallen asleep with his arms around her. He had kissed her on her head and shoulder. But in the morning they lay there, back to back, cold air through the window pricking up the hairs on their necks.

It was good sex. It had been sweet and hot and made Bobby feel woozy after. But it helped him forget the night before. It stopped him feeling ill when he thought about slamming that man down for no reason, for nothing. For Mikey. For fucking up his hands again before his fight. He felt his right fist, swollen and sore.

Now, everything felt curdled. The room, shaped just like his own and like every flat on this estate, was lemon yellow and cream. Tidy and soaked in all her sweet smells. Yellow frames held pictures of her and friends posing outside clubs and pouting on streets. Around her mirror dangled yellow silk butterflies on fairy lights, which twinkled against the glass as they drunk-fucked through the night. Theresa had white blinds and fake yellow daffodils in a china vase on the windowsill. And like her lemon-pie room, with her cheap bottled hair, and her cheap sunbed skin, Theresa was beautiful and sickly.

Bobby felt ill. He had training for his fight and he wanted to leave before she woke. But he was tired. He needed ten more minutes, staying on his side. A gap in the bed between them. She made a moaning sound and Bobby's eyes opened again, to gaze at the nape of her neck and the two gold chains that had caught onto to some of her bleached blonde hair and made a little knot.

He tasted her on his lips. The lotions displayed like his trophies on a shelf. Deodorants, hand lotions; all market stall, sugar-powder crap.

He'd drunk pint after pint. And then more, until he was eased back to himself. Until he stopped thinking about the man's face, all shocked and frightened as Bobby went to smack him the third time. The drink had not been enough. She'd let him in, like she'd been waiting for him. He did it because he could. Because he'd won the fight at the canal. He'd won Theresa and he could sweat out the shame of another fight in her bed.

Theresa's people made Bobby nervous, but he never let them know. Some of them were on the estate. Bobby knew a few from growing up around the way and knew many put those brogue accents on. Bobby knew that if she wanted to, Theresa could run to them and Bobby would be hunted down.

She turned and moved into him, all skin and bone and bacon-smells from the fake tan she used morning and night.

He moved a hand and went to touch her shoulder. She turned round to face him. Her mascara had smudged. The covers had slipped to her midriff, her breasts pointed up to the ceiling, she snored quietly with little half-sleeping sighs

67

that moved her ribcage as she slept. Bobby put his right hand, battered at the knuckles, on her tight tiny stomach. He left it there, dead and unmoving. She stirred again and opened her left eye. She made a small sound and pushed her bum deeper into the pit of his gut and he held her there. His left arm around across her hip bones. Her belly in his arms. He kissed her on the top of her head, smelling the night's sweat on her scalp.

'Morning.'

Her mouth was dry and the words were mumbled. She scratched her face and yawned. Her lips were pink and dry from where they'd been kissing.

'What time is it?'

Bobby took his hand away. Then put it back again.

'It's some time in the morning. Early.'

Theresa sat up on her elbows. Her nipples pale pink and small. A tattoo of black orchids stretched from armpit to the vein that throbbed just above her hip bone. She turned to him, drawing her face up to him, pulling his neck to her. He kissed back.

'Pass us my phone.'

It was flashing and vibrating, on Theresa's bedside table. She leaned over, picked it up and looked at the screen.

'It's your mum.'

Bobby knew why she was ringing. To wake him up and get him to the club. Get him ready for training. Bobby didn't need reminding there were only four days to go.

68

He let it ring. It rang twice.

It was an excuse to leave.

'Got to go train.'

Bobby sat up. She put her hand inside his leg and ran her fingers up and down the soft skin. He felt slow and sleepy and turned on.

'You nervous about the fight?'

'If I was I wouldn't tell you.'

Theresa held tighter. Keeping her hands on his body for as long as she could before he left, she bit him on his shoulder. A small nip that left teeth marks for a second. She left her mouth there and kissed where she'd bitten. Her lips a soft, light balm. Bobby smiled, looking down at her as she put her head back on her pillow and stared at him. He searched for her face under the make-up.

She had always been prettier than any girl Bobby had been with. You could see it when she turned fourteen and started singing in musicals at youth club. When Bobby played snooker, he'd hear her in the back room with a piano. All the boys turned up to watch Theresa. Just to see her in heels and tights.

Then her dad stopped her singing. They were blood and she was their baby.

She looked like she was trying to wake up and yawned.

'Do you want a cup of tea?'

Bobby shook his head. He was looking deeply at her face and put his arm across her body to keep her in bed. He was beginning to stir for her again. 'How come you don't want a baby yet?'

A blush crept over Theresa's cheeks. She

frowned and it began to fade.

'What you want to know that for?'

'All your friends walking round with prams. Never you.'

Theresa looked at Bobby's face and saw the boy she'd always known. Straight-talker. Quick temper. She had watched him get better with age and knew he would get too big for the estate soon. He would leave it, and her in it.

'And get stuck here for good?'

She scratched her chin with an acrylic nail and shrugged.

'I don't want to speed it up.'

'What?'

'What's going to happen to me.'

He took her hand, sitting up a little to look at her nails, and changed the subject. 'Why you get your nails dressed up like that?'

'Like what?'

'All long and painted up.'

'I think it looks nice. I sit there for a couple of hours and talk to the women. We chat about life.'

She held them out in front of her. The green nails and the gold tips.

Bobby made a face.

'Can you still do normal stuff with them?'

She moved over to face him again. 'I can do *everything* with them.'

She gently drew a nail across his chest, her hair flat on one side and her eyes swollen with sleep. He couldn't help himself. He was morning-hard and this would be quick. As he knelt over her, he knew the price he would pay for this would be high. But he fucked her

70

quickly, to the sound of kids play-fighting
outside, and all the while he couldn't shake off
the feeling of trouble. Afterwards he got dressed
quietly. Looking up every so often to smile at her
leaning up on her elbows and looking at him, he
couldn't wait to leave. In her bathroom he
splashed some cold water on his face and soaked
his hair, hanging his head over the sink as the tap
ran. Wishing he could just keep away from her.

Back in the room she had her head to the
pillow again. He kissed her on the cheek and
then her lips to say goodbye. A sour, wet, messy
kiss that put her back to sleep. He left her place
with his heart still beating a little bit. Bobby put
her to the back of his mind as he headed home
in the cold and sun.

★   ★   ★

Maggie answered the door with a bright breezy
smile. Her dressing gown snug around hips that
had been curvy when she was younger, and were
now bulky under the silk. She carried a mug of
tea in her hand.

'Alright.'

'Hot water on, Mum?'

'It is, love. Where you been, out with a girl?'

'Sort of, yeah.'

'Not that Theresa, I hope?'

Bobby didn't know how his mum knew so
much. Everyone round here knew so much.

'Yeah, her.'

Maggie made a face.

'You can do a bit better than that, love.'

71

Bobby shrugged.

'Don't worry, Mum, I'm not gonna marry her.'

Maggie raised her eyebrows. 'You'll wanna tell her dad that?'

'Her dad doesn't have to know. Nothing to know.'

Bobby wanted to put Theresa to the back of his mind now. He knew his mum was right and it made him uneasy.

Maggie went to the kitchen and put the kettle on. At the click, she called out.

'He's a horrible bastard, Bobby. She's from a horrible lot of people. Don't be flirting with stupid trouble. If it doesn't need to be there, don't start looking for it.'

Bobby jogged up the stairs.

'Not a problem.'

He heard her still going.

'She's got half mad in her you know, and the half mad always comes out. You mark my words. You watch that half mad in her blood come out to play . . . '

Bobby left his mum talking and went straight to the bathroom. In the shower he let the water run hot, on the verge of scalding. With the strongest-smelling soap, he washed away every single trace of the day before and tipped his head back so that the water smacked his face.

On with his white T-shirt, his club tracksuit. Shiny and black. And his trainers: white and perfect. He messed up his hair. Wax and a footballer's nose blow in the bathroom sink and he was done. He looked up to the mirror and smiled.

He bowled out of the flat with a piece of toast, his mum blinking behind him as he clicked the door shut. He blew her his Saturday-morning kiss, and stepped out in the squealing, rattling baby-crying sounds of his estate, bursting to life. Geraniums on balconies and wheels on walls in the wind. Dogs and cats and Union Jacks and a smell of sour drains and laundry. Bicycles and washing lines, dishcloths and sheets, chequered and cream and blowing, blowing quietly in the middle of it all. And the dark bass from a bedroom.

Bobby walked through. All the time walking, never stopping, with his bag over his right shoulder, his shoulder blade straining underneath, and his eyes ahead.

As he walked by Theresa's he saw the yellow daffodils move, the blind shift to the left and her face appear at the window. Her left hand waved. He smiled. She pressed her naked chest to the window and watched him walk away. Bobby smiled again and walked on, and did not look back.

He'd give her a good cuddle later. Next week, after this fight. Keep the mad half of her quiet.

He wanted the gym. The gym was real. He ran for a bus, his heart pounding too hard. His breath was short. His Oyster was short. He paid his pounds and sat down. Right at the back. With his bag down, he put his hands on his lap, exhaled and looked out the window. His hands felt tight. His knuckles stiff. The row of bones on

73

his right hand were pinker than usual, underneath the hair. He wondered about that man, collapsed and alone in the toilet, if Vanessa had found him. He had to stop fucking up his hands before the fight. They'd be too stiff to pound Connor's jaw. His knee began to shake. Nervous and tired. At the lights, Bobby got off the bus and walked the rest of the way. He needed air. He needed to walk off the smell of that bedroom and the pain in his head. He looked over his shoulder, thinking he saw Denny at the betting shop. But it was another big man in a grey tweed coat and sideburns. He walked faster.

The club kept them civil. It made them friends. Outside it was different and Bobby had gone where he shouldn't. Best he could do was knock Connor out so hard in the fight he'd forget there was a war between them.

Bobby put his bag on his back and began to run. He ran through the streets, working up a new sweat by the time he was at the gym.

9

Bobby skipped quickly in the early morning
quiet of the gym before the younger boys started
piling in. Empty apart from a couple of trainers
and a faithful old heavyweight, Mo, who moped
around waiting to spar with anyone who needed
him.

Bobby skipped until his heart began racing
fast and his blood pumped hard. Staring at
himself in the mirror as he bounced on his feet.
He looked slow. He picked up the pace to feel it
burn. He was still fit enough to move through
the pain. His body broke through the tiredness
until it started looking sharp again.

He asked Mo to get in the ring and take shots
at his stomach, shoulders and jaw. A couple
rocked his head guard, but he stayed tall and
blocked most of the others. Then he let them in.
He began to sweat as he shifted and twisted at
each punch, taking them in the stomach.

'Harder, Mo.'

Mo hit deeper and Bobby felt the glove in his
organs. Mo was a low, dopey slugger, but they
could hurt if you didn't get out of the way.
Bobby didn't get out of the way. He stood in the
fury of them all. Straight in the middle of each
one.

The two carried on this way for several
minutes. Bobby curled up when it got too much
and Mo slowed down. Then Bobby moved his

arms away and raised his gloves and let Mo keep punching. Stomach and shoulder, stomach and shoulder. They kept coming and Bobby kept taking them and each time he did, he saw Connor standing in front of him, his scar ripe and pink under his head guard and his fists quick and dangerous. When his torso was red and beaten, Bobby moved back to the corner of the ring and leaned back on the ropes. Panting and in pain, he wanted to train every muscle to remember how to come back from a big hitter like Mo. He felt like his insides were on fire. 'Enough now.'

Mo grinned and cuffed Bobby around the side of his head with his glove.

'You took a few hard ones there, Rocky, you alright?'

Bobby nodded, out of breath. The good fighters could see Mo's punches coming. But he was good to spar with and Bobby needed a noisy, grunting heavyweight to build up his tolerance. If he could get ready to take some of Connor's big ones, he might be alright. He wondered where Connor was doing his training. Before a fight he used a different gym near his site. Denny liked it that way.

Derek walked in and blew his whistle.

'Who's been stinking out my gym this time of the morning?'

Bobby, still out of breath, lowered himself out of the ring and walked towards his trainer.

'Sort this out for me.'

Derek undid his gloves as Bobby felt a sickness rise to his throat.

'You alright?'

Bobby shook his head and tried to laugh.

'Nah, think I've gone and fucking winded myself.'

'You been sparring with Mo again?'

Bobby hung his gloves round his neck and nodded.

'You won't beat Connor by taking his knocks. It's a head game with you two.'

Bobby didn't want to think about it and went to get his bag.

'I know.'

He went towards the shower rooms, dripping with sweat. He'd just knocked open the door with his shoulder when he saw her out of the corner of his eye.

She was standing in the corridor, more beautiful than when he had first seen her, eyes bigger and blacker. Her hair, a little bit down, a little bit up, curled at her neck. Chloe smiled when she saw him, and her stare fixed on Bobby. He felt embarrassed. This was the second time she'd seen him in need of a wash. She was in jeans and a dark grey T-shirt, her hair tied up and silver bracelets on each small wrist. Clean and fresh, and warm from the sun. He could smell it on her.

'Bobby?'

Straight to the bull's eye of each black pupil, seeing the other in the shine of their eyes.

'I was just about to go and clean up. I'm a mess.'

Bobby was also in pain. He needed to wash up and sit quietly and let his body get over Mo's punches.

Chloe turned her head to the side. She nodded to the corridor.

'Devlin's just getting changed.' She smiled and Bobby saw there was a tooth sharper than the others like a fang and he realised how easy it could be to fall in love with all the little parts of someone.

'You aren't going yet, are you? Mind if I have a shower and come back and buy you a cup of tea?'

Chloe shrugged. 'I don't mind you looking like that. It doesn't bother me.' She turned away, shy.

Bobby heard his phone go in his bag, rumbling on vibrate. He rubbed a hand across his sweaty face and hoped again that he didn't smell as bad as he thought. Next to her he felt ugly. Too big and battered to be near someone as pristine as her.

He pushed back the curls in his eyes with sweat on his hands. Then Bobby motioned to the coffee machine. Quiet now, without the children smacking it.

Chloe nodded. She watched him walk, each stride at ease in his body.

'Wait here.'

He took change from the pocket of his jacket and put his bag down. He set the gloves down on a chair. Chloe sat next to them.

Bobby went to the machine. He fumbled with his change, dropping coins on the floor. When he picked them up he ached and breathed through the hurt that reeled in his body. Two PG Tips in plastic. The tea gurgled its way to the top.

She had sat down on a table by the window.

Bobby took his phone out of his pocket. One message: Theresa. He put the phone back in his pocket and took the teas over to Chloe.

His hands began to burn holding the plastic cups of stewed tea. Bobby didn't know how the tea came out old every time. It was just hot water and a new tea bag, but it always tasted sour and rotten.

He threw down some sachets of sugar. Chloe took her tea, and he could see her hands were shaking slightly.

'It's okay, I don't take sugar. Thank you.'

'Wasn't sure.'

'Thank you for thinking.'

Bobby felt unusually shy, self-conscious. He realised he'd never really sat down like this with a girl before. Not in broad daylight. Not face to face like this, with eyes and smiles. Not with one who spoke so gently either. He was suddenly aware of his hands, and didn't want her to see his scrapes. He didn't want her to think he was an animal.

He watched her teeth bite her lower lip. That wolfish tooth on the left side of her mouth.

Bobby put three sugars in his tea. He only needed one. He kept stirring it round. He'd spent so long growling and nodding and listening to bullshit, he'd forgotten how to have a conversation. He shook his head. Unable to find words, Chloe tapped her right hand on the table, a ring on her middle finger, with the emeralds and the white gold.

Bobby could tell Chloe had seen the lovebite, a savage little tear on his neck. She was looking at it when he sat down and he wanted to cover it up. The telltale mark. His hands had been in and over Theresa's body and he was embarrassed about them.

There was a small silence. A pause as both tried to think about what to say. They both sipped their tea, too hot in their mouths and on the tongue, to give them something to do in a room gone quiet.

The howling of boys could be heard as they raced to win, muffled as punchbags, from gymnasium rooms across and down corridors. Occasionally, a big booming voice, Derek's, would tell them what to do. But Chloe didn't hear what it was he instructed.

'When you see Devlin, will you sort of, you know, look after him a bit? But in a way that doesn't make him look like he's the weak one.'

Bobby was pleased she'd asked him a question.

'He doesn't really know anyone here.'

'Who is he anyway?'

'We have a neighbour, Fiona, who works a lot. We've been babysitting her kids since we were thirteen. She helped us arrange the funeral when my mum died. We help her now.'

Bobby didn't know how to talk about death. He could watch a man's head get stamped on and a glass-shattering, neck-breaking car crash, but Bobby could not do death. Draining the last bit of tea, he kept his eyes on the cup. Bobby had only once seen a body; he was twelve. He didn't know if it was dead or not. By the side of the canal, smashed and smashed again, there was a lot of blood. Bobby had called an ambulance from a phone box hidden in the dark, and walked away. Stepping in a puddle so he didn't tread red footprints on the way home.

Bobby could take that. He could take seeing a body that had been in a fight. Watching a man's face slip on one side after a hit or a body go down unconscious was okay. Bobby understood the language, he knew everything would heal. But when Mikey's brother had died, walking in front of a lorry, drunk, Bobby had only been able to mind his own business. Death was not his currency.

'I'm sorry about your mum.'

It was all he could say and he hated that he didn't have words that were good enough for this.

'Thank you.'

Another silence. Chloe drummed her right hand and her green-gold ring on the plastic, marble-effect table.

He needed to give her more.

'How'd it happen?'

'She had a heart attack. A big one that killed her there and then.'

'When?'

She blew on her tea.

'A few weeks ago. I don't think it hurt her for more than a second.' Chloe sighed. 'We didn't really understand it. She smoked a lot, but she wasn't, you know, unhealthy. She was tiny, actually. But she wouldn't have told us if she was ill. She ignored herself in that way.'

Bobby nodded. He wanted Chloe to stop

talking about death. But she didn't. She spoke with ease and intimacy.

'It's funny the things you do when you're sad. I went and tried on all her dresses the other day. My sister can't fit into them. So now they're all in my wardrobe.'

Without knowing what words to use, Bobby felt a need to hold her right hand in his. He couldn't quite get there, and instead touched her knuckles with the fingers of his left hand, warm from where he'd held the cup of tea. He touched her lightly and let go again.

'Sorry.'

Chloe said what she had said to so many since it happened.

'It's okay. Really it was the best thing. It was a quick big one that took her in the moment. If she'd recovered she wouldn't be herself. She'd need looking after forever and we weren't going to be able to do that.'

He struggled again to find words that would help her. He wanted to get to know this girl, this Chloe. She had lived a life Bobby didn't understand. One where people died. And she had that look in her eyes which bore into him and made him feel like he wanted something good, for once.

He tried again to hold her hand, and put his little finger on her small, white knuckles. He touched the gold ring with the tip of his little finger; then let go and put both hands on his empty cup.

Chloe breathed in deeply. Bobby thought what the world would be like without Maggie and found he could not think of a world without his mum.

'So. Tell me about the fight?' she said, lifting the mood.

Bobby grinned and the lines around his eyes crinkled. Girls always wanted to know. Everyone wanted to know.

'The North East Divisions. All the amateurs from round here compete. Different clubs. I got to fight someone from Clapton because we're the only two in our weight.'

'So you have to fight someone from here? Who?'

'He's called Connor. He's come here since he was a kid. Like me.'

Chloe grinned. 'Who's better?'

Bobby scratched his head.

The question made his gut turn. They'd won and lost about the same.

'Me.'

'And why are you better?' She spoke with her stare. She spoke straight.

Bobby met her gaze. 'Because I know I'm going to win.'

Bobby winked and broke the glare between them.

Chloe put her hands up and made two little balls with her fists.

'I could never hit someone, I don't think.'

She made Bobby laugh.

'You would if they hit you first.'

She put her hands back on the cup of tea.

Bobby stood up. He could have a shower later. It wouldn't hurt him to train a bit more. 'Shall

83

we go and check on Devlin?'

She seemed happy as she scraped back her chair and stood up. Wiping his palms down on his tracksuit, he felt something ripple inside him, nerves or excitement, he didn't know. The day was bright through the window. The day was bright because of her.

Chloe had to look up at him as he walked her down the corridor to the gym they'd met in, listening to him tell her about the day he'd first walked into the club. Though he'd walked down here hundreds of times, today he felt dazzled by the heat of the place and found it hard to focus.

'My dad took me when I was old enough. My granddad went here too.'

Chloe looked at all the photographs as they walked.

'I can't find you here.'

'You won't.'

'Why not?'

'It's a mug shot, isn't it? Anyone can walk in and see me up there and point me out to anyone they want.'

Bobby picked up his pace a little bit and Chloe hung back.

'You know, if I ever got in trouble.'

He laughed.

'I'm joking. I'm on some of the posters in the gym. They framed me by the trophies.'

He liked telling her that. He was their trophy boy and they'd put him in a special place. Chloe was silent, though he turned back to see her smiling.

'Where is he? The one you're going to fight?'

Bobby looked at the wall of photos. He knew where Connor was. Top left. 1994. He knew because he was in it too, next to him. Two ten-year-olds with their gloves up and elbows in.

Bobby pointed it out.

They were both grinning for the camera. Bobby had a black eye and Connor a shaved head. They both wore white cotton vests and black shorts. Both big for their age, they stood with sweet menace, sharing a secret. The way young angry boys could stand when they had a place to take their anger out.

Chloe stared up. She put her hand to it and moved her fingers around Bobby's face that had none of the jaw and stare and toughness of him now.

'You both look so *sweet*.'

Bobby put a hand on the small of her back and moved her away, gently. She turned round to look at the photograph again.

'It must be hard fighting someone you've grown up with.'

He was walking away. The photograph was from another time and Bobby had moved on.

10

The canal attracted strays. The black ribbon that tied everyone together. Tonight it looked after Joe. He cut a lonely figure at night, which was when he liked to go. The buzz of people going out and coming back and all the time he stayed still.

From the Blitz to the gang wars, this canal had seen it all. It had kept company with all the hookers and dealers and deadbeat mad-eyed, yellow-toothed crackheads. Its arches had been hideaways for the homeless and sick. And it had been a friend to Joe. A long, loyal friend. It had kept its banks lush and wild, the swans and ducks coming back and the swanky barges cruising up and down. He laughed at them as they moved slowly past, living their lives on old, London sin. The dirty muck of London underneath them as they slept; the ghosts of the canal whistling to their ears. It sat in its own special gloom. Its own graveyard, ribs and teeth buried below. Black and secret. Hushed, peculiar. In this dark, two men sat opposite Joe, their heads turned towards each other, muttering. But Joe could not hear them, and they were only blots by the bank.

Joe sat on an upturned crate. His old fishing line on the floor and his hands on his lap. Not drinking tonight. He would if he could, but he couldn't afford to. Joe's eyes looked into the shiny water and could see nothing. He stuck on a cassette in an old Walkman he'd always had and pressed play on Beethoven. Boxing and Beethoven: Joe was always a bit better; a bit different. It's how he'd got Maggie.

He'd taken Maggie here, all those years ago. Just the two of them, sitting in spring sunshine, full of bloom. Their first few dates had been near here, having two drinks in the Park Hotel Pub, and cradling each other as they walked down under the bridge, to their spot.

If he was lucky he caught something. Thick, black eels weaved along the edges of the banks, under the water, through the moss and crap. Once Joe and Frank had picked up a couple of them.

'Look at the teeth on that! It's a fucking anaconda.'

Laughing as Joe grabbed it by the throat and watched it struggle. It struggled until the end. They'd cut it in half and the thing had pulsed on, fighting for life even when it was just cut up in four thick blocks. The head moved the most, spitting that it would not die.

'How you gonna cook that, then? Couple of onions and butter?'

Joe had laughed.

'I ain't eating that. Would you eat something that come out of there?'

Frank had shrugged.

'Dunno. Once you fry it, food's food.'

'You'll get cancer eating that. Anything that's come out of there is rot.'

'We could take it down Angel. See if the pie

and mash shop'll have it?'

'You can't eat this junk.'

Joe had kicked each piece of the dying eel back into the canal, chipping each bit back to the water.

He'd seen a carp, but no bodies. Not yet. He'd heard stories of them slipping down the canal and getting caught on the locks. He'd heard of prostitutes being cut up, like this eel, and found in bags. But he'd not seen one. And he hadn't seen any prostitutes either since the dank, canal strip had been cleaned up a good fifteen years ago. The glue sniffers too; they had wandered to the big park, finding new corners to twitch and get beaten up in by boys off the local estate. Boys like his son. Boys like Bobby. Drugs changed. Places changed. The boys changed.

Once they'd drained the canal, black oil stuck to the sides and turned to quicksand. Bobby and Mikey had thrown injured pigeons into it, just to watch them sink. Joe had watched, wincing from the bridge to see his son so cruel and told them both off even though he remembered stoning pigeons on the pavement years ago. He didn't know if he was proud of the son he'd raised or sad. He supposed he was proud. He was a strong boy and, deep down, Joe knew he was a good boy. They weren't bad bones that held Bobby together.

Always at night, frightened of very little in his old age, he enjoyed soaking up this black stuff. This storytelling water. Joe took out his earphones to enjoy the silence, his hands a little shaky.

There was the sound of heels clicking down the stone canal bank. A girl. Joe turned and looked to his left; through the fog he could see no face. No eyes. Just shape. She was small and maybe blonde, but it was hard to tell either way. She would have blended into the night silently if it weren't for her shoes.

The men coughed, and in the dark it made fog and noise. She was getting closer. Joe kept his eyes on the canal. He wasn't sure what kind of woman walked under the bridge at this time of night. He didn't want to help people, and he didn't want to be helped.

The clicking heels stopped.

'Excuse me, got a light?'

Without bothering to look up, Joe smiled and the wrinkles on his old face deepened around his dark eyes. He glanced only at the girl and kept them to the ground, hardly taking her in at all. Joe knew best. Never look at a woman when she's on her own; they didn't like it. He put his right hand into the breast pocket of his green parka coat and felt for his lighter. He took it out with the same tired smile and held up a small flame, still with his eyes away from her stare. She bent and leaned down to spark up and he couldn't resist a quick look. In the dim flame-light, Joe saw her.

Little Theresa.

'What you doing here at this hour?'

'Shit, Joe. Didn't know it was you.'

'Your dad know you're walking around so late?'

Theresa tugged on her cigarette and blew into the cold.

'I'm just coming home from a few drinks.'

'And you're taking this way home?'

He could smell the spirits coming off her hair, her breath and skin.

'It's a way home.'

Joe shook his head at her. 'It's a bad way home.'

Joe had known Theresa, just as Bobby had, since she was a little girl. She'd always stayed little. A tiny little girl-woman.

'And in what you're wearing . . . '

Joe had worked with Denny, moons ago, sifting yards to pick up valuables and sharing their profits. Both young, fit and cunning, they'd used each other wisely. Until Denny had been out of turn with Maggie, following her into a toilet and scaring her in the dark as she turned around and saw his big bulk of a body leaning by the door. He had made it hard for her to leave. He said he never knew she was with Joe. Maggie had never liked Denny, even before he'd made a pass at her. She said she hated the way those travellers talked to you. Like they were barking dogs, she'd said. Talked at you rather than to you. Joe and Denny had given each other a hiding in front of everyone in the pub. Two different kind of men fighting the only way they knew. A brawler and a boxer, bashing each other until Denny limped away. Joe had made Denny a local bogeyman for a few weeks. Children and women crossed the road to avoid him, looking away instead of at his ugly head. For years there had been man-to-man

90

handshakes and more drunken punch-ups as they circled each other around the manor.

Now here was Denny again, closer than ever. Joe was messing with Daphne and Bobby was messing with his daughter. Denny had ignored Theresa until she turned sixteen and he saw he had a pretty girl that seemed to be getting a lot of attention in the pub. Then Denny felt he had to pay attention too.

'You gonna let her dance with the fella like that, Denny?'

Denny would say it was the non-traveller part of her that was slutting herself about. He'd shout at Daphne in the street, telling her to stop buying Theresa the clothes and make-up and to keep her indoors. He made no secret Theresa was a mistake.

Didn't matter how like strangers they were now, Joe and Bobby kept bumping into all sorts of trouble just the same. Joe could see why his son went with Theresa. She had a way. A skinny swagger and a hard face, but it was a beautiful hard face. There was a reason Bobby found it hard to leave her alone.

'Give us a fag would you, Theresa?'

He had tobacco, but he had been finding it hard to roll one with his shaky hands.

'Hold on.'

He looked her up and down. The mottled pink skin of her thighs and the polished bones of her shins. All wrapped up in a tiny denim skirt and ankle boots studded with huge skyscraper heels that propped her up another three or four inches. The black leather jacket zipped up to the collar. Joe had time to see her thick, black false lashes blink slowly before the flame went out.

'How's my mum?'

Joe didn't know. He hadn't seen Daphne for a few days. They'd had a little bit of dinner at the weekend and then she'd moaned that her muscles were hurting and that she was getting a spot of tummy trouble. She said it was all the pickled beetroot she'd been eating.

'Not sure, love. She was alright last time I seen her.'

Theresa shook her head.

'Flesh and blood, Theresa.'

She threw her fag end in the canal. Joe smiled again, happy to stay quiet.

She looked up and blew her smoke out. 'Where's Bobby?'

'He'll be somewhere. His mum rang me to see if I was coming to his fight.'

'You wouldn't miss that.'

''Course not. Neither would you.'

A silence before Joe spoke again.

'His mum was warning me not to do anything to upset him. Said he's getting his life together. He's got a date with some nice girl. It's got Maggie all excited.' Joe laughed in the dark.

But Theresa was quiet, looking at the water. When she spoke it was soft, almost a whisper.

'With who?'

Joe could feel her hurt and shook his head.

'You could have someone good, Theresa. You're a good girl, those aren't your choices. Leave this place and find someone not like the rest of them.'

'You don't think Bobby's better?'

Joe shrugged. 'He's just better looking.'

Theresa sniffed and stared at the water. Not moving, and saying nothing. She began to sway slightly. She looked hard into the canal for a few more seconds, frozen, cold and silent.

'You've went and made your world too small. All you got to do is leave here. It's all anyone needs to do and no one does.'

'And go where?'

Joe laughed. His voice sore. 'A fucking mile. Two miles. Get on a coach and fuck off somewhere. You're knocking two boys' heads together, and for what?'

She played with her hair extensions. Curling them in her fingers to make sure they didn't tangle up. She spoke so softly, almost to herself.

'I can't just leave.'

Joe shrugged.

'He pays your bread and butter, doesn't he? Your dad?'

Theresa stared at the canal. She hesitated.

'When I was young, I heard your name batted about so much. It was always you on my dad's nerves, always you and him stepping in each other's corners. A proper loud, flash bastard, always making drama with my dad.' She looked at Joe to make sure he was listening. 'Bobby walked straight into all of it.'

'What you mean?'

'You and my dad brought me and Bobby together.'

Joe coughed and spat phlegm. He looked out into the dark, his eyelid tucked into its craggy scar.

'Two shadows, eh?'

They both felt the chill in the night and Joe shifted on his crate as Theresa wrapped her jacket tighter around her little body.

Joe laughed. Theresa didn't say anything, moving her foot and bending her heel back and forth until it looked like it would snap from the sole of her shoe.

'He's not the answer, Theresa. You know that, don't you?'

She shook her head.

'Who's looking for answers?'

Joe coughed and felt cold.

'You ever hold my mum's hand?'

Joe sighed. 'I dunno. Probably I do. I must hold her hand sometimes. That's what you're looking for?'

Joe felt a sudden sadness for Theresa. A skinny little fighter in her own strange war.

She spat and her head spun round, out of the dream, back to the night. 'Not looking for anything.'

'You're two shadows, like you say.'

She lowered her voice again. 'No, you said that.'

Joe would have got up if he could. He would have held her and told her it would be okay.

'The world isn't just Bobby and Connor, you know.'

She was looking in her handbag. She didn't want to answer him, she'd said too much. She took a cigarette out of her box. 'I'm drunk. Forget it.'

Joe tried to get up. 'Let me walk you back home.'

Theresa looked through her bag, taking out three cigarettes. She handed them to Joe.

'I'm fine.'

He smiled.

'I'll see you at the fight.'

'Yeah, yeah.' As she turned she muttered. 'Fucking old drunk.'

Just loud enough for Joe to hear.

She turned on those high heels. Walking quickly back the way she'd come, to wherever she'd been before. All Joe could see was the light of her phone guiding her like a torch, in the canal's black tunnel. And across the water the men went from muttering to talking. And now Joe could hear them.

'There she is. Up and down like she has no home. Like Denny doesn't give her enough pocket money to stay indoors.'

The men were travellers. Joe kept his head down, and put Beethoven back on. He kept quiet and sat back in the night, before struggling to pick up his crate and grab his line, his aching, wobbling legs finding it hard. He headed in the opposite direction to Theresa. Towards the cemetery, towards the red of the turning traffic lights. He'd tried to tell her what these men were like. What he was like. He threw the line into the canal. There was nothing to be caught there anyway.

11

Bobby was nervous. Three days before the fight and he was waltzing about on a date with a girl. He was going out for a drink with Chloe.

The beer on his bedside table was getting warmer every time he sipped it, as he looked through his wardrobe, worrying about what he was going to wear. He knew he shouldn't be drinking, but he had to. So much harm already done to this fight. He told himself he would train harder and faster tomorrow, but he knew it didn't work like that and he knew he'd fucked it up.

Shirts were for weddings and funerals. He wasn't some boy from Milton Keynes out on a Friday night to Equinox; he was Bobby. Bobby-Bobby. London-born, big smoke, big streets, big men.

Laid out on the bed was his outfit. A pair of dark jeans and a dark jumper. Navy and soft. He'd decided, after they had stood, arms touching, watching Devlin fall down and get up again in the gym, that he wanted to take her out. Standing next to her, watching the vein beating close to her collarbone, he knew he wanted to see more of Chloe. He'd had the balls to ask her, as he showed her round the club.

Bobby stood in the middle of his room in his pants. This was too difficult. Parties were easier, when you looked at a girl at the start of the night, and she looked back at you, and you knew it was on. It was just about waiting for that hour. The drunken hour. When all the chemicals of the night bubbled up to your brain and balls and you got what you needed. Girls you didn't want to see again.

Girls happened to Bobby. They met him and found their way in.

Maggie hovered outside on the landing.

'Mum. Get us another beer from the fridge, please.'

Maggie's feet moved down the stairs. He heard her open it for him when she walked back across the landing.

Her head popped round the door.

'I hope you don't drink more than this tonight. You'll not be right for your fight, you know.' She started to laugh when she saw Bobby standing in his pants.

'I hope you're going to wear a little bit more than that?'

Bobby was too nervous to say anything. He looked at the clothes on his bed.

'This dressed up enough?'

Maggie went back down the landing, still laughing and muttering to herself. 'It's fine!'

He swallowed from the can and felt it in his guts, bringing him back into the world.

Some box-fresh boots. Everything had to look like he didn't walk in the same gutter as the rest of the world. Aftershave-fragrant, with his mum's laundering. That's how he had to step out.

His face looked polished, freshly shaved and shining with aftershave balm and lotion. The curl in his hair waxed and pushed out of his eyes.

'Mum, another beer please.'

'No. That's enough.'

'It is just a beer.'

He had a half-hour before he had to go and pick her up and he needed a couple for courage, but he was being careful not to get too drunk. He had asked his mum where to take her.

'Take her somewhere nice but not too nice.'

Bobby had said that wasn't helpful.

'Your dad used to take me dancing. Why don't you take her dancing? Soho or something like that. Somewhere fun.'

'Soho isn't like it was when you went dancing there.'

Maggie carried on. 'How about a pub then? Simple pub for a few drinks. But you don't have any. She'll understand why.'

His mum had always kept it simple. Too simple. She did herself down. Bobby knew you could teach yourself anything. That had been his mum's life: knowing her place. He had felt sad for her then, and given her a little squeeze.

In the end he'd gone for a pub that served dips and pitta and fake cockney muck like jellied eels and pickled eggs. It was posh-ish, but it was still a pub.

He'd get a minicab to hers. He could get her to come out of her door then and be ready so he could drive them both off. Or the Moroccan behind the wheel could.

He got out his phone and started typing out that he'd be with her in twenty minutes. Once he'd sent it he wished he hadn't. Because it

98

sounded keen, and he'd done kisses, which made him look like a boy.

So he rang her.

She picked up after two rings.

'I was just texting you back.'

Bobby's voice had got thin. He had to take a breath before he spoke.

'Just ringing to say I'll pick you up in twenty. You'll be ready, yeah?'

He was being too cool. Too hard on the phone. He hadn't even asked how she was.

'I was texting you back to say I'll see you then. I'll be ready.'

There was silence.

'I'll see you in about twenty minutes.'

'About fifteen now.'

Bobby didn't laugh.

'Bye, Bobby.'

'Bye.'

Then she'd hung up and Bobby was left with his mouth to the phone. He blinked it all away, took a deep breath, a sip of his beer. He asked his mum if he could have a cigarette in the kitchen.

'Yes, but only with the window wide open.'

They sat opposite each other with a pot of tea between them and Bobby's half-empty beer on his right. The kitchen was spotless with white scrubbed tiles and bleach fumes steaming from the floors, the kitchen surfaces and the sink. The silver toaster squashed them in its reflection and the washing drying on racks and radiators around the flat gave the room a smell of fresh linen.

On evenings like this, Bobby wanted to stay in with his mum. It was calm.

She was in her jeans and a jumper; her hair pulled to each side with combs. Maggie still dyed her hair a bright platinum blonde. As long as Bobby had known his mum, she wasn't sure what her real hair colour was. She poured two mugs of steaming tea and stared at her son.

'Who is she then? She must be special to make you drink again. And smoke. Is she good enough to wreck your body for?'

Bobby exhaled, turning his head away from his mum so the smoke didn't go in her face.

'Girl I met down the gym.'

'What she do?'

'Dunno. Grieving at the minute. She just lost her mum.'

Maggie tilted her head and pursed her lips. She made a hissing sound and shook her head.

'Poor girl. You be careful.'

Bobby reached for his tea but wanted his beer. 'Why do I have to be careful?'

'She'll be soft.'

'She doesn't seem soft to me.'

'Soft. Raw. Be careful.'

'Don't know what you mean.'

'When I lost my dad, I didn't know what I was doing for a bit. It's like you're in a very bad dream. Why I went and got pregnant so quick.'

There was regret now, but the wedding day picture still stood on a shelf in the sitting room, in a frame. Maggie hardly ever opened up and Bobby felt awkward listening to her talk about her own feelings.

'You saying she's going for a drink with me because she isn't thinking right?'

'No, I'm just saying you should walk carefully around each other.'

Bobby reached for his beer and finished it in a few big glugs. The taxi rang his mobile.

'Am off, Mum.'

She winked at him and he left her sitting there, still a beauty in middle age, with the humming fridge and fresh air from the kitchen window. He winked back, bursting with a son's love. She had her paper in front of her, and she reached for it when he was gone.

As he was going to the car, Bobby saw Theresa walk by. He had sent a half-arsed reply to a message she sent him. But he had kept forgetting to call her back, forgetting, because he didn't want to call her back, because this easy fucking was getting him into trouble. News of the fight by the canal had spread, shared in conversations over a few days and now everyone knew the reason behind it. His mum had heard people talking in the shops. Mikey heard the talk in the pubs. And their upcoming fight took on a different edge.

'They want to hurt you a lot, Bobby.'

Bobby didn't care. He knew he was better. Being better always made people talk. There was no need to be scared in the ring if you were better. You were trained to fight. There was art and style to it. You didn't just make someone bleed. Bobby would balance it all out. He was annoyed that talk was making this a fight over Theresa, though. She wasn't worth fighting over.

But she was waiting up for him. She'd spent the best part of the afternoon walking up and down his bit of the estate. Her head was turned to his kitchen window and, although she was in a tracksuit, she had her hair straightened like she was going out, her lashes thick and false.

She raised an eyebrow when she saw him.

'You look well.'

Then to the car.

'Taxi?'

Bobby played it as cool as he could. It was none of her business.

'Just off out. Meeting a mate for a drink.'

'In a taxi. Must be far away. Where does he live?'

To any other girl, Bobby would have told her to mind her own.

'Highbury.'

'You back tonight?'

Bobby shrugged. He hated living on this estate. Everything was everyone's business.

'Theresa, slow down, yeah? You're asking too many questions.'

Theresa took the telling-off calmly. Again she nodded, trying to look into Bobby's eyes.

Bobby had the door of the car open now.

'So you definitely aren't coming back round this way later?'

'Not sure.'

He'd given her a small something, a glimmer of hope, and she was pleased with that. She smiled.

'You know where I'll be.'

And as he got into the car, he heard her say:

'It's never too late to wake me up.'

He slammed the taxi door shut on her voice.

He hated living on doorsteps and in pockets and around the lives of so many others.

The cab drove off and Bobby didn't bother looking behind him. Through the back window, as the sun was setting, Theresa would be watching. Her head at a tilt and her face in a scowl that would turn into a sideways smile. Her hands gripping, pulling, playing onto the sides of her top as she looked at him leaving her again.

12

The pub was done out in dark, pansy-covered wallpaper with stags' heads hanging on the paint-cracked turquoise walls. Dripping, lop-sided candles and jars of pickled eggs and pork scratchings sat on the bar. Bobby didn't like it. The beer was expensive. But he'd chosen it because it was a little bit fancy and out of the way.

Pulling up outside her home he'd thought about her getting ready inside. Nervous, he'd asked the driver to go round the block two times before finally parking and knocking on her door. He glanced at the upstairs window and saw a girl's face that wasn't Chloe's look down at him.

When she opened the door, Chloe wore a black dress with pink flowers, slim at the waist, skirting out a little. It stopped just above the knee. When he'd held the minicab door open for her he saw the shape of her hips in that dress. She was wearing black tights and black heels. As they stood next to each other in the pub, he noticed her eyes were lighter with creamy liner around them. They smudged as the pub got hotter, as she drank more. Honey in black, they stunned Bobby into a brand new shyness. Her nails were as pink as the flowers on her dress and Bobby thought she hadn't needed to do that; hadn't needed to paint herself up so much.

He felt the same knotted-up thrill he got when

he stood in the ring, when he knew he would win. Except this night was softer and kinder. He only had to be here, he was free from his fights. Bobby could stay still with Chloe; she had nothing to do with history. This was the beginning.

They talked about his boxing to start with. It seemed like a good place to start. He told her about the difference between a fight in the ring and a fight outside it: a real fight.

'There's respect in the ring. A kind of love between you, like you want to hurt someone you love. I can't explain it. You're together but you're not.'

Chloe nodded. She didn't understand what he meant, but it kept her interested. She looked at his strong, worn hands, on show even when he sat down. He seemed aware of them, stretching his fingers and balling them into fists as he spoke, his knuckles flattened from the punches they'd thrown. She listened to stories of bodies getting broken and coming back alive and angry. No one died; they lived on and fought on, round after round. In the ring there was life.

She thought of home.

'Our dad used to have the boxing on sometimes, but never too loud, my mum never liked it.'

Bobby couldn't think of a reply good enough when she mentioned her mum, and he held his right hand up, rotating his wrist. 'It ruins your hands.'

Chloe looked at them again, the nails cut short on each finger and thumb. She put her own hands up and Bobby thought she was going to touch him and was worried his palms were sweating. But she brushed hair away behind her ear and put them back in her lap.

He laughed. 'Ruins a face too. I used to be pretty.'

'Your face isn't ruined, there's not too much damage done.'

Bobby looked down, shy, he could feel a redness. A shame at his body in front of her. She saw his rough fingers touch the ridged bridge of his nose. She smiled, lightly.

'My mum used to beg my dad to turn it over, said she could never understand it.'

These men, Lynn would shake her head, leaving Chloe on the sofa, hypnotised by the guts and glamour of each round.

'He loved his boxing. He loved all sports, even though Mum would tell him it wasn't.'

'Wasn't what?'

'A sport.'

She crossed her legs and Bobby looked at her left ankle, tiny and coltish. She went quiet, thinking of something to say and Bobby tilted his head to get a better look at her.

'What do you think it is?'

Chloe could feel his eyes were on her when she looked down.

'Boxing is boxing.'

'You ever seen a street fight?'

'Not since school.'

Bobby laughed. 'Not in the playground. A proper one.'

He hadn't meant to make her feel stupid, and

as soon as he saw her look down, he felt bad. He didn't want to preach violence.

'I mean one where people had no one there to break them up.'

Chloe looked back up calmly, her voice suddenly a lot colder. He had made her feel like a child and she wasn't.

'Are you asking if I have seen fights or if I have seen people hurting?'

He had made a mistake; already Bobby was fucking up, right at the start. Bobby was embarrassed, jittery. He wiped his hands on his jeans. Her eyes still watching, waiting for an answer.

'I don't know.'

Chloe had flushed pink. Angry, maybe. Or a cider-bloom had started to creep over her cheeks. This was her second pint.

He needed to change the conversation.

She glanced at him from over her cider glass, her eyes catching him in full focus before starting to sip at it.

Bobby's right eye throbbed. Tired, excited. He wasn't sure.

'Want another drink?'

He had drained his. He'd been trying to pace himself but had finished his pint fast. Slow down, Bobby. He knew how he got. He wanted to avoid the trigger pint, the one that turned him.

Chloe shook her head, still holding the half-full glass in her hands. 'I'm still working on this one, but thanks.'

The way she was looking at him made him

want to grab her and kiss her. But he couldn't. She was too far away. He wanted to pull her body near and touch her polished hair. Straight down tonight, iron-flat and shining.

He stayed looking at his empty pint glass. The place was getting busier, noisier. A couple of men in suits hovered over their table and, seeing the space on the sofa next to Chloe, one of them asked Bobby if he wouldn't mind giving up his seat so that they could sit down.

The man wore a cream linen blazer and a blue shirt. Bobby moved over to the sofa and sat, trying to find ways to place his body and look comfortable. Chloe angled her body to him a little bit more, her crossed legs wrapping her up.

They were closer to each other now. Bobby could smell himself: cigarettes mixed with Lynx and Armani.

And they smiled together. Shy to see their knees touching. She put her hand on his arm and left it there.

'Are you going to get another drink?'

His eyes locked on to hers. Pace yourself, Bobby.

'Not yet.'

She put hers down.

'So, what do you do now, then?' he asked.

Chloe looked at the floor.

'Well, before it happened, before she went, I was a classroom assistant in a primary school. Saint Augustine's, do you know it?'

Bobby shook his head.

'I'll go back when I'm ready. Kids know when you are weak. They can sense it, you know?'

She put her hands in her lap.

'My sister asked if I wanted to help her.'

'Doing what?'

Chloe rolled her eyes.

'She stands outside clubs and hands out flyers in a dress.'

'She like a model, then?'

Bobby had slept with a girl who called herself a model. But all she did was stand around Ferraris in a pair of knickers smiling with her big hair extensions and La Senza tits. She never got into it in bed, either. She'd perch on top of him, arching her back and porn-starring herself up. Playing with her horsehair extensions; flicking them around his face and stinking of pigskin fake tan.

'No. Not really. She's really pretty though.'

Bobby thought he might as well say it. It rolled off his tongue. 'You could be a model.'

He didn't really think she could. She was better than a model. She had a glow about her. She crackled black and gold, and she looked him in the eye with a cold look that licked Bobby's bones clean.

'I couldn't, but thanks,' Chloe said, smiling.

'It probably isn't much of a life anyway.' Bobby chewed on his lip.

She looked away and finished her drink.

He took a risk and put a hand on her knee. In the same way he'd brushed her fingers in the gym canteen, he did it softly. When he did, he stirred at the way she looked up at him, straight into his eyes. She had a grip on him, a spell that held him in awkward moments he couldn't get out of. He wanted to kiss the bony part near her ear and the tip of her nose. Chloe let out a sigh — bored, awkward, or tired, he couldn't tell. Stuck for words and with that moment slipping away, Bobby pulled his hands back.

The pub was packed full now. Bobby could feel his back sweating up. He'd waited a bit; he'd be alright sipping another one slowly.

'Another?'

Chloe looked up at him with her big smudged eyes and nodded. Then she smiled and her whole face lit up, and Bobby felt an electrical impulse course through him, so strong he needed to stand up and shake her off for a second.

That's what she was like. Like one of those poster girls in the Indian shops on Brick Lane. Petite and big-eyed. When he stood up in the heat and chatter, his eyes felt hot and his body moved too quickly for the rest of him. He mumbled a couple of pardons and put his hand on the waists of a few women as he passed them, squeezing shoulders and arms. He wasn't trying to feel them up, it was just instinctive to Bobby: to put his hands where he shouldn't; to put his hands where he liked. They moved out of the way immediately, jerking away from a strange man's touch.

At the bar he stopped himself getting a round of shots. Each one would tear up his body, would make his arm slow. His punches soft. He would suffer in the ring on Saturday night. He waited his turn to order, pushing the feeling away.

He looked back. Chloe was playing with the strands of hair that had fallen from her topknot.

'Two of them.'

Bobby pointed at the pump.

He looked behind him again. Some man was leaning over and talking to Chloe. An office type. Full of beer and bullshit. Chloe was looking up, but Bobby was happy to see her leaning away from him.

The women he'd brushed his hand against smiled as he walked through again and let him pass. Men let him pass too. Because Bobby was Bobby. Because Bobby looked the way he did. People let Bobby have room.

The man was still hovering over Chloe when he got back to her.

'Was just saying to your lovely friend that a friend of mine runs this pub, which is handy because our offices are just there. Across the road.'

Bobby smiled thinly. 'Good to know.'

The man smiled. He knew his time was up. 'Nice to meet you.' He put a hand out.

Chloe looked up and shook his hand when he offered it. When he was gone she turned back to Bobby and made a face.

'They never know when they're not welcome, do they, those sorts of men.' She grinned to make him feel better and Bobby tried to smile back. He didn't know why he minded so much. The fact that the man was well spoken, maybe; that he hadn't cared enough when Bobby returned to fuck off back to his friends. Maybe it was because Bobby wanted to be the only one to have discovered Chloe; to have found her in the middle of all this chaos, when the world was

111

flinging out all sorts to pick and choose from. Bobby realised then that he was not the only one to see how beautiful Chloe was and he put his hand on her leg again as she turned to him. Not hard, but firm and strong. He sat closer to her and he felt her lean into his body.

Trying to get himself back, to feel like a man again, he said something he thought would impress her. He would ask her to the fight. He didn't normally like girls going but she wasn't like other girls. She wasn't there waiting for blood or other boys to notice her, she'd be there for him.

'What you doing Saturday night?'

Chloe smiled.

'I would love to.'

'You don't know what I was going to say!' Bobby laughed.

Chloe blinked. She put her hand on his and, although the pub was hot, her hand was cold and she put her fingers through his.

'I want to see your fight.'

'How do you know what I was going to ask?'

'Because you know I want to see you win.'

* * *

They kissed in the minicab home.

He had been stroking her thigh as soon as she'd sat down, and was lighting a cigarette, drunk, in his seat with his left hand. Trying to light a cigarette. Bobby was drunk and clumsy.

'Mate, do you mind?'

The minicab driver had looked over his

shoulder, sized up the situation and shrugged.

'Open window, please.'

'Cheers, mate.'

She supposed, in a way, the taxi back — to wherever it was going — was the biggest part of the date. Her head was spinning and her legs brushed up against his. She liked his hand on her thigh and he liked the feel of it. He could grip the tendons above her knee and hold her still, almost.

When he leaned towards her, cigarette still in hand, she could smell the smoke in his teeth, but it wasn't bad. Just bitter. Like bitter chocolate.

He moved his hand from her leg to the back of her neck and kissed her, just a small, slight one, and his thumb rubbed her jaw.

Then he pulled away, took two drags and threw the rest out of the window.

'Your dad in?'

Chloe nodded. 'Always.'

Bobby made a face. 'No chance of a cup of tea then . . . '

'Not this time.'

Chloe looked out of the taxi window, at the switching traffic lights and the April shower falling on the glass and she heard herself breathe, his kiss coming off in her sigh. He put his hand back on her leg.

'Can I walk you to your door?'

'Yes, okay. But just to the door.'

Bobby overpaid the cab driver with fresh notes from his wallet. Notes he'd got out of the bank that morning, and kept pressed and crisp all day.

The driver put his hands together in prayer in thanks.

'How are you going to get home?' she asked him.

Bobby felt the spitting rain on his face.

'I'll walk . . . it's not far.'

'Where do you live?'

Bobby laughed. 'Actually, it is quite far. But I don't mind the rain.'

And then, up against her door, he put his hands at her waist, and her head bumped against it a little because he'd moved her too quickly, and did not know his own strength. It didn't matter because it wasn't hard enough to hurt and Chloe didn't feel anything but those hands at her waist, encircling her, and in his kiss she was swallowed whole, letting him do all the tonguing around in her mouth. Until slowly she was able to do it back. Trying him out, letting her hands sit on his shoulders.

It was not a sweet kiss. It was a breathless, slippery melting kiss that moved his hands up to her ribs, where it felt like he was pushing two sides of her together. And then he was over her top, pushing the cups of her bra up with his hands. Pulling her body close to him with a grip that left pink marks on her skin.

They both smelt of the drink, and he felt her slightly push him away from her. Bobby moved back and gave her space.

He kept his eyes on her as he walked backwards down the steps one at a time. He stopped when he got to the bottom of the steps and with his arms at his sides, breathed in and out, heavy and deep. He shook his head.

'You're beautiful.'

Chloe went to put her key in the door, smiling to herself. Before she opened it, she turned to look at him walking away. When he was a few yards down the road he turned back to her, just before she'd locked the door shut from the other side.

Chloe crept in quietly so she wouldn't wake her dad up.

From the hallway, a curl of smoke. Polly was sitting up late, smoking.

Chloe leaned on the wall and walked alongside it, glad of the support.

'Where have you been, then? I leave you alone with Devlin for a week and you've hooked up with some thug.'

'How'd you know?'

Polly sat back.

'Devlin told me.'

Chloe was still smiling. 'What does he know, he's eleven.'

Polly smiled.

'You know what . . . '

'What?'

'Whatever makes you smile like that.'

'He's just . . . him. I like him.'

Chloe went to the fridge and took out a can of Diet Coke, feeling hot and tired.

'Have another drink with me.'

Chloe took a nail to the can and heard it hiss.

'No, I think I have to lie down.'

Polly was dolled up from her night out on the town.

'He married?'

'No.'

'Does he have any kids?'

'No, he's single. It's just him.'

'Who does he live with then?'

'His mum.'

'Oh.'

'What's wrong with that?'

'I just don't think that's very healthy. How old is he?'

'Twenty. I think.'

'He should have moved out by now.' Polly smoked some more.

'We haven't moved out. You haven't moved out.'

'It's different when you're a girl. You slept with him yet?'

Chloe shook her head.

'But you will.'

'How much have you drunk?'

'Not enough. Come and drink with me.'

Chloe's head spun. 'I can't.'

Polly opened the fridge and took out a half-bottle of rosé. She reached into the cupboard and grabbed a big wine glass, filling it to the top.

'Come on, just a little one.'

'No, really, I think I'm done.' Chloe was already starting to feel a bit sick.

The butterflies were the slow, acid fizz of the cider coming back up. Chloe didn't drink often and when she did she got drunk fast.

'Polly, I'm off to bed . . . '

A slow mumble. The last little bit of sentence

116

she had left to say. She couldn't say more.

Polly watched her little sister shuffle slowly up the stairs.

'They can lash out, you know. Those kinds of men.'

Chloe turned around. 'What do you mean?'

'Men cooped up with their mums, they turn. I'd stay well clear.'

'He has his own life.'

'I went out with a man who lived with his mum. It was why he was always fighting. He hated her. And then he turned that all on me.'

'How can you just assume that? You haven't even met Bobby.'

Polly swallowed the wine. 'You aren't as strong as you think.'

The drink kept Polly talking and feeling free with it.

'Do you even like boxing?'

'I've watched it with Dad.'

'No, but do you really like seeing one man beat up another?'

Chloe could feel the cider rising.

'I am going to see Bobby in a fight. But he isn't like that. He seems lonely, actually. He seems lonely and nervous of stepping over lines.'

Chloe was keeping her cool and it made Polly keep loose-talking.

'You might want to ask yourself that. If you like seeing men batter the shit out of each other on stage for you. You might want to ask yourself what it is you see in boxing boys. You going to dab him up after every fight?'

Chloe stared at her sister. In a clear and quiet

whisper she held her stare.

'I met a boy. All the rest, the stage and violence and the kicks out of beating someone up, you can keep. All I did was meet a nice boy. I don't know what's upsetting you.'

Polly was hot and her cleavage spotty and red.

'You don't get men.'

Chloe sighed. 'You're drunk.'

Polly poured another. 'Well, he got you out the coffin anyway, didn't he?'

'Fuck you,' Chloe muttered under her breath and turned, walking to the stairs and up to her room.

She switched on a lamp and fell on her bed. Her make-up on, the kiss on her lips still there, and the Diet Coke in the weak grip of her fingers, about to fall. Her stomach swimming with cider and Bobby. His push against her, against the wall of her door. Hands and stubble on her face.

And then those butterflies came back. Chloe had just enough warning to sit up and put the can of Diet Coke on her bedside table before getting to the toilet and being sick.

It was still in her hair when she woke, fully clothed, the next morning.

13

Flats lit up like little white boxes. As he turned into his estate he saw Theresa's bedroom light was on.

Even without the sound of wheels and the flash of headlights, she knew he was coming back. The world of his estate was quiet this time of night. The older kids had gone out for a longer club night and the kids who raced up and down on a motorbike they'd somehow got hold of, had grown tired and gone to sleep.

Bobby walked in a drunk, happy swagger. The glow like honey off Chloe's skin made him happy. She was clean and soft and she didn't know how much he'd hurt people. She looked at his hands as if they weren't broken. She looked at his face as if it hadn't been hit. When she held his hand in the taxi he felt his body grow quiet and still.

Theresa went to her window. He looked up at her and she waved down to him.

He was stuck, not sure whether to walk on, or wait to see if she would come down. Bobby thought about going up there too. He wasn't with Chloe, was he? He didn't feel ready to have sex with Chloe yet.

The face went from the window and the bedroom light went out. In seconds the hallway lit up. And then Theresa was at her front door, dressed up like she'd been out too. Gone were the slouchy, off-the-ass track bottoms and baggy top. She was dressed in lace shorts and a vest, and looked whiter than normal. No sunbed glow.

They looked at each other in silence. The beam from the doorway washing them out. The drink swilled around Bobby's head and with the rain still spitting he switched on. Chloe had left him horny, and while he liked that she didn't let him in, he felt raw, his body alive. Sex with someone you don't love doesn't count.

He walked into the light. Into Theresa's arms, his right hand in the back of her shorts. She giggled, and stood on her tiptoes and kissed him.

'You stink.'

Bobby pushed her against the wall, harder than he pushed Chloe against the door. He held her face, pushing her head into his. He felt the scar on the back of her head, his thumb pressing the throat.

She laughed.

'You always come back.'

Bobby kissed her like a bulldozer.

'I know about her.'

Bobby didn't want to hear her. He kissed her again. Kissed her harder and harder until Chloe had been driven out of his mind with every angry press of his mouth onto Theresa's lips.

'I bet she won't fuck you yet.'

Harder still, Bobby drove his tongue in Theresa's mouth until he'd pulled it apart. He didn't want her smiling at him. If it wasn't for the wall, she'd have toppled over.

'You keep coming back here because you want

to. Stop trying to pretend you don't. You belong here.'

Two blocks apart. The same brick and sawdust. Nothing before or after mattered to either of them. He pushed at her shoulders and put her hand to his belt to undo him, grabbing at her neck and holding her head there until she spluttered and gasped.

Pulling back he said sorry. And looked at her as if for the first time.

'Shit, Theresa, your neck.'

It was red. Deep, bruising red.

She smiled and took his hand. 'Doesn't matter.'

Upstairs he was led; nothing he did could ever take him away from this creaking staircase.

Chloe would never know. She wasn't his girlfriend. This was fine.

Bobby closed his eyes and let it happen. Like the fight in the toilets, this wasn't all of him. He let her touch him and he touched her back. And when Bobby woke the next morning, and saw Theresa in the same position she was in last time they'd slept together, he got dressed and left. No sour kiss. No sticky morning sex to say goodbye. Her knickers that he kicked off his jeans were white and small.

He walked away and closed her bedroom door. Creaking his way to the bottom of the stairs and clicking out of the front door. He didn't care anymore, about Denny and the lot of them, sticking to their plot and to their own. He didn't scare easily.

And if they did start getting noisy, then this

121

fight would keep them quiet.

The morning was young. Dawn, still. The sky quiet and milky. No one on the estate but Bobby. The morning would have been bliss if it did not tick off another day closer to Saturday. Bobby was a tired fighter. Sick of the sex with Theresa. Sick of that room. Sick of himself. Sick of his body and his body was sick of him. Bobby knew a fight was won before it happened in a ring.

In his shirt and jeans he collapsed onto his bed and was out like a light. He had an hour before he was back training. He slept a dead, dreamless sleep.

14

Joe peeled off the Blu-tacked flyer from the window by his table in the cafe and smiled as he turned it over. A glossy picture of his boy and Connor squaring up. He put it on the table and smoothed it down to have a good look.

To Rest is to Rust.

The ink he'd paid for. Dug in deep to his boy's biceps. If it wasn't for Joe, Bobby would never have even heard of Jack Dempsey. He'd let him get the tattoo at fifteen, after his first real fight. He thought it was nice, how Bow had printed out a few flyers to hype up the club. They had it as the Gypsy against the Jew. Star of David against the Shamrock. Cartoon drama. Bobby was as Jewish as the Pakistani boss of the post office. He knew more about Irish pubs than he did his own lot. That was his mum filling his head up with tales of his granddad.

But it had been Joe who'd got his son in the ring.

It wasn't so long ago that Joe had been the one holding up his hands in the back garden so that Bobby could pummel his palms. Stroking them, like a broken jaw. Bobby's right had always been better than his left, but his left wasn't too bad at all. He'd come a long way since then. He didn't need his dad.

Joe was meeting Daphne for lunch. His weekly spend had just come in, and as soon as it had, he'd withdrawn it all and put it in his pocket. Now it was just paper. Now it didn't count. He could throw it away. But first he could treat Daphne to lunch.

She walked in, all smiles. The happy grin of a drunken woman.

She was immaculate, always was. Her hair, a tough, lacquered black chignon, the sparkling stars in her ears and a red polyester blouse, tucked into the elasticised waist of her blue jeans. Her pencilled eyebrows, after years of over-plucking, looked startled. She'd made them look too happy, too high and rounded. She saw Joe and raised them even higher.

He lifted himself shakily out of his chair to say hello, but only an inch. His weak knees needed the seat back. Joe'd made an effort too. His trousers had been washed: the bottom half of a suit he'd found down the back of a wardrobe. With his hair creamed down and a half-arsed shave, he looked, at least to him, almost presentable.

She came over, nervous, glamorous and thin. He lifted himself up again and kissed her on the lips when she went to him; their dry lips poking at each other.

'Been waiting long?'

Joe shook his head.

When she sat she put down her little leather bag, smoothing it and making sure the strap didn't dangle over the table.

Grease lay in a thick, cold film on the walls and ceiling: this place was a dive. Daphne, her perfume poured over thin skin before she left the

124

house, sat with all the ladylike self-respect she possessed. Joe saw she had put pearls around her neck too.

He put his left hand, shakier than hers, on her knuckles to comfort her. Her eyes darted around in blinks and twitches, her nose crinkling at the top.

'Nice here, isn't it?'

Joe shrugged.

'I wish I could take you somewhere nicer.'

Daphne moved her hand away from Joe's.

'What would I do in somewhere nicer than this?'

Joe felt sad for them both.

He had already had his brandy-tea as he waited, and was okay sitting there for the moment. Daphne seemed bright, her face healthy and her cheeks pinkish; he knew that she had downed her mid-morning nip too.

She picked up the menu.

'All Day for £2.99? That can't be right. I wouldn't trust those sausages, there's got to be something up with them.'

Joe smiled again at her.

'Have something more expensive, Daphne.' And then Daphne smiled too.

The waitress came over. The same, sloppy-eyed lady who always waddled over with the same rude manner she'd used every day Joe had been there. She said nothing and stood with the pen in her fat hand.

Daphne looked surprised, though Joe did not know if this was her eyebrows.

'Omelette and salad, please.'

Daphne said please loudly and slowly. If there was something that Daphne had, it was manners. She groomed them herself, said it cost nothing.

'All Day Breakfast for me.'

Joe didn't say please. He was less bothered about airs and graces. Joe did not care whether people were nice to him anymore.

He also did not want the All Day Breakfast. He'd chosen it because Daphne had gone for the one thing on the menu that cost over a fiver, and he only had about a tenner to spare on this. He was worried, thinking of the teas and coffees they might order and what that might add up to.

The waitress went away with their order having not spoken a word to either Daphne or Joe.

'Manners cost nothing.'

Joe pushed the flyer forward an inch.

'You seen this?'

Daphne lifted it up and peered at the picture of Bobby and Connor. After a few seconds she grinned.

'Oh, it's your boy. It's Bobby.'

Joe nodded.

Daphne carried on looking at the picture. 'Think I've seen them in the butcher's window.'

'I think he looks good, don't you?'

'Your boy always looks good.'

Joe folded the flyer slowly. He found it hard with his shaky hands. He was proud.

'And it's with that Connor boy too. I know Connor. Since he was a round and rotten little boy.'

'We all know Connor.'

Daphne shook her head.

'He has my Theresa and he nearly tore her to pieces. I don't know why she stays. She's got scarring on the back of her head from what he done to her.'

'What he do?'

'He tried to bloody bottle her.'

'For what?'

'For *what*? What do you mean, for what? There's no reason to bottle a girl's head.'

Joe had never gone with a bottle, but he remembered rage.

'I'm just saying. What set him off? Either he was off his nut or she went with someone else.'

'I can't believe you think there's a reason for it. The boy's a maniac. There was no reason. What's the matter with you?'

Joe looked out of the window and tried to change the subject. He wasn't saying Connor was in any way right; he knew how young boys could switch. That was all.

'Denny know about that, does he?'

A huge sigh.

'Oh, I don't know . . . '

Daphne looked up.

'This was years ago. I don't think he cares.'

'No, I wouldn't think so.'

Daphne's hands went back to her handbag.

'Them lot would think Theresa deserved it anyway. It's alright to whack her if she's big enough to take it. That's Theresa's problem and will always be. She thinks she's big enough to take it, and to give it back. The size of the gob on her. She wouldn't back down from the biggest

127

bastard in this city. Not ever. That girl will be snarling back until she's deep underground.'

Joe thought of her little legs in the huge heels, strutting into the mouth of the canal's black tunnel.

'Am sure she'll be there watching.'

'At the Hall, isn't it? Tomorrow?'

Joe nodded.

'I daresay a fair few will show their faces, Joe. Could get messy.'

Two local boys. One from each side. Of course people would show. Joe wondered if Maggie would be there. That's what Daphne meant when she said that. She was talking about Maggie, and Denny too.

All the families would be there. Everyone liked a fight.

Joe hadn't seen Maggie for a good while, not since the one day she let him pop over to see his son in her house; once their house, the one Joe had got for them to start their family. The only time in the year she let him sit at her table, drink her tea and, if she was feeling kind, she'd put the hot water on and let him have a bath.

'You can use Bobby's stuff if you want to shave.'

Usually Bobby was never in, having gone out the night before his birthday with Mikey and boys from the club. A wasted trip. Except Joe always left feeling like he'd got something out of it. That he'd got a little closer to Maggie. When she left him in an empty kitchen, after making his tea, there was something there.

He saw that she kept the wedding photo out.

When he'd asked after the photo, she said it was because she wanted to remember how pretty she used to be; that every woman wanted to keep the picture of herself as a bride, never mind how it ended up.

'The man you marry isn't important when you look back. It's that you wore the white dress.'

Joe still thought that Maggie was beautiful. They weren't even old. They had just got tired and didn't smile anymore. It added years. Maggie was still a good-looking woman. Daphne, Joe thought as he looked over at her reapplying some more brick-house red to her lips, never was and never would be as beautiful. Not even close. Both Daphne and Joe knew this. Maggie too. And when Joe found company with Daphne, Maggie found her revenge. She'd thrown him out and all he could get was the poorest, palest, broken version of the woman he'd married: her plain best friend.

Their food came too quickly. Already made, it had been heated up behind closed doors and was also too hot. Steam came off Joe's fried eggs, the yolk, dead. Daphne's plate looked no better. The edges of the Spanish omelette curled and the salad piled on to fill up plate space was just an emptied bowl of diced cucumbers, tomatoes and sliced white onion in vinegar.

Daphne dusted on the powdered pepper. Joe did the same. Adding salt to the beans, the black pudding and the bacon. He'd seen his son eat this so many times. It did the job, filled you up and tasted good in the moment. The stomach upset happened later, but Joe was never sure how

129

much that had to do with the fried rubbish or the sloppy drink rotting away his gut.

'When was the last time you saw her?'

'Theresa?'

'Yeah.'

'Weeks ago, when she wanted some money. She knocked at the flat and started roaring her head off, drunk. Just like her dad. I took her in, gave her a cup of tea, which she drank. I was pleased about that. You know, when your baby comes to the table again. It's nice. And then she was gone with my tenner in her pocket.'

The whole time she'd been talking, Daphne had been playing with one chunk of potato that had broken away from the rest of the cracking omelette.

'She and your boy still courting?'

Joe laughed. 'I don't think they're courting, Daphne.'

Daphne looked up. 'Well what are they doing then? From what I heard, it sounds like courting.'

Joe spooned beans in his mouth, with shaky hands and only a couple made it in. He didn't even really like the taste of food.

'They're doing something, but it ain't courting.'

'She talks about him like he's her boyfriend.'

Joe shook his head in his belief.

'Don't be stupid. My boy's a brute just as much as the next one. Tell Theresa to bin him. I already did.'

'You already did what?'

'I told her to get someone else. They say

130

Bobby's off with some skinny thing he found in the gym. Someone a bit away. I don't know if it's the truth or if Maggie's making up some sort of drama to make me feel like I don't know my own boy.'

Joe pushed half his food to the side of his plate. It disgusted him. And the warm air outside was making his feet sweat. His long toenails sore in the too-small leather shoes.

'This is what I mean about Theresa. She'll sniff around the man who doesn't want her. Just like her stupid mum.'

Daphne shot a look at Joe, and he realised she hadn't just topped up; Daphne was drunk.

And then, as if the door of the cafe had a bell to turn their heads, both Joe and Daphne looked up at the same time and watched Bobby, hot in the face, sweating from his throat to the belly of his soaked cotton vest, walk into the cafe and take a seat, his own flyer in his hand. At his table Bobby studied the flyer, his arm bearing that tattoo. Joe smiled, and pulled himself up to go over.

15

Joe had told his son to start taking his top off when he had his fights.

'When someone wants to fight you, the top comes off first. You understand?'

'Is it to stop blood getting on my top?'

'It's to stop someone pulling it over your head. You can't fight blind.'

Joe stood over his son. His arms bulked up and tanned. Bobby could smell his dad's sweat, nutty and sweet. He could see his dad's white vest soaking it up at the chest.

'Especially with those sneaky bastards.'

Bobby learned the hard way, when a boy on his estate, bigger and tougher, hooked Bobby's collar over his head. Beaten, Bobby learned. From then on, every fight he had in a street, outside a bar, or at a party he did it topless. Summer and winter, it was raw and ready. Old-school, bare knuckle, straightforward, skin-on-skin fighting.

Bobby had seen his dad when he walked into the cafe and knew he was going to come over. When he did, he straightened out and tried to look pleased to see him. He hadn't seen him face to face since he'd raged out at the park. He'd watched his dad, around and about. But his dad had not known this. And Bobby had liked it that way.

Because there was nothing much to say

between them, and his dad was an embarrassment.

'Alright.'

Joe hobbled over and took a seat. He sat smiling like Bobby was the best thing in the world.

'Excited about your fight?'

Bobby stooped his shoulders. He hadn't mentioned it because he didn't want his dad there.

'It's just my turn.'

Joe grinned.

'You're the one people really care about.'

'Yeah?'

'Yeah. 'Course you are. You got someone in your corner?'

'Derek. Derek's always in my corner.'

'The big black fella?'

'That's the one.'

Bobby looked over in Daphne's direction and nodded. He gave her a big smile. Daphne's tongue licking around her fork for bits of omelette made Bobby feel sick.

'What do you see in her, Dad?'

Joe looked over at Daphne too. And then he looked back at his son.

'Something warm.'

Bobby had a flashback of Theresa moving up and down on top of him. Bobby felt his face, full of stubble. He stared back at his dad and saw a nose that was just the same as his. Except his dad's was covered in veins and whiskers.

'You nervous?'

Bobby was. But Joe didn't need to know. 'It's just my turn.'

'He's a good fighter. Nasty little boy, though.'

Bobby looked at the flyer and at Connor's face. 'I'm not there to like him.'

Joe leaned in. Dribble and spit on his lower lip.

'But you can take him though, can't you? Between you and me, son. You'll take him.'

Joe stank. He stank so badly when he went in close that Bobby had to pull back. Leaned away and turned his head to the side to stop himself feeling sick. It was dirt and drink. But old drink. Drink that had been resting on his dad's gums for days. Sinking into his hair and skin. And piss. There was something pissy about his dad. He looked at Daphne again. Her hair up as if she'd made an effort.

'Yeah, I guess I can.'

Joe could see his son turn away from his stink, but still, he carried on.

'Might put a little something on you. Would you mind? Just a few local bets. See if I can get a score or two off you.'

Joe was and wasn't joking. If he could make money off his son, he would. He could probably get at least a one-er if his son played the fight right.

'Dad, do what you want.'

Joe smiled. He loved it when Bobby called him Dad.

Bobby stared into Joe's watery eyes.

'This fight means as much to you as it does to me.'

Joe looked to Daphne, checking to see if she was okay. She was playing around with her food, most of it still on the plate. He faced his son again.

'Never forget, whatever you are told by your mum. I brought you up 'cos you were my own. You're my boy, Bobby.'

Bobby felt an odd feeling. One of those feelings he buried in the base of himself. Far at the back. The flip-side of his anger.

Joe carried on. Bobby wished he wouldn't.

'I was there. However it seems that I wasn't, or am not now. Don't look at this. Those muscles you got come from me, my family too. My dad and his dad, and his dad before him. We were part of all this. We all got the same right hook. The same dig.'

Joe waved his hand in the air. Around East London.

'We got our history. Our bones are from the earth round here. Don't forget.'

Joe leaned back, staring deep into his son's eyes. Bobby felt lost and picked up the flyer again, giving himself another look at Connor's mean and mangled face.

Then Joe went forward and did something he hadn't done for too long. Caught in the past, he touched Bobby's hand, his right hand with his left, and then he held it in cold, dry palms. He held onto all of Bobby's grazes and cuts. He held it as tightly as his shaking hand would allow.

And Bobby let him. Too stunned to shake his dad off. Too tired to move it. Bobby's head was sore. He sat while his dad gave him a talk, like a child. Like a son.

'Things happen. They always happen.'

Bobby had no idea what his dad was on about. Always drunk and never to the point.

'I was such a good-looking thing. They always thought I was a soft touch because I had the face. Because I was such a looker, they all wanted to wipe the smile off my face.'

Joe trailed off. His eyes to the table, filling up as he thought about who he used to be. Then in a start, he looked up again and carried on.

'Know what Maggie would call me?'

Bobby shook his head.

'Boxer handsome. Said I was boxer handsome. Isn't that lovely?'

Joe smiled and sighed. Gently and softly laughing.

'I couldn't keep it together. Fine, I hold my hands up in court and they can judge me. But I brought you up. Remember how I told you to take your top off? You kept fighting with your top on and boys would just laugh at ya. Pull it over your head so you couldn't see.'

Bobby nodded. 'I was young, Dad.'

'But I taught you right, didn't I? I told you that early on so you knew. Without me, what would you be? I made you strong.'

Joe's voice was becoming high-pitched and excited. Little bits of spit spraying off his lips.

'You never forget where you came from. You're a good, strong English boy. Never walk into a ring thinking you can't fight. Or that you don't care. You got lions on your chest.'

His dad did this; went on about his Englishness, tearing Bobby away from the Jewish in him. Like the two weren't the same thing;

could never be the same thing. Bobby frowned hard. Frightened of crying. This reminded him of when he was younger and his dad held his hand when he'd got in trouble with his mum.

'It'll be alright, son.'

Now, even with his dad's shaking skinny fingers, Bobby felt that things might be alright.

But only for one second. Because Joe then began to splutter and cough his lungs up and Bobby felt stupid for feeling like a son. He took his hand back and frowned even harder. The dark, thick crease in his forehead getting deeper. Bobby looked at the table until Joe stopped.

Joe smiled through a cough. 'Alright boy. You gonna win the fight?'

Bobby used to get excited about fighting. Used to love these fights. He lowered his head. 'Yeah, I'll win it.'

But Bobby was almost afraid of seeing Connor again. For the first time in his life, he wasn't so sure if he'd win this and he wished his dad could fight it for him. Not his dad now, a shaking mess, but his dad as he was back then, back when he was Maggie's handsome boxer. He didn't want Joe to go just yet. It didn't matter if he was coughing. He wanted five more minutes.

Joe started to get up.

'Dad.'

Joe tried to focus on his son.

'You worried, boy?'

Bobby's eyes clouded over with something like fear. And Joe, even with his mind hazy, could see his son was frightened.

'You never been knocked out in your life, boy. Not once.'

He tapped Bobby's hand once more for good measure, and went back to Daphne. Walking slowly. Scared of his steps and how far his feet could carry him. He left Bobby looking at his own flyer.

'How is he, alright?' Daphne whispered. A mouthful of white onions and iceberg.

'He's a champ.'

Joe sat back down to his plate of cold food. He couldn't stand to eat it. He would not let himself turn to look at his son. It was better for Bobby.

'I hope he hurts that Connor boy. I hope he really hurts him,' Daphne whispered.

Bobby looked at them both grinning without any sense between them. He held the flyer in his left hand, sniffing and ashamed. He heard the noisy clutter of workmen eating their yolk-stained toast, laughing with their mouths full. Him on one table; his dad on another.

He got up and walked over. From his pocket he pulled out a scrunched-up twenty and he put it by his dad's plate.

'Stick that on me, Dad. You'll get it back.'

Joe looked up with his mouth open, and Daphne stopped moving her cutlery.

'Hello love.'

Bobby smiled at her and watched his dad take the note and hold it in the same shaking fist he'd held Bobby's hand with.

Joe kissed the fist that held the money. Making it lucky.

'We'll split it. How's that?'

138

Bobby left with his head down, until he was outside and round the corner. He held it all in until he found himself on a side street with nobody in it and rested his head on a graffitied wall. His right hand gripped the flyer and the other held onto his gym bag tightly.

And then the tears came, suddenly and unexpectedly. Disgusted with himself for doing it, Bobby cried. He called himself a cunt and spat at his own feet.

He stood head to the wall, letting his body shake. He snarled and spat and swore. He was so close to the wall he could have kissed it, but instead he butted the brick until he was sure he had made his head bleed.

For the first time though, Bobby didn't head to Theresa's doorway. To the yellow, sick room he had fucked her in so many times. Instead, Bobby walked it off, heading down the street, taking deep breaths. He tried to let his heart go back to normal, and wiped at his eyes with his knuckles.

When he was sure that his voice would not break, he picked up his phone.

16

Chloe answered the call when she was walking Devlin around the park on the way to the gym. It was warm enough for ice cream and she'd got him a Mr Whippy from the van that drove down their street. It jingled through estates like Santa's sleigh. Chloe had liked her Mr Whippy trips, running down the stairs and begging her dad to hurry up and cough up coins from his jeans pocket so she could catch the man before he got away.

The tremble in Bobby's voice sounded like he'd been crying.

'You in today?'

He didn't even ask how she was. He was urgent. To the point.

'Yes.'

But then, he knew she was coming in. She'd told him yesterday.

Chloe said nothing else. Bobby spoke again.

'When?'

She put her hand on the back of Devlin's neck as they walked. Everything about him was thin. His head was bowed to the ice cream.

'We are walking there now. Are you okay?'

Bobby breathed deep. He felt shaky and needy. He didn't like it.

'Just seeing where you are.'

He heard himself, heard how nutty he sounded.

Chloe could see the crossroads ahead.

'I'll be there.'

'Okay. I'll be in soon then.'

Bobby hung up without a goodbye. Reassured by her voice. Reassured that he'd see her face soon. He walked slowly to the gym.

Derek thought it was a good idea to get the two boys together first. Any two boys about to fight. He said it taught them sportsmanship. How to be men. That there were two worlds: in the ring and out of the ring. And in the ring you gave each other a little decency and dignity before you bashed each other up.

He didn't know that Connor and Bobby had fought already. He had heard about the 'straighteners' — those score-settling fights — that went on beyond the club, out there, but he didn't talk of them. Only once had he pulled Bobby aside to ask him.

'Tell me how they end.'

Derek was tough. But he had always performed for people. Always had managers, people moving him around, negotiating on his behalf. His fights were all man-made; they didn't come from fury and long-running feuds. Derek was a sportsman. From puppy to dog, he'd trained to fight. But only in the ring.

'How do these things end, Bobby? How do you stop it if there's so much space to keep doing it in? And so much time. How do they end?'

Bobby had swung his gym bag over his right shoulder and turned behind him to answer.

'They end because they have to. Fights always

141

end, Derek. They always stop at some point. When you know that, you don't get scared of them. They are always gonna end.'

'What do you mean 'end'?'

Bobby laughed.

'Well, someone always loses.'

Derek had asked him to sit down. To explain the rules. Derek knew the ring: the inside, the ropes. What happened outside of it was nothing to do with the way Derek fought.

'So it sorts things out, for good?'

'Mostly.' Bobby nodded. 'Except you can be out of shape and still do it, if you think you can win. Some of the men that call it are fat as fuck and heavy-breathing like they're going to die. Some are warriors. It's about showing up and seeing it through. If you win you get nothing but the end to an argument.'

'And if you lose?'

Bobby shrugged, it wasn't an idea he spent time on. 'If you lose you shake hands and fuck off. You lose.'

Derek still didn't understand. 'But how do you know if you win or lose?'

'The shadow between, Derek. The referee. He keeps up and calls time when someone's had enough.'

'When's enough? When is the last punch?'

'When you just can't fight back.'

His tears behind him, Bobby walked fast. He touched his head where he'd banged it against the wall and wiped down the little bit of blood. He wore them well: bruises, breaks and blood. Some faces looked better a little bashed about.

142

Bobby had always said it stopped him looking too pretty.

He didn't know who he was more nervous about seeing. Him or her. And suddenly his hangover kicked in and Theresa's little knickers were in his mind and he had to heave himself out of it with a big, long sigh and break away from his tears and his dad and her, Theresa, and he had to put his hands in fists, smile and bang through that door.

Red hair under the canteen lights. Sitting with Derek, who was trying to make jokes, was Connor, his face still like cold stone, stopping only to look up when he heard the door open. His pale arms marked with a mix of coloured tattoos and biro-looking outlines. The light, strawberry-blond hairs thick on his pink skin. The purple scar on his left cheek. Bobby's scar. He looked big in the light; solid and strong. His hair short and his eyes fixed ahead. He tapped his foot as he listened and looked just once at the door for Bobby, then back at Derek.

They would never shake hands again. When a bad kind of blood had been spilt, there was nothing to say. Bobby looked at the scar and felt shame. Connor and him used to walk into this gym together and they'd lean and chat against the machines. Not about anything, but that wasn't the point. If they'd had a good spar they'd say so. Always wary, but always in awe of each other's punches. They'd even stood together when a gang tried to get into the club to start on a boy who owed some money. Years ago. Bobby had gone out first to get rid of them and their knives. Connor had been at his side. Maybe it was because he just liked to fight and didn't care who it was with, but he'd been there and the two of them had been enough to scare off the fifteen-year-olds.

Bobby tried not to look at Connor for too long and scanned the rest of the canteen. He saw her sitting by the machines with Devlin, who was in need of a haircut. It hung straw-like and messy over his eyes. He sipped his Ribena and Chloe had her chin on her hand and looked bored.

He walked over and he could see Devlin shudder with excitement as Bobby approached him. His eyes getting wide. He put down his Ribena and stood up, full of sugar and plum and fun and fight.

'Check this out. Check this out. Look what I done last week.'

Devlin jabbed the air. Bobby held his palms out for Devlin to hit. He smiled and for a second his frown disappeared.

'Come then. Whack one on here.'

Devlin hit out. It was a little spark. A tickle.

'Hey, slow down fella.'

Bobby dropped his bags and shook his hand out as if Devlin had done some serious damage.

'I got a fight coming up. You're gonna cripple me.'

Devlin laughed, and kept hitting Bobby.

Chloe stayed seated, unsure where to put herself. She didn't know how to say hello. Bobby liked this about her. He lowered his head and held her jaw with the fingers of his right hand, and he kissed her. He kissed her deep, wet and full of tongue, cleaning the taste of Theresa away. When he pulled away she was smiling. It had been better than their kisses last night. He crouched down. Devlin had stopped punching and was drinking his Ribena, out of breath. Having to stop sucking to breathe in and get his oxygen back.

'I got to talk to him over there. Then I got to do some training. You're going to be sparring with someone else today, okay champ?'

Devlin nodded.

'You want to get lunch with me later?'

Chloe did. She nodded too.

Bobby kissed her again and turned back round to Derek and Connor. He didn't want to show Chloe he was scared.

Denny opened the doors and made a noise coming in. His sideburns as long as the last time Bobby had seen him. His cheeks red and hot and his shirt collar up. His brown, nylon shitty shirt. Denny's nose had been broken more than any nose Bobby knew. Bobby kept his stare. He kept his hands in fists and his back straight.

Denny grinned wide. Missing teeth and brown fillings. He winked.

Derek, who was good with the naughty young boys, could not sit himself comfortably at a table like this. Especially not with traveller boys. At the gym he let the other trainers take care of Connor. Sometimes Denny would drop in. He was going to be in Connor's corner. Derek belly-laughed too loudly and patted Bobby on the back too hard.

Everyone looked at Bobby, who could not

smile. He glanced at Connor's eye, at the fresh scar. He sat nervous in his seat. Connor smiled back at him. The boys would never train with each other again. This fight would put an end to that.

Derek knew this too. He talked on, fast and excited.

'I just wanted us all to meet quickly so we all know where we're at. Keep it nice and tidy outside. You're both strong boys, we got all sorts of crowd coming down to see. It'll be a good old time. Remember to represent the club, okay?'

Denny was chuckling to himself. Derek looked at him and carried on. Bobby and Connor were rock-solid silent.

Derek lowered his voice. 'You've both always done the club proud.'

There was a silence and Bobby waited for someone else to speak.

Denny took a pouch of tobacco out of his shirt pocket and licked his lips.

'It will be a good old fight, Derek. Don't worry about that.'

17

Joe found himself back on the bank of the canal. Late afternoon and Joe could see faces in the daylight.

A small group of Polish men with shaved heads, coming from or going to work in blue boiler suits, were sitting, some standing, by a bench. Drinking their white and red cans, deep in serious conversation. Snake-whispering to each other. Joe smiled and walked on. They turned and gazed through him with tired, glassy eyes before spitting out their Polish even faster.

Joe had never got on too well with this new influx of Poles. Or the Lithuanians. Or any of that Eastern Bloc. Too young to know his London with them in it and too old to have ever been able to work a job with them. They were part of a city he didn't know at all. Like most things above this canal, Joe didn't get it.

A blue plastic bag of beer in one hand, Joe found a patch that was as away from everyone as he could find. He went for a little strip of green that was shared only with a row of ducks, lined up along the bank together. He'd used Bobby's twenty to get a four-pack. Cans this time. The money was a bonus and Joe thought he'd treat himself. He set the cans on the bank beside him and watched lazily as the blue plastic bag flew into the canal. It skimmed along down the left side of the bank, towards the two traveller fellas.

There were always two sitting about, day and night, like guard dogs.

Joe took one of his beers, cracked it open and swallowed half. So cold it hurt his throat and froze his empty belly. That was just how he liked it. It wasn't so much the fishing that brought Joe here, it was the space. His line was on the grass, though Joe wasn't ready to start trying to catch anything yet. Instead he felt like drifting for a little while longer and hoped the fifty or so yards between him and the two men to his left was enough to keep out conversation.

Joe hadn't felt right in himself since seeing Bobby at the cafe. He'd been drunk because his giro had come in too. And Joe always spoiled himself a bit on giro day. He hadn't meant to rant on. Seeing his son excited him, it made him feel young again. As if he was going to have a fight too; seeing his son made Joe remember he was a boxer.

He could see Bobby had taken the betting the wrong way too. It was a compliment, not an insult to their pact as father and son. It was the way Joe showed faith in fighters: you put your money where your mouth was.

He'd always loved it when people put money on him. He'd found a nice little slot for himself in between the Irish and the Jewish East End corners. It was and had always been his home and he had less to prove than those who'd come in after. This wasn't their home. It was Joe's. English born and bred. Cheapside to Clapton Pond. Roast potatoes, pints and piccalilli; salad cream and a boiled egg for breakfast. Never a penny yet always a pint. A good home boy. He'd gone in the ring with all of them.

He'd taken a few knocks, but he loved that too. Seeing the County Kerry boys getting the rages, their black eyes getting darker and darker, their faces redder and redder. Marked by their silver crucifixes.

He finished his can and stretched his legs out a little. They shook. Joe looked at his bony ankles peeking from below his trousers, his knees up and arse cold on the dewy floor of the bank. His black slip-on shoes worn and sore on the heel. He put his tongue to where his back teeth used to be and could taste the rot. All his beautiful body broken down into bad breath.

The air was warm and breezy. Joe felt himself starting to relax. He and this canal were friends; they'd been here a long time and were going nowhere. The soul of East London was here. The pregnant underbelly.

Joe missed the little old doxies that used to work this damp path. He'd had some nice blow jobs by nightfall in the crooked turns of the canal. And in the dark, the faces of the women sucking him off disappeared. Headless prostitutes of the night. The canal was once a place of chaos, lust and flesh. Bellies and breasts. Not anymore. There was the odd one, here and there. But they looked lost, far away from home. Eastern European virgins. All Catholic of course. The inexperienced prostitute new to the game, heading to where she thought she ought, asking for business like she was asking for directions.

I can't afford you, Joe would smile sadly.

He hadn't the heart to tell Daphne about little Theresa scuttling up and down here, breaking through the darkness with her blade-like heels.

I can't afford you. I can't afford anything.

Joe turned to his left. He was getting pissed.

The same two old Irish boys. Same two travellers who were here at night; who were always here. The ones he'd seen out and about for as long as he'd known.

Joe wondered. Then thought the better of it. It was a bad idea probably.

Joe opened up another can.

They were sitting and drinking and staring out to the canal too. Occasionally muttering to each other. There was a bark about the way they spoke. A coil of lead was set on the grass beside one of them, just next to his feet.

Joe went to his pocket and felt the twisted-up ten pound note.

He started to walk. One foot in front of the other. Careful now, Joe.

Back in the day, men got their guard up when Joe came near and would be ready for talk to take a bad turn after a few too many. Now he didn't scare anyone. He was just there to be mocked.

The two men looked Joe over and waited for him to come closer before they nodded. They knew who he was too. There was village history between them.

'What about ya.'

'Alright there, Joe.'

Civil but not pleasant.

As much as no one was scared of Joe, Joe was

scared of no one. He smiled his gap-tooth smile and bent his body a little to shake their hands.

'You having a nice afternoon?'

The two men frowned up at him. Their hands double the size of Joe's. They were sat on chairs meant for fishing. One wore his slippers with white socks, suit trousers and a white cotton shirt. The other, who was meatier than his friend, wore a grey tracksuit, like an old prison-boy trackie, with a pair of workman's boots. They both had gold watches on their wrists. Their faces pink and clean shaven. Dark-haired and dark-eyed. Both had the familiar round, red noses, pimpled and scarred and broken over time.

'Not bad. Yerself?'

Only one of them was doing the talking. The one in the grey tracksuit.

'Not bad. Caught much?'

'Not today, no.'

They spoke in lilting London-Irish. Like music. Joe listened.

''Course, 'course. Lovely down here.'

The man turned back to the canal. Both were turned from Joe, neither knowing why he had come over and neither too bothered.

'You know about the fight, do ya?'

The grey man turned back. 'One with your boy in?'

Joe swelled inside. Yeah, his boy. His Bobby boy.

'That's the one.'

'Aye, what about it?'

Joe had to reel them in like eels. They'd

wrestle with him like eels too. 'Well, I'm reckoning my boy's gonna do it quick. No offence to you lot, but your sort are alright between a couple of cars, on gravel and that, but you've not got the art of the ring down.'

'You telling me our Connor can't fight?'

Joe fluttered in excitement. 'I just mean, you know, Bobby's the real stuff.'

Now the other man turned around. He had big busted lips. He leaned into his friend.

'He's just a drunk.'

Joe kept on.

'Bobby can take anyone on, anywhere, under any rules. He don't care. I'm saying I don't fancy your boy's chances against him. He'll be stopped in two rounds.'

The men laughed.

'You ever seen Connor fight, have ya?'

'Nah, but I heard what he can do. I heard what he's done.'

'Aye, he's a vicious little fucker.'

Joe's legs were growing weak.

'Look, I got to back my boy here because he's my boy, and I am willing to put real money on it.'

Grey tracksuit coughed.

'Money on that fight? How much?'

Joe went big. He was going to win this. 'Two hundred.'

The men cocked their heads and squinted into the sun.

'Sure, that's piss-up-the-wall money.'

He smiled and looked them both in the eye.

'Bring it to the game.'

The man in grey held out his big hand covered in Claddaghs and sovereigns.

They shook hands. Joe could feel the hard metal press against his fingers as they squeezed his hand tight.

'We'll find the money, Joe. So make sure you have it. It wouldn't be a fair fight between us if you didn't.'

Joe grinned.

'Don't worry chaps, I will.'

And Joe turned. Shuffling back, his rickety legs creaking in pain as he stepped one foot in front of the other, wondering where Daphne might be so he could ask her for the money. He could feel the trickle of wee coming down his right leg and willed himself to get back to his chair quicker. Not from fear. But from standing too long, and because he was an old, sick man. He was fading, Joe was. He could feel it.

18

He and Derek had started early, before anyone else got in. Bobby was already soaked through from his run when he walked into the gym. Beer, sweat, snot, steam and fat, all crackling hot and wet on his skin. He'd woken to the same sweet smell he'd fallen asleep to. The fresh, clean laundered sheets done by his mum. It was like she knew just how to make things good again when he needed. He stank now. In the gym he trained hard and made it hurt. It was too little and too late, but he had to catch up. Breathless from his run and out of practice, he took the rope with a banging heart and skipped with heavy feet. Connor did his training with Denny. Said he didn't want to come in until the fight was over.

'Lighter.'

Bobby tried to push the weight from his ankles and toes upwards, into his gut, his carriage and to his shoulders. He tried to dance. He bounced and bounced. Feeling a burn and a pain in his chest that he ignored. He was thirsty.

'Two more rounds and you're done. Take it easy now. You want some left for tomorrow.'

Derek sat in a chair with a cup of coffee and gave his orders. The gym, clean and polished from the late-night cleaners had air that was thick with bleach and Bobby breathed in the fumes as he skipped. Nimble, straight-backed,

154

neck thick and still, his eyes at the wall.

On the floor. Crunches. Deep rods of hot pain through his belly. Stitches kicking in. He'd not been paying attention to his body and it was playing up. All those cigarettes, fluffing up his arteries in soot and crap. Turning red to black. Like old, drying blood. He felt he was filled with it.

Bobby thought about those soldiers who were fighting in the war. Boys his age. Boys he knew. As he sweated and strained, he imagined them crouched down in deserts, shot at and bleeding. He thought of all those coffins being carried back home and he felt like he should be fighting real fights like that. Guilty for not being there, he trained harder. This was his war.

Keep going Bobby.

'Okay, stop for a minute.'

Bobby did three more and laid his body flat. Panting, he put his hands to his heart.

'Fuck me. I'm fucking dying.'

Derek laughed.

'You used to be tougher than this. What happened?'

'Fuck knows.' Bobby's voice was broken. He could hardly get the words out.

Derek walked over and put out a hand. Bobby took it. Derek was a big old beast of a man and hauled Bobby up no problem.

'You can't die out there. Not if you want to go through this tournament seriously.'

On his feet, Bobby shook out the sweat from his hair like a dog.

'When you've had some water we'll get in the

155

ring for a little spar.'

'It won't be a long fight.'

Derek frowned. 'I wish it wasn't you two fighting.'

'I already beat him once.'

Derek gave Bobby a towel. 'That's why I'm worried.'

Bobby wiped at his face.

'You know what they did back in the old days?'

'What?'

'Back in the day, they'd blind the big, strong bear. Blind him and make him go crazy by putting fire in his ears and on his back. Then the people would try and whip him. And the crazy bear had to wait until these little men got near before he could rip them apart. But they never got near to him, you see. They just whipped him and the bear would go mad and crazier and crazier. Because he had no one to fight.'

Bobby stared at Derek. He wasn't getting his trainer's poetry.

'Derek, what the fuck are you talking about?'

'Don't go mad or crazy. This fight isn't going to feel good.'

All these years they'd worked and sweated together, Bobby forgot Derek cared about him. It made him feel shy. Derek hadn't let him put a foot wrong in the ring and where he could help it, outside of it too. When Bobby came in to train after a Friday night fight, it was Derek who'd dress the cuts, bandage him up and set him straight on the road again. A few words of care. It stuck in Bobby's head. It didn't stop him

156

getting into fights out there, on streets, but it stuck in Bobby's head that this man cared enough to hold his hand now and again.

'You're the only big bear, Derek.'

Bobby leapt right on Derek's back and wrapped his muscled arms around Derek's thick neck, holding on as Derek spun left to right, letting out a strange little giggle for a man so large as he tried to shake Bobby off. Bobby clutched onto his big back and laughed with him.

Derek's forehead was shiny with fresh sweat. 'Glad you're not a heavyweight.'

He strolled up and down outside the ring, trying to get his breath back.

'I mean it, though. Don't get crazy no more. I never won a fight being crazy. This is a big fight. It will lead to bigger and better fights after that.'

The sounds of the gym starting to come alive.

'Just win. It's all you have to do.'

Bobby ducked, his body perfectly lowered, gliding under the ropes and standing up again, tall, inside the ring. Derek finished lacing up his gloves.

The big man moved as elegantly as his bear-shaped body would allow, and Bobby skipped around him, dancing to his punches. Ducking and weaving and jabbing the air. He could feel the blades in his back move. He liked this bit. The bit where he danced. When he could smell his sweat and knew he was getting rid of the poisons he'd been carrying. It was a relief forgetting, even putting Chloe out of his mind. Sometimes he felt it was just much better to be by himself and away from the blinding lights and heat of a girl, even a nice one. That was the heat that made you crazy.

They struck silent air-punches at each other without talking. Their eyes focused and their glare heavy on keeping away from the moving fists.

Bobby was nervous about his mum and dad being in the same room. Maggie would've never missed her son's fights, even though she hated seeing them. She'd been going to them since he was a little bean of a boy, sharp elbows and bony, bruised knees, weighed down by the gloves. She'd been there when he'd had his first cut. Some tough little kid had managed to catch him on the cheek and had split it. She'd rushed to his side, right into the ring, in front of everyone. Derek had to gently take her back out.

'It's alright. We got it. He's got to learn, Mags.'

But once Bobby had seen her crying, he'd felt his own start and he knew she'd seen the tear come out of his eye. He'd turned from her, desperate for her not to see him crying. It was her face, as pale as his. She worried so much about Bobby.

Joe had taken her hand and taken her out of the little gym.

'Maggie you can't do that to him. He sees you upset and he'll cry. You can't do that to the boy.'

'*Wake up!*'

Bobby had started to daydream and Derek popped a play jab on his jaw.

'Wake up or next time that will hurt.'

Bobby shook it out.

158

'Hit the bag.'

Bobby ducked under the ropes again and went to the bag. He stroked it with the same pressure each time. Again and again and again and again. Then harder. Then harder and harder.

'Good, that's good, Bobby.'

This was good. He liked to keep punching. You could never do this to someone's face without destroying them. Wasn't possible, to just keep hitting them. Their cheek would cave right through, like a mine explosion. Hollowed and full of rubble. He'd only ever come close once. It was outside a club and it'd been brewing all night long. The old stare-outs. Someone knew someone's girlfriend and someone didn't like the way he'd done something months ago and was still sore about it. It was all bollocks. He knew from the way the air got quiet for a second that he was going to be set upon. There was always a moment in the air, where it went still and quiet, and the nerves through the spine began to tingle and flutter, sending bolts of energy to the neck and arms, down to the fists. When the back got straight and the jaw got stiff and the tongue pressed tight against the roof of the mouth. So he went in first. Grabbed the man by the neck and smashed him there and then before anyone could tear him off. He pummelled until the blood was a pretty purple.

'I haven't mentioned the girl.'

Bobby stopped and held the bag. 'You what?'

'The girl. I don't think you should bring her.'

'Why not?'

'Because you won't fight as hard.'

'She won't change the way I fight. No one can change the way I fight.'

Derek shook his head. 'You like her, don't you?'

Bobby, still holding the bag, felt awkward talking about this with Derek.

'Yeah, I think she's okay.'

'So don't bring her.'

Bobby knew he'd feel a bit nervous with her there. But he thought that might make him fight harder.

'You see that crazy fire in your ear? She's your crazy fire. Don't bring her. Trust me. I know.'

Bobby smiled.

'Ah, Derek, you been stung by a woman?'

Derek leaned his big body on the ropes and smiled. The ropes sagged.

'Stung like a bee.'

19

Maggie was laying the place out all nice. She'd done her shopping. Filled her basket with sausage rolls, mini pork pies, pizza and some crispy spring rolls. She'd got lemonade, some lime cordial for lager and lime, and fresh orange juice. Bobby liked that. She didn't want him drinking tonight. Not the night before. He'd already let himself go.

She went to the airing cupboard and took out a white tablecloth with lace edging. Smoothing it over the table, she put down place mats for the hot dishes and set down the bowls of crisps and cold snacks ready for when they arrived. The sausage rolls and pork pies she left cold. The spring rolls she'd heat up later with the pizzas. She put the huge chocolate cake in the fridge, next to the four-pack of lager. She chose not to buy any more than that because, while she had never been able to stop Joe drinking, she didn't want to supply him with too much of the stuff. There'd be a can each. And if Joe wanted more he could use his own money, which he didn't have.

She had Bobby and Chloe and Mikey coming round. And Joe too. She always had a little get-together before Bobby had a fight and she didn't want to break with tradition. Bobby had never been knocked out, or hurt too badly, and Joe had never not come round beforehand. Only then would Maggie keep it together and be nice. She had her superstitions.

She had a bottle of white wine in the fridge they could share if they wanted. Maggie took the daffodils from the TV room into the kitchen and put them in the middle of her spread.

It looked nice. It looked very nice. With the place to herself for a short while, she went upstairs to run herself a bubble bath.

In her dressing gown, sitting on the edge of the bath and watching the hot water getting higher and the bubbles get foamy. She wondered what this Chloe was going to be like. She'd never met one of her son's girls before. He'd never really set his eyes on one long enough to want to bring her home.

She was pleased he wasn't with that Theresa, with her nasty mouth and black little heart. Maggie knew damaged goods when she saw them. She remembered the night Daphne had gone off with Denny. Not that she was one to talk given her record with Joe, but she had looked at her friend just before she let him buy her that first drink and told her with her eyes to keep away. Maggie didn't believe in curses. But she thought in this case, Theresa was all that Daphne could ever have hoped for.

She put in a little cold water and started to undress, hanging up the dressing gown on the back of the door, and leaving her slippers at the side with her white cotton nightie folded in a perfect square over the top of them. Without looking into the mirror at her body she stepped into the water. Letting her skin adjust to the heat she lowered herself in. She turned the cold tap off and lay back. Her whole body covered by water and foam except her belly, which after Bobby had never fallen flat again, and as she had got older the skin had become parched and sack-like, like an empty apricot. She rubbed a hand over it in a circle. She remembered being bruised there by Joe. He'd thrown her to the floor and her stomach had struck the edge of the bed before she fell completely, turning her belly purple.

There'd be no chance of a baby now. Look what you've done, she'd said. No brother for Bobby.

And there wasn't.

Days later, she wiped at something red on the toilet. Days after that, something the size of a golf ball fell from her in a thick bubble of blood as Bobby played downstairs. Maggie stood staring at the thing until afternoon fell into evening, looking for a face. Until Bobby called for her. Then she flushed it away, washed her hands and went downstairs to carry on with the dinner.

And hadn't Joe cried when she'd told him. Hadn't Joe always cried and said sorry when he'd ruined her life.

As long as she didn't have to be in a room just the two of them she'd be okay today. But this Chloe. Maggie worried about a girl who'd lost her mum. That was a lot for a boy like Bobby to get his head around. Maybe it'd be the making of him. Maybe he'd learn to love someone.

She soaped her body and scrubbed at her face

hard. They'd be here soon. She hoped Bobby would get here first. Sitting with Mikey was almost as bad as sitting with Joe. The boy was a sweetheart, but he could hardly string a sentence together. He'd smoked so much of that stuff he could only talk in a stupor or with this mad in-your-face energy that frightened Maggie. And it went from one to the other too quickly. Still, Bobby liked him and he loved Bobby.

She left the bathroom to the sound of the water gurgling down the plughole. Hidden in her towel she hurried to her bedroom and dried herself off in a rush. She dressed how she always did when she had company: her black trousers and a cream knitted jumper with the gold trim. Thin enough for spring. She untied her hair and held it back on each side with hair combs and put tiny pearls in her ears.

Not much make-up. A touch of powder and some brown mascara. Maggie looked at her skin in the mirror. Dry as old bone. Old as she'd ever looked. And she used to be so pretty. She draped her damp towel over the end of her bed and made her way downstairs to carry on with the snacks.

She emptied another packet of crisps into a bowl, just in case. It always looked better to have more than just enough. Maggie also poured herself a small glass of white wine and sat at her table waiting for people to come. It was a little early for her to start drinking. Four in the afternoon was still light and Maggie didn't like a drink until after dark. But she was nervous.

The wine felt nice and cold and, by the end of

the glass, Maggie felt relaxed in time for the key to go in the door.

Bobby. And Chloe. Here they were.

She stood up at the table and tugged at her sleeves.

'Alright, Mum.' Bobby was nervous too. His voice was too loud.

He came in to kiss her on the cheek.

'You alright?'

Bobby's eyes lit up at the table. 'Starving.'

He took a big handful of crisps.

Chloe hovered at the doorway, just behind Bobby. She came up to his shoulder. Maggie took her in. She was pretty, and she had a nice neck. It was thin and long and with her hair up, she had the gracefulness of a ballerina.

Maggie beamed. 'Hello, love. Come in. Bobby, let her get through.'

Chloe moved forward, careful where she stepped. Maggie watched her son leave a hand on Chloe's back as she walked into the kitchen, letting her know he was right behind her.

Maggie took Chloe by the shoulders and gave her a hug. She was a delicate thing, smaller than Maggie, even.

Bobby went to the fridge and took a jug of water out. He offered a glass to Chloe, who shook her head and smiled.

Maggie had never been good at being sociable. She expected people to talk to her and that way she could reply with short answers. Bobby sat at the head of the table drinking and Chloe sat at the corner next to him.

'I got you some orange juice too,' Maggie said.

'You want orange juice?' Bobby asked Chloe.

Chloe shook her head and looked around the kitchen. It was cleaner than hers, with less fuss and things put away. It smelt of a hospital ward. So clean it was quiet.

'Let me get you both a plate of this and that, shall I?' Maggie said.

Bobby nodded. He stared at Chloe, sitting in his kitchen. He still couldn't work out how it had happened. Here was someone so rare and tender, and somehow she had let him near her. He watched her looking around the room and suddenly felt embarrassed by his mum's dull and lonely neatness. By the silly flowers in their plain, white vase.

He nodded to Maggie.

'Please. Derek had me going hard today and I'm starving.'

'Glass of wine, Chloe?'

'Yes please.'

Her voice hung in the air.

'I'll get the bottle out of the fridge. Let me just warm these little bits up.'

'Lovely, thank you.'

Then there was a silence as Maggie pressed buttons on the microwave and took plates out of the cupboard.

'Good workout?'

'Yeah, but tough.'

'I told him he needed to look after himself a bit better, Chloe.'

Maggie took the spring rolls out and put the pizza in. She started doing Bobby's plate first and halved the portion for Chloe.

'Thank you for having me, Maggie.'

Her voice was calm and soft. Maggie felt aware of the way hers twanged and curled around the vowels.

She went to the fridge and took out the wine, filling glasses up for Chloe and herself.

'Here you go. Bit of wine for the girls.'

Chloe smiled. She had a nice smile.

With the food set in front of them, Maggie sat down with her drink and picked at a pork pie.

'It's just a few bits. Nothing special.'

'Got any salad cream, Mum?'

Maggie went to the fridge and gave it to her boy. Chloe had drunk half her wine but not touched her food.

'When's Joe coming?'

Maggie felt a shiver. 'I don't know. He said from now 'til whenever. It's up to him to get here.'

Bobby gobbled his food. The thought of tomorrow stopping him tasting it.

'I seen Mikey. He's on his way up.'

The door went. Maggie could see Chloe stiffen, shy of more company.

'Speak of the devil . . . ' Bobby put his pizza down and went to let him in. Mikey bowled through loudly, a can of Foster's in his hand. He'd put on some weight.

Maggie turned her smile on again. 'Sit down, Michael, I'll get you a plate too.'

Mikey sat in Maggie's chair as soon as she'd got up. He stared at Chloe.

'This is her, is it?'

Bobby frowned and gave him a cold, hard stare.

'Watch your manners.'

Mikey put his hand out.

'Sorry, sweetheart. My fucking manners. You alright? Nice to meet you.'

Chloe gave him a firm handshake and looked him in the eye. If she was offended, she didn't show it.

'And you.'

Maggie didn't bother telling Mikey not to swear. It was easier to just let it go.

She put a plate at the table for him and leaned against the sink smiling dumbly at Chloe.

'You sorted it out with the missus yet?' Bobby spoke with his mouth full. Mikey shrugged, his mouth also full. 'She got sacked so she's back at home again.'

Mikey winked at Bobby. Bobby looked down at his food. Chloe bit into a spring roll and chewed it slowly. She'd finished her wine and Maggie topped her up.

'You all ready for the fight then?'

Bobby shrugged.

Mikey laughed, putting crisps in his mouth.

'Can't you just wallop the geezer and you're done? He's blind anyway, isn't he? What I heard. You fucked his eye right up.'

Bobby's eyes darted towards Chloe. She sipped at her glass of wine. He hadn't told her about the fight by the canal.

Maggie remembered Chloe was still nursing her grief for her mum and felt a wave of pity for her.

168

'Mikey, if that's all boxing was about even you'd be able to do it.'

Mikey ate on. 'I reckon I'd be alright.'

'Mikey, you couldn't jump out of the way if my mum tried to punch ya.'

Mikey put his arm up and squeezed Maggie's right arm. 'You'd never hit me would you, I'm a better son than him.'

Maggie laughed. She'd hoped, actually, that they'd all take a few bits from the table and go sit in the other room. That way she could at least sit next to Chloe on the sofa and get to know her a bit. Maggie watched them all eating and talking, until she couldn't really hear them. Mikey's laugh was loud and unkind. She watched the bowls of food being eaten. Still no Joe.

'Chloe, want to give me a hand with this cake?'

Maggie didn't need help, but she could see the girl was rigid between the two boys.

Chloe got out of her chair and stood quietly at the fridge.

'If I cut it, can you just pop a slice on a plate and give it to these two?'

'Of course.'

They shared their duties in silence for a moment.

'You alright here? Excited about tomorrow?'

'I think so. I've never seen a fight before. I don't want to see him lose.'

Maggie looked at her, amused. 'Oh he won't lose. Never does.'

She put the dirty knife in the empty sink. 'I

can't stand the things. For most of Bobby's fights I've had my eyes to the floor or in a napkin.'

That got a smile out of Chloe. Sweet girl.

'Tell you what — let's sit together, shall we?'

Chloe smiled again. 'We can look after each other.'

Joe still hadn't turned up. Bobby would leave soon. The wine Maggie'd been drinking made her feel warmer now. She ruffled Bobby's hair as she went past him and went back to leaning against the sink.

'Right, Mum. We're off down the pub for a couple.'

'But you haven't seen your dad yet . . . and you shouldn't be drinking.'

Bobby looked at the clock. 'He's late. I'm going to be on the water, just need to take my mind off.'

Bobby needed company tonight. The fight began to choke up every room he was in like fog and he needed to step out for air. Thinking of Connor, Theresa and Denny made the walls close in on him.

With chocolate around their mouths, Bobby and Mikey got up and kissed Maggie goodbye. Bobby hung back and gave her a longer hug too.

'I'll be back later, Mum.'

Maggie held Chloe's hand.

'Lovely to meet you. We'll have a girlie chat just us two next time.'

'That would be really nice.'

She walked in front of Bobby, who hovered just behind her, so close he could smell her neck.

He whispered into her ear and she turned round to laugh as they left.

Nice girl.

Her home was still again. Joe wouldn't be coming now. She wasn't too surprised. His drinking was getting worse. He was getting worse.

Chloe hadn't touched her cake, so Maggie finished it for her. She took it to the TV room and switched the set on. It was getting a little dark outside and she curled her feet under the cushions. It was nice, being on her own. Eating her cake. It was peaceful. She'd leave the tidying up until later and enjoy this. Each mouthful was rich and sweet and she licked her lips to keep the taste for longer. After she'd thrown the leftovers away and drained the last bit of wine, Maggie went to bed. It had gone last orders, but Bobby wasn't home yet. As she dozed, her face free of her powder, Maggie heard the knock at her door.

'Maggie you old tart, let me in!'

The drunken messy drawl of a drunk Joe.

'Got held up, let me in please.'

He knocked again. Feeble. Tired knocks from a hand that had no strength in it.

'Let me in, you old bitch.'

Croaking out the last little whisper of abuse.

If Joe hadn't aged into such a weak and wasted man, Maggie would have been scared lying there in the dark. Just like she used to be. But Joe wasn't the man she married. He was just a drunk now and wouldn't know how to punch. The knocking stopped.

Maggie sighed. Joe was so stupid and drunk he'd forgotten she had a bell you could ring. She was pleased he had though, and, turning her head on the fresh, white pillow, Maggie closed her eyes and went to sleep.

20

'Come and sit in the sun.'

She went over to him. They'd just got their first flat on the new estate. Not the first of its kind, but bigger and better than those Sixties blocks. It wasn't theirs, really. But they could make it theirs from the inside.

It was 1984 and they'd just got married and the radio kept blaring on about the miners' strike. Maggie's dad had been glad he had done most of his hard work as it was a rotten time to be young. He also said he was glad Joe wasn't Jewish. He thought it had caused their family too many problems, too many chips on shoulders. He remembered Jewish boxers from Russia and Poland heading to America and turning their native surnames into Irish ones. Just so they could get treated with respect by real fighters. Real bare-knuckle Boston boys.

'They had to get rid of the Yid in them. We're too holy to be trusted. That's the problem.'

They were lucky enough to have a garden on their ground floor one-up, one-down. They were in love with each other enough to want to grow flowers in it. They were blessed that the sun was out today.

Maggie pulled her skirt up and let the heat get to her thighs. Joe was topless in his pants, turning a lovely conker colour. Where he got his olive skin, Maggie didn't know, but he turned brown in the summer quickly. Turned into a little Turk. She'd put lemonade on the small table for them both and she handed a glass to her husband. Joe downed the whole thing in one.

'Lovely.' Then put his face back in the sun to burn.

She looked over at him fondly. Honeymoon bliss. Neither could afford to take a week's or even a day's pay cut for a holiday so they'd just decided to spend a weekend together in their very first garden.

'I'll probably have a go at doing some tomatoes over there.'

Joe leaned up on his elbows and imagined a cluster of plants in the small stretch of soil by the wall.

'Be nice, wouldn't it?'

He looked to his new wife and she smiled and nodded.

'And I'll do some nice sweet peas over there.'

Joe was lying down again. He hummed some song and tapped the grass. 'Yeah, we can make it into something, this place.'

That was what she loved. How he was happy in his own head; she loved how Joe kept it simple. He had his wife, he had his garden, and he had the tunes in his head ready to hum.

Maggie admired his sunbathing body, from his tanned feet to the legs, too skinny for a boxer, he was much more of a dancer. His lean stomach that dipped at the gut, not letting on that he liked a drink. He had a scar across his waist where he'd fallen off a ladder and scraped it on an iron nail. He had another; a newish, baby-pink fleshy scar on his shoulder from falling off a motorbike. It had burned and bled at the same time, ripping skin off like wet paper. Maggie didn't like the feel of it when she stroked his chest at night.

Maggie looked up at his face. The nose broken. Some huge black chap with long arms, Joe had said. Joe was a different weight, had no chance of winning. Joe was feather. This man was heavy, Joe had said. His arms were like a spider's, so quick it was like he had eight of them. 'We should have never been in the same ring.'

And his left eye, twisted just slightly, the lid closing and slanted from a fight with the traveller lot. The stitches went in and came out, and the eye was never straight again. Joe was what they called a bleeder. When he was cut open, he was hard to close up again.

Maggie loved and hated learning about his scars and where they came from. Joe's body was a story.

His hair had gone a light peppery brown and was greased into a rockabilly quiff, and his nose, that leaned to the left, freckled in the sun. From here, he looked like a pretty boy.

Joe hated that he was so pretty, so nippy and light; almost dainty. It was a mystery to Maggie why he'd had a go at fighting. Stick thin as a kid, his strength must have all come from inside, because although Joe had muscle and a shaped body, he wasn't a big man. Despite this, he'd win fights with men twice his size. Maggie didn't know how he did it. But he nearly always did.

She lay down too, happy in their little garden. Excited to dig up the old earth and put in new bulbs, seeds and plants. Her little skinny legs turning their own shade of honey. She wiggled her red painted toes with the nails that matched the swimsuit she was wearing underneath her denim mini and yellow T-shirt, her silver-blonde hair tied up with a big bow. She could smell Imperial Leather soap on her skin, and could hear the kids outside playing with footballs and having water fights. Yelping as buckets of water were thrown over their small bony bodies. She liked the sound of children playing; it was a friendly noise.

Maggie put a hand on her belly to warm the heartbeat inside her.

Four months and she had a good bump. He was going to be a big boy, this one. Maggie had a feeling she was going to have a boy. She didn't think Joe would have it any other way. They'd call it Bobby. They'd settled on that. It was an easy name; a name the world would like.

21

Chloe had got drunk. She was in a pub she didn't know with men she'd just met and the drinks slipped down easy. Bobby had stayed true and drank water all night. He could not afford to lose anymore.

He thought about telling her to slow down, but it wasn't his place. Not yet. Instead he made sure they got a taxi home and led her gently back to his. Bobby put his hands on her lower back and guided her through his front door. She sat back at the kitchen table again, now spotless, shining and clean. Not a dish on the table. Maggie had tidied the evening away.

Bobby took out what was left of the chocolate cake. With his hands he broke off chunks and took huge mouthfuls. Then, with icing still on his fingers, he took Chloe's face in his hands and pulled it towards him carefully. He kissed her.

She wiped her mouth when he pulled away. Wiping away his spit and the chocolate icing.

'Come upstairs.'

Chloe was weak in her legs and she fell against Bobby.

They tiptoed up and she giggled when a step creaked. Bobby watched her ahead of him. She looked back and grinned. Her hair had come out of its knot and fell down her neck, straight and black. He put his hands around her waist, so strong it was like he was lifting her over each stair. At the top he kissed her again.

'Is your mum asleep?'

Bobby nodded but even so they walked quietly as they could down the corridor to his room. He switched on the light and she looked at his bare white walls, at the nakedness of the room. It was like walking into a doctor's surgery. Chloe sat on Bobby's bed and waited to be seen. Her head running with drink and dizziness, she was excited.

Bobby looked at her. His deep frown gone and his face open and kind. He sat down next to her and held her hand.

'You want some water?'

Chloe shook her head, smiled back and sighed. Smelling the beer-bitter fumes of her own breath. His cold, white room was spinning a little.

'Here, lie down.'

Chloe lay at the foot of the bed on her side. Bobby lay next to her, and rested his hand on her stomach.

He took her hand with the ring on the finger. He kissed it and she laughed, pulling it away from him and rolling onto her back to kick off her shoes. Bobby sat up again to take his own off, then the rest of his clothes. He stood in front of her for a few moments. Chloe stood up too and stared at his statue of skin, muscle and shape. She took her right hand and pressed it on his chest.

'You nervous?' She grinned and he saw her wolf-tooth.

Bobby towered over her and smiled. He

undressed her, leaving her knickers on, and bent down to kiss her neck and stomach, ticklish as his mouth met the sides of her waist. She lay back on the bed, bringing his face to hers. Bobby bowed his head, obedient, and moved down her body. He stopped, his fingers pulling at her knickers.

'Can I?'

She nodded.

'You don't need to ask.'

But Bobby wanted to ask. He took her knickers off with his big hands with a gentleness he wasn't used to and felt clumsy.

Chloe swallowed, she felt the white wine and beer repeating in her mouth as she lay there. He moved his way up again and kissed her on the lips. He knew he was heavy and was trying not to be, propping himself up with his arms. Chloe held onto the back of his neck with both hands to bring his full weight to her. She kissed him hard. Bobby stopped to catch his breath and lifted his head to look at her. Chloe kissed him again. Even harder. She slipped her body from under him, so she was on top. She pinned down his shoulders. She lowered herself on him. The muscles inside her thighs stretching, her head back, her stomach tense and strong.

Bobby's hands held her waist. Holding on as he moved with her. Their bodies dipping and rolling together. Fitting into each other for the first time. Every time she pushed down on him tears of relief rolled down Chloe's face. She was breathing again. She put her fingers over his mouth before balling her hand into a fist he could bite. He turned them over and for a second she let herself feel the comfort of his big frame and heavy weight on her body as she locked her legs around his back, her skin damp in the dim light of his room. She dug her nails into his sides and then in a new breath she switched them round, her legs still wrapped tight around him. He gazed up at her, unsure of himself. Turned on because he was unsure of himself. She stared at him. She made him keep his eyes on her.

'Keep looking at me.'

Whispering into his ear as she bent to him, holding tight to the nape of his neck. His breathing choked and dry, his body seizing up stiff, his eyes rolling to the ceiling.

She stayed on top of him, searching his face. He put his left hand out for her, blindly, and she slid off to lie next to him. He turned and held her, kissing her messily on the side of her face and on her mouth, before his head sank into the pillow and he fell asleep. Twitching and dreaming as his fingers loosened and let go. Chloe closed her eyes and put her hand back in his. Her skin hot. She moved closer and he draped a sleepy arm around her. She fell asleep to the rhythm of Bobby's breathing.

*   *   *

Bobby woke up to a girl he wanted to hold. He held her, squeezing her to him as she stirred awake, trying not to hurt her. He nuzzled his nose in her neck, feeding off her, before he had

180

to get out of bed. As the morning of his fight glowed through the window and shone on Chloe's face, he shook off the dream he'd had about being a bear in a cage, with Connor lighting fireworks from a bridge and them landing on his skin. Skin which had no fur and was human; it was his skin and he wasn't a bear anymore.

But it was not Chloe in his dream, it was Theresa. Connor was dangling her over the bridge by the knots in her hair extensions and she was laughing, her skinny little body in flames.

22

He'd asked Chloe to stay for breakfast, but she said she wanted to give him space before the fight.

Shy and sweet around each other the morning after. He watched her get dressed and smiled, noticing the chipped colour on her toenails. He'd held her hand before she left and when she went to leave he held it tighter. He sat down to porridge made by Maggie. It wouldn't go down his throat.

Maggie knew better than to talk too much on a day like this and moved from one side of the kitchen to another in silence, handing him hot toast and new mugs of tea.

Bobby's hands were shaking and he felt sick as the clock ticked on. Nerves. He needed a cold shower. Cold to get his heart going. Bag packed and body clean, raw and hard for his fight, Bobby kissed his mum goodbye. She smiled, keeping it light for him. No nerves from her.

He had his head down low when he left the front door.

The sun had gone in now. The estate, a grey mess of tall buildings, a box of concrete, tilted towards Bobby and he felt dizzy. Kids cycled around each other, turning before they crashed wheels. He walked to the strip of shops: the newsagent, the Coral, the corner pub that belonged to their estate; the mosque that stood a few streets down. The pub they'd gone to last night. Pint glasses stacked up on the window ledge and on the ground.

He thought he'd walk today. Walking was real and his head needed to be clear. As he walked, he tried hard to push the memory of last night with Chloe to one side, and by the time he turned the corner Bobby had got into mode. He pushed back his shoulders and felt his body tense and harden. He walked like he meant it. Mikey was waiting outside for him at the top of the stairs. Sunlight and shadow on the old bricks of the hall. Ghosts of the boxers still there.

Mikey stood in the shadows. He was hungover and puffing away on a cigarette. But at least he'd made the effort to come and walk in with Bobby. His personal entourage. Mikey opened the door for him.

'Move that smoke out my face.'

Mikey smiled. 'You better win this quick so I can go home to bed.'

Inside, Bobby felt the same sense of belonging he always felt when he boxed here. A grand, theatrical home. Plush, big and special. Where his granddad had once rocked against the ropes. His dad too. When the lights went up and the people sat, waiting for a good fight, Bobby felt the lovely hunger and fear. He wanted to and would win this fight. He could feel the footprints of champions and hear the sounds of knockout punches on tough, concrete jaws. The sound of the shouting trainers; the sore limping losers wobbling out of the ring, grabbing onto ropes to keep them up; the winners filling out the four corners with their swelling eyes and pride.

Bobby loved this place and he loved all of what it meant.

'There he is.'

Derek was waiting for him inside like he said he would. He took Bobby's body in his, holding him in a big bear hug. He shook Mikey's hand. Mikey could barely look up but grinned as big as he could.

'We're going to feel it out, Derek.' Bobby winked at Derek.

Derek nodded and laughed. 'Either way I got a Clapton boy through today.'

Bobby led the way, carrying his gym bag, with Mikey trailing behind.

Bobby could have been here all day, watching everyone else, but they were nearly last on the card and he liked his own time before a fight. He liked to walk around the building first, breathing in and owning the space. He could hear other fights happening in the hall, trainers firing the boys up.

Mikey leaned back on the wall of the corridor, taking his hat off and rubbing his balding head.

'Your missus is a bit quiet, isn't she? Nice though.'

'I like them quiet.'

'Not your usual type though, is she?'

'That's what I like about her.'

Bobby looked at Mikey.

Mikey shrugged. 'Don't get me wrong. I'm not

184

talking bad about her. Just didn't think you'd like someone like that so much.'

Bobby shrugged. It was none of Mikey's business.

'Just never seen you like this.'

Mikey sipped his coffee, his eyes meeting Bobby over the cup. 'She good in bed? Is that's why she's done you over?'

He let out a throaty laugh. Bobby didn't smile. Instead he walked over to his friend and whispered in his ear.

'Shut your mouth.'

Mikey stepped back and yawned. 'I thought you're not meant to fuck before a fight.'

He took another cigarette out and started to head outside.

'When's this fight, anyways?'

Bobby paced up and down. Jabbing and punching the air, quick-quick-quick. He wanted to stop Connor by the second. He wanted to win and he wanted to go home.

Bobby picked up his bag and went to change. A troop of London boys walked tall out of the changing room, filling the building with heat and noise. Bobby moved in and around them, into the empty space they'd left behind. He found a quiet spot for himself on a bench. The same bleach-clean smells and the same hard loneliness he felt before every fight. He had no real cause behind hurting Connor. No cause other than to keep people coming to the club, for boys to see what it was all about. Roping in some ginger gypo because everyone wanted to see a gypo bashed up. Same way everyone used to love seeing a white boy do a black boy in the ring at the time when his dad was fighting. Same English pride. Same English nonsense.

Bobby got undressed and sat for a while in his boxer shorts, just breathing. His head down between his knees. He rolled his shoulder blades and tilted his head from side to side. He put on new, clean tracksuit bottoms and a new hoodie. Dark grey on grey. Prison cell kit. He put the hoodie up and his socks and running trainers back on. He'd wait in here for a while, until it was time.

Bobby closed his eyes and felt his fear.

The changing room door banged open against the wall.

Bobby opened one eye and saw it was Connor.

Already in his kit, he had nothing else on him but a crinkling smile and a box of cigarettes in his hands.

He sat on a bench opposite Bobby.

It would have been so sweet and easy to do Connor now. But Bobby didn't have the rage and he didn't have the fire. Bobby simply couldn't be bothered to even swing for Connor, even if he was sitting there staring at Bobby trying to rile him up.

'We allowed to smoke in here, are we?'

Bobby waited before answering. Doing everything not to react.

'You know we aren't.'

Connor took his first drag and blew the smoke into Bobby's space, staring through him again with his mismatched eyes.

All this pre-fight showing off. Bobby sat calm and still and smiled. He looked at Connor's body and the tattoos on his lower arms that looked like he'd done it himself with a stencil and bottle of blue ink.

Connor kept blowing the smoke into Bobby's way.

'I don't blame you for having a go on Theresa. She's a good ride.'

Bobby said nothing.

'You went a few times with her, didn't you?'

Bobby stayed still.

'You know you're not the only one though, don't you?'

He'd heard people saying things. It was a nasty way to keep her down. He knew Theresa moved around, but not in that way. Whatever else he thought about Theresa, he knew she didn't do that.

'She's not like that.'

Connor laughed. 'You care a bit more about her than you think.'

'I couldn't care less about her.'

'You care less than me, but you care. She's got a piece of you.'

Connor leaned forward, his baby face gone bad, sounding blocked up as he held smoke in his mouth.

'When she was fucking you, did you ever feel that lump at the back of her head?'

Bobby had. He'd heard different stories about how Theresa got hurt.

Connor smiled.

Bobby licked his lips, trying to keep his manner cool.

187

'Why you smoking before a fight?'

'Because I can.'

'The fight mean nothing?'

Connor looked around. He grinned big and wide, messy and sprawling.

'It means a lot to me.'

Bobby looked up at the clock. Not long.

Connor threw his cigarette on the floor, next to Bobby's foot. They both looked at it, the smoke curling up into Bobby's eyes. Connor winked. Bobby stamped it out and went back to looking at Connor. At his freckled face, covered in nicks and cuts. The cut Bobby made had gone the deepest.

The clock ticked on and they looked keen at each other, ready. 'Can't use your gold in the ring.'

Before Connor could say anything, the changing room door opened again and Derek filled the doorway, smiling and clapping his hands.

'The two big lads. The warriors. Look at you sitting here all calm. Like proper Clapton boys. You wouldn't get many sitting together before a fight.'

The two boys turned to look at Derek.

He frowned.

'Smoking?'

'That's me, Derek. Sorry, I was just feeling the nerves, you know?'

Bobby picked up his bag.

'You know that's madness before a fight, son. What you doing?' Derek warned.

Connor shrugged.

188

'I need what I need. My body's different to other people's.'

Derek knew he'd lose one of his best boxers today and hoped it would not be Bobby.

'It's time. Come on, boys.'

23

About four hundred had shown up at York Hall. Most had been here all day for the show, but some had come just to see Bobby and Connor. For an amateur fight, there was the dark weight of a professional bout in the air. An anxiety about these two meeting. Those who knew Bobby and Connor as fighters knew they both threw punches and liked giving a good fight. They could go professional if they kept fighting. Though it was harder to do in amateur, and unlikely, both could end fights by knockout. The first stage of the North East Divisions. Two boys from the same club. It was unlucky and it was unfair. But it would also end the bad blood. This would finish one of them. The crowd looked unsettled in their seats, their eyes burning the canvas, waiting to see someone get hurt.

When he got checked Bobby wasn't sure if he'd get passed through. The cigarettes and the drink and the rage had made him toxic. Derek had carefully wrapped up Bobby's hands, taking care to make the gauze a second skin, whistling as he did it to calm Bobby's nerves. The lights were bright and the talking loud. The rows nearest to Bobby were full of local faces. Bobby's name had been called and he'd walked alone to the ring. He smiled at those he knew briefly, before keeping his head down. He held a blue glove in the air, ignoring all the heckling and abuse that echoed round the hall. Some of the travellers' boys stood up to say their piece until finally one of the old trainers got up out of his seat and told them to shut up and let the boys fight.

'They're from the same fucking club.'

Bobby couldn't help but look for her. In the middle of the faces. In the middle of the threat and noise, he wanted to find something still. Chloe and his mum sat above, in the balcony, side by side, his mum's handbag on her lap and a cream headscarf in her hands to blindfold her against anything she didn't want to see. Men shouted around them, but they both said nothing. Chloe sat with a straight back, her face a blank calm as she looked around her. Head to toe in black, her silver cross hanging over her jumper and her hair up in her ballet-dancer bun. Her face turned to stare blankly into the ring waiting for it to begin. She caught his eye and smiled. He nodded and smiled back, and for a second wished he hadn't.

Joe was on time for this. The one thing he'd have the get-up-and-go for. Lapping it up like he was the one fighting. He sat with Daphne, the two of them reeking of drink and giggling like children, in the same row as Maggie and Chloe. Mikey sat next to Joe, still tired, taking his hat off to dab at his brow, sweating out last night's coke. Mikey had never called time on his friendship with Bobby's dad, he still had a soft spot for the man who'd taken him out to play football as a boy. Bobby could make out his dad's leg shaking. Joe was alive, in his zone. He sat jabbing the hot air. Shadow-boxing in his seat. They said the mighty Joe Louis once fought with concussion. Some boxers could keep on going, with all the courage of a headless chicken.

A row was filled with the old boys from the club. Other trainers and old fighters who'd come to wish Bobby luck. They sat with grace and weight, sizing up the travellers like a mafia. The two kids on their bikes from the park were at the front, grinning up at the ring. Hairlines pushing their dark hair forward under their hooded tops. Lots of leather jackets, even though the evening was warm. Others in plain collared T-shirts with jeans. Rows of skinny wives glittering in gold and diamanté, skittish like colts as they yapped to each other on show. Their faces made up like pharaohs. Shimmer on their lips and curls strung up in sparkles.

The referee itched about the ring in his white shirt. Bobby looked up into the lights, blinking and breathing as he felt his body stiffen up as he moved his mouth guard around.

Connor had been called first and stood in his corner. Same weight, same height. Bobby in blue shorts and Connor in red.

When Bobby walked into the ring, Connor came towards him smiling. Bobby kept a straight face.

'You'll remember this day, Bobby.'

Bobby's body stiffened and he spoke quietly. 'You fucking won't. You'll remember fuck all.'

Connor squinted, his scar a flash of lightning on his cheek-bone. Bobby looked at his childhood friend and remembered Connor before his face filled out and hardened like cement. Cracked by different fights, put back together in lumps and bumps. Connor said nothing before he moved in closer and put his gloves at Bobby's waist like he was hugging a brother. The hall already so hot Bobby could feel the steam between them.

Connor tapped the stitched-up skin on his cheek.

Bobby kept a fixed glare on Connor. You never looked away.

Connor skipped back and jogged in circles, at ease with the hall, playing up to his people. His body inked and scrawled over with one tattoo after another. Some fading out over time, some so smudged you couldn't see what they'd ever been.

He bent low to have words with Theresa through the ropes, turning his wide back to Bobby, then moving his head to catch Bobby's eye. Bobby caught his stare and held it before Connor finished talking.

He had tried not to see her, but she stuck out. Sitting between two old men. Her mouth pouting and glossed up. Her big fake mane piled high and her clingy blue dress cut low. She dazzled in the bright lights and Bobby found it hard not to stare. He smiled to himself and wondered if Connor had worked out who she was there to support as she nodded, vacant as he talked at her.

No Denny yet. Bobby couldn't make him out anywhere and he wondered why he wasn't in the ring, with Connor.

He shuffled a little on the canvas and jabbed at nothing and no one. Keeping busy; blocking out the chants. He leaned back and sprang up from the ropes, letting his body feel at home.

He watched Connor, hardly blinking, shutting the rest of the world out. Derek rubbed Bobby's shoulders, but he could hardly feel his trainer's hands. He heard Derek whisper to him about playing it cool and not rising too quickly. To make sure he had this fight with his head.

'Make him come to you. Make him reach for you. Safety in distance. Stop him in the third if you want.'

Though Denny was late, he walked in slowly, like it was his fight, with four other sturdy men, in his smart suit especially for the fight. Every other trainer wore the club's tracksuit. He chose his jacket with the fraying sleeves and a Whitechapel Market sheen across the lapels. Denny's big boozy gut leaving gaps between the buttons on his cheap shirt as he launched his large frame between two ropes and stepped inside the ring. He grinned at his crowd. Bobby moved forward towards the middle to stop himself feeling cornered before the fight had begun.

'Sorry I'm late, boys.'

Then ring by ring, Denny took off each gold band on his fingers and put them in his pocket, before taking off his jacket and handing it to a small boy, who took it ringside. Denny was already sweating. Big patches on his back and under his arms that came through the thin cotton.

Connor paced like a bull. His legs were strong and muscular and could stand shots well. His jaw a slab of concrete. Bobby knew because he'd tried to knock Connor out before and it was hard to do. It took more than power. It took a kind of discipline and quiet beneath the temper of the fight. The right moment. When all the pieces came together. It was something Bobby would be waiting for.

Bobby met Connor's gaze and stared again at the scar he'd made.

Denny took himself out of the ring, leaving the two boys alone again. But not before turning to look Bobby solidly up and down and giving his audience a bow.

'This will be a grand old fight.' Denny sang like a circus ringmaster.

There were yells.

'Kill him, Connor.'

Bobby looked one last time at his dad. Joe was taking in the sights and smells of the crowd, drinking up his son in the ring.

The judges sat at their table, their scorecards blank, ready to take down points. The lights went low outside the ring, brighter inside it. The voices got louder. The cheers, the yelling, the swearing became one long loud chorus. Bobby could hear his name.

Bobby wished his dad was up here, sober and strong. Bobby wished his dad would fight for him.

The bell.

In the middle they met, fists up, moving around each other. Waiting before they hooked onto each other. Bobby held back from throwing anything and covered his chin as he sprang around Connor's body and blocked a left. As much as each could throw, the fight was about getting the other to make mistakes and defending the blows. It wasn't enough to clump hard and hope for a crash landing. Connor would try to make Bobby's hands go up to protect his head so he could land a good body shot. And he would be looking to trick Bobby into moving his hands from his head so he could bang hard at his chin. Bobby knew this because he was going to do it too.

But Bobby was also a prettier fighter than Connor and first he made the two of them dance. He wanted to slip those punches in. He didn't want to go toe-to-toe and battle every punch. Bobby was a better kind of fighter.

At first it was nothing but a few jabs, skimming shoulders and skin. Bobby needed to lead. Make it move to his rhythm. Their eyes buried beneath their head guards, eyeballing each other with early nerves. Connor kept stepping towards Bobby, but his big legs were slow and Bobby saw him coming. Bobby side-stepped out of the way and flicked a couple of rights at his chin. Moving forward, scoring some points.

Bobby moved back and shuffled, relaxed, free on his feet. Stepping quick and light. He was calm, he was dancing, he was jazz. His skin gold, his back twisting, muscle by muscle, as he kept ducking and weaving his body away from Connor's jabs.

He tried to keep Connor throwing and thrashing like any meat-headed brawler. Bobby took a step back to his own corner and kept his feet moving but his body still, arms up, gloves ready to shield his face. He knew he could get trapped. But he wanted Connor to step close to him. To let him lose his control. To work himself up.

Connor didn't lose control. Not yet. He was close and took it too easy when he threw a punch. Bobby blocked it as easy and calm as it was thrown. Connor threw another and Bobby blocked it again. A rage deepening his red face, Connor moved back and licked his mouth guard.

Bobby took two body shots and the third bounced off his guard. He stepped to the inside of the ring. He could take it.

Quicker and hotter now. They shuffled round each other, jabbing and moving. Bobby made contact with Connor again, the shoulder and stomach. Then another right-left-right combination that struck temple and neck and cheek. Connor stepped backwards, his arms across his face. He was shaken.

Bobby moved towards him, his elbows in tight, and landed two clean shots to either side of Connor's chin. He was enjoying this. Connor kept guarding his head and staggered back. He gave Bobby the space to send more to the gut. More to the soft fat of his sides.

The bell.

Denny's lot were starting to pipe up a bit now. Cheering for their own and getting restless in their chairs. A couple of babies were crying in the laps of those women.

Derek dabbed and smiled.

'Lovely. This is your fight. On points alone I'd say you've won this, though he gave you a few in the corner there.'

Derek checked for cuts and nicks.

'If you carry on throwing like that you'll stop him, son. His legs will go. They aren't as strong as they look. He isn't as fit as he was, I can see that.'

Bobby blinked and spat. He nodded.

'Time your left a bit better though. Use your jab, use your jab.'

Blinking again, Bobby turned. He looked to see if she was still there. For just a second. He tried to find her face.

Derek shouted.

'Who you looking at?'

Bobby blinked again. He shook his head.

'No one.'

'Not a mark on you. You're good, you're good. See if you can get him to his knees in this one. Let him get tired. Let him in and let him get tired.'

Bobby nodded. Slightly stunned from Connor's punches. Hyped up, his blood burning. Ready to take more.

And back out again.

The bell.

Bobby saw Connor coming at him and ducked. He took him back against the ropes, covering his body and face with his arms and taking blow after blow. He had her in his bed again. The way her body was cold when she took

198

off her clothes. The way she pulled her legs up to make herself smaller when she slept. The way she sat on top of him and didn't let him go.

'You okay?'

She'd nodded.

And he'd held her hand first, before he did anything. He'd held her hand and sat next to her, whispering in her ear as he kissed her neck and she shivered.

She had wanted to. She had known exactly what she wanted.

A huge punch came from nowhere. A punch as hard as Bobby could ever give.

His head ringing, another caught his chin. His body blasted from his feet. The sound of the punch still beating against his cheekbone, his eyes blank. His head spun and his nerves shook.

Fucking hell. Connor had found his moment. Bobby's brain tried to tell his body to keep up, but the wires were crossed. In a daze he felt his left leg wobbling and his weight fall back on the ropes behind him. He tried to hit back with his right, but he wasn't steady or quick enough and he hit air. He tasted sweat and blood. He was seeing stars. Then he saw Connor's glove again.

Bobby tilted his head and tried to put his feet in line, missing another big one. Then all he could do was duck and cover and block the best he could until his nerves were steady. Defend and duck and wait. Stuck in a rut, trying to hold out, trying to take the hits as hard as they came. This wasn't how he planned it. He wanted grace. Pushing himself forward, Bobby got his control back, landing clean jabs at Connor and building his points up. He threw quick combinations that dazzled and duped, and used his left to connect with a heavy blow to the right side of Connor's head. This time Connor stumbled backwards and Bobby charged in.

They got up close to each other, a blur of fists, Bobby going in hard and fast and leaving Connor to block until they were in a clinch, holding each other in the middle of the ring, coming together in a slow, waltzing stagger. They locked horns and leaned on each other. Arms wrapped tight, noses in each other's necks, breathing in the sweat of each other's skin, kissing sweat. Tired, they used each other to breathe again, each supported for a second by the other's weight before twisting their way out.

The bell rang out again. Bobby was happy the round had finished and both boys went back to their corners.

Derek put his hand out for the gum shield. He washed it out and let Bobby have water. Bobby spat it back in the bucket and smiled, his skin gleaming and bruised already. His eyes shrinking and his mouth smiling.

'What you daydreaming about? Your head's not here.'

Bobby shrugged. 'Don't worry about it.'

But he worried about it himself. Bobby was in shock. His leg shaking. He had not expected to be hit so hard and could feel the doubt buzzing in his head. He'd given Connor the space to hit hard. Bobby didn't want to lose. Bobby would not lose this. Derek put his shield back in his mouth and nodded.

'Don't get cocky with me in the corner. Go and fight proper out there.'

Connor was getting worked up by Denny. His body was pink and patchy with strain. Denny sprayed him down and talked at him as he smeared a token smudge of grease over the small split on his nose. Connor's thick skin hardly bled and despite the hits from Bobby, he was ready to go in the third without much tending to by Denny.

Bobby willed the daze to leave him and for the focus to come back. The hall was a blur of sounds and shapes. When the bell went, Bobby stood without power.

Round three.

Bobby's legs were tired and he knew he had to try and finish this. He got too close and faltered, losing balance and leaving himself wide open. Bobby was winning on points, but he felt he was about to go down. He was going to lose his legs. He gave Connor a free hit. Connor came with a left that hit Bobby's neck. A wasted shot. But then another so hard, Bobby felt his face twist like whiplash.

For a second he heard nothing. He did not hear Theresa stand up and scream or his mum call for the fight to be over. He did not see Chloe look away, not giving up on him, but giving up on the fight. He had to learn his body again. The spit dribbled down his chin and he checked to feel his mouth guard was still in place.

But he did still feel. And he was still standing.

He could see Connor in front of him and twisted his tired body away from another driving

201

punch. He walked in heavy steps to the middle of the ring and tried to get his body moving again. Jogging on the spot, getting the blood pumping.

There were those last, little confused breaths of strength left. Not much. But some. He put his elbows in. He shifted his weight from one foot to the other.

When Connor came back, ready to land another blow to the side of Bobby's blue head guard, Bobby inched his head away and came hard with a right, before following through with his left and smashing into Connor's cheekbone. Connor staggered.

Bobby could have left him to fall all by himself, but he didn't. Now he would finish this. Like Derek said. This was the punch the crowd had come to see. He would finish with the last hit he had in him.

In a drifting punch, so strong it tingled and came right from the back of Bobby's left shoulder blade, all the way down his arm and through his wrist, Bobby smacked Connor hard and caught him where he wanted.

Connor went to his knees, his chin drained, the fight over. His eyes looked up at Bobby, like a sinner coming clean, and he collapsed at Bobby's feet.

He tried to get up, holding onto the ropes to help claw his way.

Bobby was too tired to lift a gloved arm up. He turned from Connor's body and looked to Derek, who was smiling. He shrugged, as if to say I told you so.

People were loud and happy. The referee was holding Bobby's arm up and his mum was standing on her feet grinning; Joe too. He stood and shouted out his son's name. Bobby carried on looking at the ground, taking his arm back and tearing at the laces on his gloves with his teeth, savage and desperate. Needing them off his hands. They were hot and they hurt. He couldn't lift his arms or feel his fingers.

'Get these fucking things off me.'

He spat out his shield.

'Derek get these things off me, please. Get them off me.'

Derek grinned and patted him on the back.

'That's you through to the next stage, boy.'

As Bobby looked over at the people quickly, he caught Joe's eye. Joe was crying in his seat, grinning and crying. Not clapping, or cheering anymore. He'd sat down and was staring at his son with tears in his eyes.

Chairs started to scrape again and that lot were the first to go. Then his: the big army of old-boy trainers. They rolled by him, relaxed and regal, happy their boy had won. Big, loving slaps on the back and promises of a soft drink in the bar if he had the time. They were proud of their Bobby who had grown up in their careful hands.

Connor was stirring, being talked to by Theresa, her back to Bobby. He couldn't see her face, but he saw Denny whispering into her ear, with his hot, wet breath full of the acid of drink and bullshit. Pouring some poison down and making sure it stayed down. Denny nudged her and she picked up Connor's hand and held it.

She helped Connor to his feet, his arms slung over the backs of two large lads, bigger than Connor himself.

Bobby shivered. The sweat getting cold on his body.

As they were taking him out of the ring, Connor managed to turn his slugged head round just a small bit and catch Bobby's eye. His face was closing in on itself, his cheeks swelling at such a speed that his eyes were disappearing. Like a little ginger Buddha. And out of one of them, his left one, Connor winked at Bobby, smiling through the pain, and turned his head back round again.

'Well, look at you.'

Bobby looked down at Joe from the ring.

'Alright, Dad.'

'Not a mark on ya, as usual.' Joe grinned up, slurring and swaying and smiling too much.

'Dunno about that, Dad. He nicked a few.'

'But you nailed him anyways. You nailed him proper.'

Joe threw his fists around the air like a baby holding a rattle, his tongue out of his mouth, spittle collecting at the side of his lips.

'Like that you done him like that.'

Bobby nodded.

But Bobby knew he'd been lucky. Bobby had not been ready enough for this fight.

'Got to change, Dad.'

Joe nodded too, and kept nodding. He had money to pick up from his two friends and needed to grab them before they left. They walked past and Joe took his chance.

'About the money . . . '

The two canal travellers stopped and looked unbothered about giving their money away. They looked like they had better things on their mind.

'Fair's fair, Joe.'

One of them stuck his hand in his pocket and drew out a wad. 'What did we say, a hundred?'

'Come on, be right.'

The two men looked at each other. They smiled. 'So it was.'

They patted Bobby on the back. A couple of scorpions.

'You've got a fine left hook.'

Bobby said nothing as Joe counted out the bills with such a thrill he looked like he was going to start licking each one to see what it tasted like. Patting Joe on the back they left, oddly at ease with letting go two hundred pounds to a ditzy old drunk. Bobby watched them walk off until he was sure they were gone and Joe would be alright.

His mum gave him a hug and kissed his face twice, making sure she didn't hurt him. Chloe hung back, looking nervous. Bobby was nervous too. This was a different role. He was a thug. A big brute, and Chloe hadn't seen him like that before. He felt conscious of his body and held his gym bag in front of him.

'Well done, Bobby,' Chloe whispered, afraid to touch him, afraid to get too near.

'Thanks.'

'I'm glad you didn't get hurt.'

Bobby shrugged.

'Am going to get cleaned up and changed,

alright? Meet you in the bar.'

Bobby took Chloe's hand and held it for a second. It was cold and dry in his big, sweaty grip.

'I wish you hadn't come. Wasn't good for you to see it.'

Chloe smiled. She shrugged. 'You won it.'

But she looked sad.

Joe, who had been standing quietly took five twenty-pound notes and held them out for Maggie. She looked down at the shaking wad of cash and back up to Joe's open, pleading face. He needed Maggie to take this money.

'What's this?'

'I won it. Our son won it. Half is yours. You can get yourself something nice, go to dinner or something. Go away for the day. Anything, Mags,' Joe stuttered.

Maggie made fists and crumpled her cream scarf. She tried to smile.

'More devil's money, Joe. I can't take it off you.' Maggie smiled. A genuine, gentle smile as she looked her husband up and down.

'Joe, get yourself a good meal. You need one.'

She tiptoed and kissed Bobby on the top of his head and patted Joe on the shoulder.

'And it's money that's come off the back of my boy's blood. I'll watch him fight, but I won't make a business out of it.'

Bobby watched her go and could see that his dad looked ashamed for saying anything in the first place. Always getting it wrong. Joe fell silent as Chloe and Maggie walked away.

With just him and his dad left standing there,

Bobby led Joe out to the corridor.

'Give me it here, Dad. I'll make sure she spends it on something nice for herself.' Bobby took the notes and stuffed them in his gym bag. Joe let him, looking up with tears in his eyes. It was all too much for him, being here, seeing her, looking at Bobby be a champion. Slowly he nodded.

'I'm gonna go home, I think. Or to the pub.'

'Alright Dad. Don't spend that all in there.'

Joe shrugged. 'Like she said, it's the devil's money. Better out my pocket, it will only drag me quicker to the grave.' He shuffled away, stopping to stare at the photos on the wall as he did. Looking up close to recognise friends, or famous faces.

'When you gonna get on here?'

Bobby smiled.

'Soon.'

Alone, Bobby could feel his heart still beating hard and fast. Although he was exhausted, he throbbed with adrenalin, but it made him feel sick and weak. The fight had meant nothing. Like a one-night stand. Like a drunk fuck that made you pant and your cock feel wet and hot before you started crashing fast into a cold, lonely low.

It made him feel the way he felt after Theresa.

With his heart slowing down, Bobby, bare-chested, bandages still on his hands and with Connor's digs making his head hurt softly, made his way to the changing room. The hall was clearing, slowly, as people headed for the bar. Denny and the rest of them gone.

24

As he got to the changing room, Bobby could smell the cigarette smoke.

Filling the doorway with his frame, his back muscles tensing and seizing up, Bobby curled his left hand into a fist, crunching out the tension, before relaxing it. Without too long a pause he pushed the handle down and opened the door.

They were all in there, packed in and puffing away in a den of thick smoke. Denny and the boys, staring up at Bobby, who stood with his fists at his side and smiled back at them. His thick neck stiff, holding his head tall.

Bobby could feel his left eye twitch under the swelling. He wanted to press his fingers to it, to ease the tightness of his skin, but didn't want to move. He counted about eleven if you included Connor, but he was lying on his back, on a changing room pew. An ice pack on his face as he groaned; one fat, pale arm sticking out to the right of him, his fingers holding onto a cigarette that was a tube of ash about to fall.

Denny stood up first to greet Bobby.

'Here he is.'

Bobby knew.

Bobby knew when he'd whacked Connor's face, when he'd walked down the empty silent corridor, when he could smell the smoke creeping out from the changing room. Why beat him up with one man, when they could beat him with ten? They didn't want Bobby knocked out. They wanted him up and awake to feel this. He knew what was coming.

Ten to one couldn't be done.

Denny finished smoking and walked closer to Bobby. He spat the roll-up on the floor and put it out.

'I can't stand the bitch myself, but she's my little bitch and she's Connor's too.'

Bobby stood still as stone and stared Denny in the eyes. Denny breathed out fumes of beer into the air between them. Over his shoulder, Bobby tried to look at the faces, trying to make out who was who; who might have it in him to hurt him and who he might be able to hurt back. Those two fuckers from the park, hoping to get their first swing at a real fighter. There were a few boys Bobby's age, tough and strong. There were maybe three or four Bobby's size, all with busted noses. There was one more chap, an older man, around Denny's age. His hands were loaded with gold rings. Bobby could make out at least three on his right hand.

And they all looked up at him with the same lopsided sneer on round, craggy mean fucking faces.

The fuckers.

Even if they came at him one by one he was going to get tired eventually. This wasn't a fight; this was a stoning.

Bobby closed his dark eyes and breathed in. He'd have it in him to hurt back a bit, but not for long. Not if they held him down and the one with the rings went for his face.

'Funny how your women come running to better men. What you not giving them?' Bobby looked at Denny. Right into Denny's eyes and he smiled. Denny sighed and nodded. He turned behind him and winked at one of the bigger boys sitting sternly in his grey tracksuit. Bobby clenched his fists and he bowed his head.

Fuck it. Never get hit first.

Bobby felt Denny's cheek crunch under the weight of his punch and watched him topple into the side of the bench.

One of the boys was up on his feet and Bobby had to step back to smack him around the face too. He fell back, onto the laps of his friends. Two he'd had now. If they kept coming at him like this then he could keep laughing. He could ping them off easy.

Except they didn't keep coming at him like that and before he knew it Bobby had three of them at him. With his head low to avoid the blows coming at it, Bobby fought hard. He thought he made contact with a couple of faces, but with his head down he couldn't see. It was all starting to get cloudy, with shots coming in at his guts, at the back of his neck, thick and fast. He used his teeth, tearing at anyone who came close. But there were too many, and Bobby was soon on his knees, face to floor, and feet were belting his stomach again and again; his face too.

Bobby's eyes began to close. Flickering at first. He'd always said to himself, once they've hit the nerve it can't keep hurting. What he was feeling now wasn't pain; if it was possible to feel noise, then that's what Bobby was feeling. He could

210

hear the hurt, but could no longer feel it. He could feel each time they kicked a rib, or the side of his face, and could taste the blood in his mouth, smell it in his nose, could feel how hard it was to breathe. But there was no more pain.

'Hold him up.'

The sound of Denny.

Bobby's body was held up, one man grabbing him from each armpit, his body like a drowned man. His head ringing, Bobby could not hold it straight, but he tried. He wanted to look them in the eye, even if he couldn't see. His head bobbed up and down. A puppet, held up by strings. A boneless, helpless body.

He lifted his head up, and from a face that was no longer his, Bobby smiled and spoke through blood.

'This isn't a fight.'

It can't hurt anymore. Bobby's nerves were dead.

Denny smiled back and with his huge, iron, carthorse fist, walloped Bobby smack in the jaw.

For the first time, in his entire fighting life, Bobby lay on the floor of the changing room.

Knocked out cold.

25

It was Derek who'd found him and called the ambulance. And it was Derek who'd sent for Joe. He had known better than to tell Maggie. Women got funny around blood, always thought it was much worse than it was. Women thought blood meant someone had died.

'Your face been bashed in a bit there, boy.'

It was his dad's voice Bobby heard first. Joe sat at Bobby's side and looked on at his son.

Bobby knew he looked a mess. Without seeing himself, without needing to see himself, he could feel from pain alone that his face had been smashed inward, meeting at his nose, which seemed to press against the bone and cartilage that had once held it together. It was hard to breathe.

Bobby tried to speak. Nothing, not a single word left his mouth. He mumbled blood, gum and spit and made a wet, smacking noise, his tongue clicking around in a slack mouth. Punched back into a baby state.

Even so, it took one to know one, and as Bobby gargled with the mess in his mouth, Joe looked up and smiled, understanding his son perfectly.

'There he is.'

Joe's unsteady hand fell onto the hospital blanket and as softly as he could, he touched it lightly over his son's forehead.

'Where you gone, then?'

Bobby moved his mouth in what was supposed to be a smile.

He tried to talk again and sounded deaf. His lips stuck to each other and his tongue was dry.

'They done me . . . proper.'

Joe frowned and tried to make Bobby laugh.

'You what, boy? You sound like you got the palsy . . .'

More gurgling and sucking from his lips.

'They done me.'

Joe understood and he nodded.

'I know, boy.'

Bobby breathed deeply and loudly. Rasping and humming from his throat. Now Bobby felt pain, now he felt his nerves hitting back and picking up on every shard of pain that had pricked at every ending in his body. It was more than pain. Morphine had sucked some of the hurt away, but it was the tiredness of simply getting beaten up so badly that was draining. Bobby felt weak. He'd been in fights before but never floored like this.

'I remember the time I got beaten up real bad by that lot. It was over your mum.'

Bobby's eyes flickered and he turned his head just slightly to look his dad in the eye, leaving his stare there.

'I hit him fair and square. Knocked him out cold in the pub one night. He and his army got me a week later. Took me apart on a street corner like I was a bit of stuffing. I couldn't do a thing. Right here. Look at the way the scar twists it up like a wink.'

Joe blinked with his good and bad eye. He stopped talking and stared at his son. Both eyes filled with tears at the sight of his face. Joe's chin started to shake and his lips quivered as he tried to stop himself crying.

'Look what they did to you. I told your mum, I said, we should have more boys. A pack of you is what we needed, to look after each other.'

He looked into his son's eyes.

'All you got is me.'

Bobby tried smiling again. He tried to talk again. Two men as crippled as each other. Hard of hearing and half awake, father and son struggled to talk.

'Fuck 'em anyway.' Just spit and blood and noise. Bobby could not make his words. He was a baby again.

'Fuck 'em?'

Bobby closed and opened his eyes to say yes.

'He's a scummy bastard. All of them. Never fought a fair fight in their lives.'

Joe huddled over his son, desperate to give him shelter.

'Fight fire with fire. Never overlook the small fella. I'll fight them my way. I've seen big and I've seen small and let me tell you, it makes no difference. Makes no difference the size and shape. You win either way if you got the will in you. If you want to win, you'll win.'

Joe looked around his pockets for cigarettes, drink, anything. He stopped looking and carried on talking, leaning into Bobby like he was going to tell him a secret.

'Fucking petrol through their door. Through

their fucking trailer window. Burn them all to dust and bone, beneath their weeping Mary Magdalenes. I'll send them straight to her.'

Bobby tried to shake his head and speak. He managed a small frown, but that was all. He opened his mouth to try again.

'No.'

And with some last reserve of strength he didn't know he had, Bobby held his right hand up and then his left, and with his right he made a swollen, scabbing fist and acted out punching his left palm. Then he pointed a finger at his chest.

He slurred like an old drunk, but his words came out and got understood by Joe. This was his fight. He needed his dad to know that this was his fight. It wasn't for old men.

'I'll do it.'

With the effort of talking, Bobby felt tired again. A nurse came to his bed to dose him up, and with the drug in his veins Bobby let his eyes close and turned from his dad. He didn't want to think about it anymore. Not for now. He hurt everywhere and there was no way he'd be able to carry on fighting in the tournament now. He was out.

Joe returned early the next morning. With only a couple of hours sleep in him, Joe was tired and found it hard walking back to his son's unit. At Bobby's side, he put his hand back on the blanket and held his son's hand. Joe studied every cut, bruise and split on Bobby's face, counting the ways it had twisted up, counting the ways he could pay people back, before falling

215

asleep in the chair. When he was woken by the nurse, he felt cold. All this time, and with all the love Joe felt for his son, he'd hardly realised he had been sobering up.

They'd told Bobby to stay on another day but he said he would heal better in his own bed. He didn't want to stick around in a hospital. Ribs could heal on their own. He needed his own four walls. When they'd been discharged, Joe found the coins left over from the score given to him by his son, and ordered a cab for the two of them back to Maggie's. Bobby had asked Maggie to call Chloe, and she was waiting in the kitchen when they arrived. Maggie, panicking from the phone call from Joe, was waiting at the door.

'It looks a lot uglier than what it really is.' Joe ushered Bobby through the front door and pulled Maggie to one side.

'Most of that's just superficial. Like make-up.'

Maggie's face was white. She nodded and bit her knuckles as her son passed.

'But he doesn't look like him,' she whispered to Joe with a soft voice and glassy tears. She sounded desperate and scared. When she had left him he was okay. A winner. Now he was disfigured.

'No, well it won't for a while. Not for some time.'

Chloe was standing at the kitchen doorway, her long neck craned towards the floor. She stood with her toes turned in to each other, her right hand clutching her left thumb.

'Why don't you go and sit with him a bit?'

Chloe looked up. Her eyes wide, black and

still. She nodded at Joe and went upstairs.

Joe, enjoying being in control for once in his life, smiled at her. Suddenly he was man of the house and it was a role he'd missed. He turned to Maggie and smiled at her, taking her hands and feeling his legs getting weak under him. He leaned against the door frame.

'It looks worse than what it is, Mags. He'll sleep most of this off in a couple days and his eyes will be back to normal again soon. He'll be Bobby again day after tomorrow.'

'But he doesn't look like my son.'

Joe needed a drink, but didn't want to leave just yet because he was enjoying having Maggie hold his hands. It felt like they were married again and he missed her.

'Yes I know, love. But it's just blood. They fixed him up now. You remember how I could look and you knew it was nothing at all. What did I always use to say to you when I came home after a brawl?'

Maggie looked up and at Joe.

'Learn to love the bruises.'

Maggie pulled her hands away all of a sudden and turned cold, flashes of the last thirty years of her life making her face even whiter.

'Yes. Well anyway, Joe. Thanks for bringing him round. We all have to chip in when these things happen.'

Joe sighed. She was gone to him again.

'He'll be alright, Maggie. If you need me . . . '

'Yes thank you, Joe. If I need you. I'll look after my boy from here. These stupid bloody fights.'

Joe coughed and went to leave. Before he could turn to try and smile a goodbye, the door had been closed in his face and his wife had shut him out of her life again.

He shuffled out of the estate, tired and smelly in clothes he'd been sleeping in for a few days. His long jacket pockets had hardly anything in them but some change from the taxi and a few stray Rizla papers. It was a long walk home. Bobby's face didn't look worse than what it was. It was bad. Joe felt an anger he hadn't known since he was young and bloodthirsty himself. He bought two bottles of good brandy with his win and sat by a wall. He'd spend it all in one go if he could, but his arms wouldn't be able to carry the bottles. He wondered how a man like him was going to get back at the thugs.

But first he'd go to Daphne's. To her little room and little bed, to hold her little body. He couldn't be bothered to walk all the way home and he was lonely and tired. She was only round the corner and what Joe needed now was a woman to give him a cuddle as he lay down to rest. Daphne would be pleased with the brandy. They could stay up a while with that before they both conked out.

26

Chloe had moved in the darkness of his room, sat beside him and tried to hold him. Up and down his chest moved. Quickly, in pain. His breathing was short and sharp, his eyes closed in half-sleep. Bobby's mouth was open, slightly, and Chloe could smell his breath, sour and metallic. Old blood and morning, dry and warm.

She bent her head and kissed him. Stirring awake, Bobby managed to move his mouth to kiss her back. She held his face in her hands, around the bruising and stitched-up skin, careful not to hurt anything raw. Seeing his body broken and healing like this reminded her that he had a tough body to break.

'What happened?'

Bobby's brain was still groggy and he struggled to focus. His face looked up at Chloe, his eyes, small and slowly blinking, were slanted and the skin around them torn, and like a little boy he burrowed his head into her chest and breathed her in. From her armpit he mumbled.

'Them lot. Them lot did me.'

'Who is them lot?'

'The gypsy cunts.'

'But you won your fight. He fell to the floor. I saw it.'

Bobby tried to clear his throat.

'That wasn't the fight they came to have.'

Chloe knew there was other stuff going on she

219

hadn't been told. She didn't think she wanted to know.

'But why would they want to fight you?'

He didn't answer and instead pulled Chloe closer to him. His left arm held her tight as he could before the hurt became unbearable and he let go. Chloe kept still and silent, staring at the bare, white walls in Bobby's room. No sign of life. Everything Bobby owned was tucked away in drawers and cupboards; the shelves neatly stacked with fitness magazines and a Tyson DVD, and a poster of the boxer on his wall. Just one photograph of his mum, Maggie, in a glass frame taken a long, long time ago. She could hear Maggie downstairs, pottering in her kitchen, fixing meals her son was too sore to eat.

Bobby groaned. After a long silence he spoke.

'Do you think I'm weak?'

Chloe moved closer to him and looked into his swollen eyes. At that moment, for the first time, she felt bigger than him.

'No.'

'You do, you think I'm weak.' Bobby sniffed.

She touched his skin, tracing one broken part to another and felt the current of heat between them.

'No, Bobby. I don't.'

There was a long pause.

'Will you fuck me again?'

Chloe looked at Bobby's face, trying to find him again through all that swelling. She looked for his eyes in the middle of it all and couldn't meet them. He was not ugly. Bobby would never be ugly. But he was unrecognisable. Dried blood

220

was still caught on the ends of his hair, making it stand up stiff.

'You need to have a bath.'

Bobby winced in pain. 'I can't.'

He held her belly. Her flat, hollow belly. She could hardly feel his hands he held it so gently.

'Do I stink?'

Chloe shook her head, even though he did. He had the stench of someone ill.

'Can you do something for me, Chloe? I need you to do it.'

'Yes.'

'Please fuck me, Chloe. Please.'

'Now?'

He nodded.

'I . . . can't.'

'Please just fuck me. Please, Chloe. Fuck me. The way you did before.'

So desperate to prove he still worked.

He was the elephant man. Twisted and brutal and beaten inside and out. The blood in the stitches sticking like tar. She wanted to look after him but she wanted to look away too.

She didn't. Chloe looked into Bobby's eyes again and they stared back at her, glassy under the swelling. He was scared by what they had done to him in that changing room. Seeing him so weak made Chloe feel strong, like a mother would feel strong. She could pick his body back up from where they had left it and make it better. She could give him his strength back. She could do this for him.

Without moving too much, she took off her top and undid her bra. She felt tearful. Wiping her eyes, she twisted the elastic of her knickers, taking them slowly down her legs and wriggling her feet from them. Naked, she lay there. Smooth and still against Bobby's rusty-coloured skin, burnished from its beatings. Her face perfect, black-eyed and shining against his rough-and-tumble face. She stood over him. She let him watch her.

He pulled her down to him and tried to roll onto his side. When he did, he howled in agony and had to catch his breath.

'Everything aches. I can't . . . ' He tried to touch her and couldn't.

Chloe nodded. As light as she could, she climbed on top. 'Stay still.'

She lowered her body so she could kiss his face. He made a small moan where it hurt to feel her lips on his sore skin. She kissed him softly, stroking his lips with hers and feeling how mashed up they were. All went cold and silent, except for their breathing. The open window moved the curtains in the breeze and she moved too, through the first tight push. She sank onto him and her breath became his. She kissed him again and sealed them together. She closed her eyes and breathed in the smell of his healing. Her hands ran over the lumps and cuts, pressing the bandages on his shoulder until she'd peeled them off. She fucked him and hurt him and made him better at the same time. Her body was strong and she swam over him like a sea.

Bobby moaned, flat and still. She stopped moving when she saw his face twisting in pain.

'Am I hurting you?'

Bobby shook his head. His eyes small in their puffed-up sockets.

'No. No. You don't hurt me. You couldn't hurt me.' His voice barely a croak. And Chloe carried on, knowing she was hurting him, and watched him wince in pain and hold her with hands that could hardly grab at her waist, could barely make a fist.

It was beautiful and it was sad. But to Chloe, Bobby's body was more outlined and hewn from the earth. It pulsed and hurt and groaned. It stank of flesh, pleasure and pain. Chloe kissed him more, tongue and teeth forgetting to be careful; bite and sweat locking her in.

When it was done his head rolled to the side and he shut his eyes. The sex had sent him to sleep. They did not cradle each other this time. It had been a dose to block things out. Chloe put her knickers back on and stood looking at herself in the mirror. She was glowing. She kissed him on top of his damp head.

She felt a beat thrum through her body as she walked down the stairs. At the kitchen, Maggie turned to her, smiling through a room full of shallow frying onion smoke and boiled potato steam.

'Not staying for tea?'

Chloe shook her head and smiled back.

'I left him to sleep.'

Maggie kept her smile.

'Good. That's good.' As she watched Chloe through the front door she put a hand on her back.

'Learn to love the bruises, darling. They're

part of it, I'm afraid. He'll be alright.'

Chloe walked out of the estate, a rush of feelings washing over her. Angry that Maggie wasn't her mum and she couldn't talk to her. Anxious that she was alone.

She needed a drink. Bobby had made her wired and she needed to feel drunk. She thought she could put him back together with her body, but she couldn't get close to his pain and only felt more of her own. Chloe felt her grief rise up so violently that she swallowed vomit.

Out of the block and back out into the open. Chloe made her way to the nearest pub. It was too empty, too close to the bones of the high-rise brick. Chloe wanted music and babble, something to fill her head and break the blackness around her. She walked further to the next pub until she was near the canal. She could hear the chatter from outside and pushed open the door.

Inside, Chloe felt safe surrounded by people. She would be left alone, but not feel lonely. She looked at the sparkle of bottles beneath bar lights, deciding what she would have. Chloe ordered a large glass of white wine and was just about to raise the glass to her lips when she noticed the red hair. Connor's red hair, striking and bright.

He was propped at the bar, hard to miss, with a huge grin from ear to ear. Drunk and wide, he took up too much space. Chloe tried to stay out the way so he wouldn't see her. But he had. He picked up his pint and came over.

'I know you.'

Chloe held her purse tightly. Connor looked

like he'd been in a fight, but it wouldn't make people stop and stare like they would with Bobby. There were two neat cuts under his eyes and swelling where the bruising had spread under the skin from Bobby's knockout punch. It looked like he'd been clumped by a heavy fist. But that was it. Nothing brutal, nothing below the belt. No ring marks or prints from cold steel bars. Connor still had a face. Apart from his scar, Connor still had his face.

'Let me buy you a drink.'

Chloe shook her head. She leaned away and he moved closer. He rubbed the ginger stubble on his chin. Grainy and growing over the place Bobby had chinned him. He ordered another glass of white wine at the bar.

'I don't want a drink from you.'

'Go on and take it.' He moved it nearer to her.

Chloe shook her head again.

'Look. Look what he done.' Connor trailed the bottle scar with his fat, dirty finger, from top to bottom. 'Go on, feel what he did.'

Chloe stared at it. Then she stared at him. Still on fire, she walked backwards, out of Connor's space, keeping her stare fixed and fearless.

'Touch it.'

He went to take her hand.

'I don't want to touch you.'

Connor took her wrist tightly and yanked her hand up to his face. He was drunk.

'Get your fucking hands off me!' Chloe's shrill voice startled even herself.

Connor began to laugh at her. Chloe stepped towards him, into his ugly laughter.

225

'I know what you did. I know what all of you did to him and it disgusts me. *You* disgust me.'

Connor's face fell dark and serious. 'You're getting a bit excited. You need to calm down, you're not at home here.'

Chloe wanted to punch Connor. She wanted to feel his nose crack beneath her fist. But she couldn't. Instead, she took her drink and threw it in his face.

'Have you seen what he looks like?' she hissed.

Connor was seeing red. Steaming up. Wiping away the wine from his eyes. Looking down his top where she'd made it wet.

'Listen to me.' He spoke hushed and breathed into her face. 'I'll give you five seconds to get out of here before I take you out myself, you silly little bitch.'

Chloe looked him up and down. 'I'd break your jaw if I had the fist to do it.'

Connor laughed his horrible laugh again. He took the ends of his wet top and took it off. He threw it on the floor. He was thick muscle and pale pink skin.

'Take a shot, you little mouthy bitch. I'll throw you through the fucking window. If you were my girlfriend you wouldn't have a jaw.'

Chloe pushed past him towards the door. Her chest pumping so much she was sweating.

Connor, bare back to the pub, put his hands on the bar and started barking at the woman behind it to serve him.

Chloe walked fast. If she could, she would have hit him. She wanted to smash a glass on his face, at his head. Her blood pumped to her face, making her feel faint. She didn't smoke but at that moment she wanted a cigarette. She could see the heads of women puffing away by the palm trees outside and went over to them.

A blonde girl turned. She was dressed in black. Her hair plaited down her back. She looked Chloe up and down, from heel to hair, and smiled with a steel that stripped Chloe's courage.

'Do you have a cigarette?'

More scared of this girl than she was of Connor. There was something cold and hard about her.

'Yeah. 'Course you can.' Walking calmly over to her, Theresa took out a cigarette and lit it for Chloe.

She smiled again. And looked down at Chloe's shoes. She was taller than Chloe. She could look down whenever she wanted.

'Thank you.'

They both smoked silently, looking each other up and down. Theresa finished hers first.

'You got him upset,' she said, gesturing inside the pub. 'What was that about?'

Chloe forgot people would have been watching. She remembered that this wasn't her world. Like Connor had said, she wasn't at home here.

'He was rude to me.'

Theresa tilted her head. Her extensions draped down her right arm, cheap and tough as a bad weave.

'In what way was he rude? Thought it was you that threw the drinks?'

Chloe smoked hard. She coughed.

'He said some things.'

Theresa's chains glinted in the pub light, harsh and metal. She spoke softly.

'But this is his pub. And you don't drink here. So he can say what he wants, can't he? You don't have to stay.' Her voice burning at its edges. Chloe could see there was some kind of war between them and didn't know why. Chloe let the cigarette fall by her shoe and stamped it out.

'Thanks for the cigarette.'

As she left she turned and saw the blonde girl with the chains and cigarettes was back inside with Connor. He was kissing Theresa on the cheek and she was pushing him away.

27

'I said *stop* fucking touching me.'

Connor sneered and tried to hold her again. He grabbed her neck from behind, holding on tightly to her mane of fake hair. He buried his big face into the curve between chin and collarbone, kissing her. She shoved him away and turned her back. Drink in hand, she looked around the pub.

Theresa didn't belong here either. She was in a room with cousins, uncles and aunts, but she didn't call them family and wouldn't have been able to tell who was who.

'Come here.'

Connor, drunk and strong. Every time she had slept with him, Theresa closed her eyes and sang songs in her head. She'd liked him once. The strong, ox body. The smile when he saw her. She'd thought he was good looking, not a beauty like Bobby, but rugged and rusty looking. But then she began to feel sick around him. Sick at the thought of being with him, of being stuck with him. When she'd had a bit to drink, she'd start screaming that she hated him. That he wasn't what she wanted. When they slept together she thought of other things and when it was over it was like it had hardly happened.

His flat nose was even flatter now, and the rim of his eyes pink and sore. The dirt of the fight still under his nails, he pawed at Theresa, pulling her to him, then pushing her away to talk to someone else or drink his pint.

She had looked at that girl, Chloe. All skin and bone and black hair. Brave. Nothing like her. Bobby had picked two girls as far apart as he could.

She saw an empty table in the corner of the pub and wove in and out of the groups of men her dad knew towards it, a drink in her hand. They nodded as she walked by but didn't speak to her.

The jukebox played rockabilly and a few men stamped their feet. Connor was laughing, telling people about his fight. The loudest in the room. Not caring either way that he'd been boxed by a better man and finished in a ring. Punch-drunk and pissed, he wobbled as he spoke to a couple of the younger boys, who gazed up at him and joined in the jokes.

The television showed a football game on mute and Theresa turned her attention to that. There were cousins at a table to the right who wouldn't talk to her. All married off with babies in prams, they raised a pencilled black eyebrow at each other when she sat down. They nodded out of respect to Denny, but left her alone like a bad apple. Theresa didn't know who she hated more, her mum or her dad. She was rotting. Neither half of her alive; both parts wasting away.

All the pub was a stranger.

She remembered when she had been small enough for the adults to find her sweet. Her dad had taken her to this pub on his shoulders after

230

her communion. In her white dress and white booties, skin scrubbed clean and hair blonde. Naturally blonde, before the bleach. He'd bought her new, glass 'rosemary' beads and walked her round the pub introducing her as his guardian angel.

Theresa finished her drink and got up to leave. But stopped when Connor sat down with another glass of whisky and Coke for her.

'Here.'

He grinned. He bent low and kissed her on the cheek. He left it wet.

'Why do you look so down?'

Theresa shook her head. 'I'm not.'

She sank the drink, wanting to get out of the pub quickly and back home. She licked the sweet whisky from her lips and looked through Connor. Bored and lonely, feeling her cousins' eyes at the next table having a good stare. She'd claw their eyes out if they weren't related. Trying to scrape out her soul with their Catholic guilt.

'She's a fucking shame to herself.' A spiky whisper. Straight in Theresa's ear. She ignored them.

Connor moved up close to her. 'You look all sad. Why? 'Cos his girlfriend was in the pub just now?'

Theresa tried to keep her face the same. She even tried to smile.

'Didn't notice her.'

'She's a pretty girl, isn't she?'

Far prettier than Theresa thought she would be.

Connor had been in love with Theresa since

he'd been old enough to drink. That she loved Bobby hurt him. He tickled her in the ribs, wishing she would laugh with him just once.

She moved her body away and Connor's face reddened with the rejection. He sipped at his pint, and winked over his glass at her. 'You should see Bobby now.'

'Why?' Theresa twisted away from his hands.

Connor put the drink down. Enjoying the moment and her attention.

'She'd have to love him a lot to stay with him now.' He laughed, dirty and throaty.

Theresa lowered her head and looked at the floor. She should have guessed they would make sure he would lose outside the ring. It hurt her to think of him beaten up. It hurt her more to think that this other girl would be able to look after him.

Her cousins were looking. She stared back at them.

'What the fuck you looking at me for, Mary?'

Mary flicked her black ponytail and made to get up, but her baby was at her side and she was rocking him to sleep and another cousin put an arm across her like a seatbelt and told her to sit down.

'Leave her to make a fool of herself.'

Connor put a hand over Theresa's mouth. Slamming her shut. He bent forward again and instead of kissing her, whispered in her ear. 'When he was knocked out, they beat him some more, just to make sure those bruises went deep.'

Theresa dug her nails into Connor's hand.

He pushed her face back harder. Then he

laughed and moved his hand away. But his leg was trembling and his breath was short. He gulped down his pint and looked at the table, frowning. He muttered to himself before getting up and heading back to the bar for another.

Theresa's jaw and mouth hurt where Connor's hand had been. She got up quickly, tears in her eyes.

Pleading with her tough streak to let her reach the door before anybody here saw her cry, before her cousin came after her hair extensions, Theresa walked quickly. The men made it hard for her to leave, slowly shifting out of the way and when they did, they moved an inch so she had to brush by each of them. The late evening had turned dark when she left the pub, and cars circled the roundabout. She stepped lightly into the road, weaving between them dangerously, until she was just a little dancing figure in headlights.

Click-clicking her heels back into the dark. Angry. Wanting to fuck everyone over.

28

Very few non-travellers came to Denny's site. To keep himself hidden, Joe waited until it was dark and he was drunk. Drunk enough to skulk into the shadows of their gravel-covered, neat and tidy village, to their rows of sparkling white trailers all lined up and shining from within, in their Lady Madonna light. Drunk enough to not think twice about what he was doing here.

Joe had waited for Sunday. He wanted it to be when they'd had a day being holy, with their families. He let the night roll on and on until he was sure they were asleep. Into the quiet and the Irish lullaby dreaming he crept, slowly and unsteadily. He knew which one was Denny's. He knew because he'd sat in there with him as a younger man in his younger days.

It was the shabbiest one. As if the smoke had squeezed itself through the trailer walls and coated the paint on the outside. The curtains were dipped in nicotine. Christmas fairy lights glittering through the beige lace, like little searchlights. Joe's heart was beating fast. This was a scary place, asleep or not, he was walking into a lawless world. Even for him. But then he thought about Bobby's face, mangled and black and blue and the way they'd done Bobby like that. With their lawless, lowlife, below-the-belt beating. You didn't take a man out like that. Not his boy.

Now, there seemed to be less feeling to anything and less care. Fights weren't what they used to be. Not like they had been for Joe. They didn't settle anything.

Joe crept around the outside of the homes, passed the stocky, chained-up carthorse snorting steam into the night. It looked cool and white in the dark, and calm, with its head bent low, over-arched for an Irish Cob, patiently waiting until morning for food and room to walk again. It was unperturbed by Joe walking by, tinkling its chain just slightly as it raised one giant iron hoof, scraping it on the ground as it shifted weight on to another leg.

As Joe neared Denny's home, he remembered the filth and trinket-cluttered chaos of it. Denny'd never kept a woman long enough to keep his home clean and the place, which had been his mum's for so many years before him, bulged with dusty ornaments and rusty pots and pans. Joe remembered creepy little figurines of ballerina girls on top of the television and behind glass cupboard doors. Black hair varnished onto shining scalps twirling in strange Victorian dresses. The settees were orange and red trimmed, with orange lampshades burning seedy, warm light into the body of the trailer.

All these men living with their mothers. It wasn't right. He worried sometimes about Bobby being so close to Maggie, the two cooped up in that two-bedroom flat; sharing the same soap and laundry line.

Joe looked around him to check if anyone was twitching their curtains or coming home. All was

235

quiet and still. From his pocket, he pulled out a scarf he'd taken from Daphne's bag. A blue silk scarf she'd worn when she'd courted Denny all those years ago. She used to wrap it around her neck to cover the bruises Denny left on her. Now she wore it around her head to hide the grey roots coming through her dyed-black beehive.

He soaked it up in the petrol he'd brought in a plastic bottle as he got closer to Denny's door and let the bottle fall to the ground. His nerves pressing him on. His left hand held the wet scarf and his right the plastic lighter, both trembling. His thumb had stopped working and couldn't push down hard enough to get a spark. Joe swore under his breath. The shakes were getting worse these days. So bad they were almost stopping him drinking: Joe couldn't open half of his bottles anymore and Daphne had to do them for him.

He kept trying to spark a flame. He could see the shape of Denny, his big wide frame and gut in profile through the thin see-through curtains. He was at a table with Connor, who'd healed well since he'd been smacked out by Bobby. But then that was a clean punch, a real proper fair hit that would heal fairly too. Not a pummelling. Connor's face was frowning and looking over a hand of cards in front of him. Denny chuckled. They were both just a rag's throw away.

His mind fluffy with drink, Joe could only see the state of his son's face and the pain he had to cause back. He didn't think about the army he was digging up to fight another round against Bobby.

236

The lighter would not make a flame. Joe's thumb began to get weaker and weaker until he let the scarf drop to the ground. The lighter too.

Foolish and with the quickest steps he could make, Joe turned and did his best to shuffle away. His fingertips sore. A knee buckled and Joe tripped, falling to the ground. He got up slowly, could feel the spit on his chin. He had just got to the horse when he heard him.

A laugh. A loud, horrible big laugh that came from the deepest part of Denny's round, tough drinking belly.

'I see ya, you smelly fucker Joe. I see you there.'

Joe froze, panicked. He couldn't move away fast enough and he couldn't fight if he stayed still.

'You creeping about my home?'

Caught in the act. Feeble and weak, there was nothing Joe could do except face his own fate. He didn't even bother turning around, didn't try and run for it. He couldn't, didn't have the legs. Instead, Joe looked up at the horse and the horse looked down at him and he kept hold of the bog-black equine eyes, inky and sad in the breaking dawn, and he smiled, hearing the thugs behind him.

'There we are. I can see you now. Trying to send me a message, eh? Thanks very much.'

Joe put his fingers on the horse's neck and stroked it gently. He put his hand to the warmth of its body and held onto the mane to prop himself up for a moment. He closed his eyes and waited for something to happen. So drunk, he was in a dream. He was the town fool, stuck in the stocks waiting for the rotten fruit to come smacking into his face.

But what they threw was much harder. He felt it catch him at the base of his skull. Although by the time he did, he was already on the ground. A brick, a can, something hard, had knocked Joe over. Joe closed his eyes and went to sleep, hearing mutterings coming from Denny and doors of trailers opening.

'No more than a bad hangover tomorrow, Joe. Nothing more than a bad hangover.'

The trailer doors shut and the site fell silent again. He was no more than a petty nuisance, and the world carried on, the new light of the morning settling over a man, face down in the dirt, and a horse, dappled and plump, standing over him.

29

It had been a couple of days of mending before the doorbell rang.

When Maggie saw that it was Theresa, she didn't know where to put her hands and held her arms as straight as planks at her side. She had come to see what he looked like. She had to know what they'd done to him. As Maggie opened the door, she saw Daphne and Denny in her. Her round cheeks, her heart-shaped face were Daphne's. She had a strong nose like her dad and long, black eyelashes. Theresa was a stunning girl. She'd got the best out of her parents and it had made something beautiful.

She was smiling at Maggie.

'Can I help you?' Maggie stood close to the gap in the door to stop Theresa looking in. She didn't want this girl knowing how she decorated the hallway; getting a glimpse of Bobby's school photographs on the walls. She didn't want it soiled and cheapened by Theresa catching a look into their private, precious world.

'I know you don't like me, but I just want to see if he's okay.'

She almost had Maggie fooled into thinking she had manners. Except she didn't say please. Maggie remembered her own, and even though she didn't want her anywhere near her son, she wouldn't have anyone, not even Theresa, saying she was rude.

With as much gentle calm as she could manage, Maggie opened the door a little wider.

'My son's been ill. I don't know if he wants to see anybody.'

Theresa stepped forward. 'I know. I just want to see if he's alright.'

Maggie frowned.

'Please, Maggie.' Theresa inched in closer.

Maggie folded her arms, guarding her home.

Theresa stepped back, giving up for a moment to open her crinkled brown fake leather handbag and took out a cigarette, lighting it on Maggie's doorstep. Her nails were a toxic green and blue, long and nasty. Maggie said nothing, watching her light up with her face at a tilt, blowing smoke into her hallway. She waited.

'I can't believe they all followed him in.'

Maggie swallowed, biting her lip and biting her tongue. She wondered when Denny would ever leave their lives.

'When they take it into their hands, they always take it too far.'

Theresa stamped out her cigarette after only a few drags, and Maggie realised she was on edge. When she tried to stand tall again, Maggie looked her up and down and nearly felt sorry for her. A little orphan child with no real home. But the pity quickly passed.

'They took it too far because of you.'

Theresa looked Maggie in the eye. She liked being the reason.

'Because of me? For other things too, but yes, mostly me.'

Maggie held Theresa's wrists. Theresa flinched at her touch.

'If you knew they'd do this to him, why couldn't you just leave him alone?'

Theresa shrugged. 'All I was doing was waiting for him.'

'Jesus, Theresa. Waiting for what?'

'I was waiting for us. Him and me to start properly. I never wanted him to get beaten up.'

A silence. A blackness filled Maggie's eyes and she thought of Bobby in his bed upstairs and before she knew what had happened she had slapped Theresa round the face. Short and sharp.

Theresa lowered her head, her acid-blonde hair covering her face. She caught her breath and smoothed her hair back, tucking it behind her ears. She smiled at Maggie, with a strange sorrow. But not for herself, for Maggie. For Maggie's loss of control.

'Why did you do that? Look at all the people on the estate who saw you do that.'

Maggie was shaking. She could see the nosy little bitches across the way having a good old stare.

'I'd have thought you were well over people being hit, Maggie.'

Maggie hated this girl. Hated her with a dark heart.

'You really are a *nasty* little tramp.'

The words stung more than the slap and Theresa shook her head.

'I wasn't a tramp to him and I swear I didn't want Bobby hurt. I never did, Maggie. I care about your son.'

Maggie went to raise her hand again, and in that moment they both heard a growling from the stairs.

'Put your fucking hand down.'

They turned to see Bobby at the top of the landing, coming out of the shadows.

His chest was taped with padding. From it, leaked cuts where the rings had opened up skin. His stomach was aflame. Dark and red and bloody from the inside. Kicked and kicked and kicked again. But it was his face that was the worst.

Maggie looked away.

His eyes had almost disappeared where he'd been punched in the nose. His nose was now lion-like, flat and wide, and two black-blooded lines of stitches zigzagged across the bridge. Under his eyes, the skin was a dark green shadow that swallowed up the slits of his eyes. The rest of his skin chequered with loose punches that had struck here and there, sparking rosy spots that were turning yellow as they healed. He looked as if he had a cleft lip. A single stitch held his top lip together and gave him a snarl. He was a monster, a beast-man, holding onto the banister.

Maggie was scared of her own son. Even Theresa watched in silence.

He walked down the stairs, slowly, two feet on each step, gripping the banisters with a right hand cut and bruised at the knuckles from the one or two punches he'd got in.

The daylight from the windows showed up the yellow bumps on his face. One eye was so bloodshot it was purple. His dark curls loose and wild, falling over his forehead.

'Mum, get yourself inside.'

Maggie stepped back, away from the doorway. Bobby stepped closer.

Theresa stepped back on her side of the door. She looked for another cigarette.

'You come to see me, so see me. Don't look in your bag. Look at me. What do you want?'

He stepped in front of Maggie.

'Get upstairs, Mum.'

Maggie did as she was told. She gave Theresa one last look of stone and marched up to her bedroom, her right hand still red from the slap.

Bobby turned to Theresa. Her cheek hot where his mum had hit her.

'What you want?'

His voice was still sore and it came out gruff and tired. A voice from a man who hadn't slept.

Theresa just stared.

'What do you want? Why are you here?'

Theresa tried to find her voice.

'You come to have a look? Here, take a good look.'

He walked up to Theresa's face. She could smell his bedridden breath and the warm, bloody smells of his skin.

'Let me tell you now. You weren't worth one of these bruises. Not one. If you were worth it, I'd wear these proud. But every mark on me makes me sick, because you put them there.'

She tried to slow down her breathing. Her chest swelling like she needed to cry, but she swallowed and kept her chin from trembling by

243

biting down on her lip. A red flush crept up her neck onto her face and she looked down until she thought it had calmed.

'But I didn't want this, Bobby.' She spoke in low tones.

Theresa moved closer to Bobby and lifted her hand slowly, reaching out to touch a split on his left eye. She put her fingers to it and frowned.

'I need to tell you something. I need to talk to you.'

Bobby closed his eyes. He hated her, but it felt nice to have cool, female fingers on his skin.

She took her hand away and he opened his eyes.

'I don't want to hear anything you have to say.'

He went to move inside.

'Wait. It's about your dad. What they've done to him.'

Bobby turned around.

Back to her bag and back to her cigarettes, Theresa took one out of the pack and lit it. She looked into his face.

'Sometimes I think I hate them as much as you hate them, Bobby.'

She smoked and looked to the floor. She waited a few seconds to get her thoughts before telling the story.

'Joe went and tried to burn down my dad's home.'

Bobby looked behind him at the hallway to check his mum wasn't listening. He shut the door a little.

'He did what?'

'He went down last night and tried to throw a

244

soaked-up rag through the window. But apparently he couldn't get the lighter to work and they saw him.'

'Who's they?'

Theresa frowned and looked nervous.

'You know who they are.'

She carried on.

'They threw a brick at him. Knocked him out cold. He was still lying there this morning.'

Bobby nodded. Humiliated and hurt on his dad's behalf. He could see Joe doing it, stuck in the mud. He was getting so tired of this war. There was no one left to hit.

Theresa paused and flicked the end of her cigarette.

'Where is he now?'

'I don't know where he is now. I just was told he was there this morning. They were laughing about it.'

Bobby could feel a nasty headache coming on. All those punches to his brain stirring. He was embarrassed for them both. Father and son both kicked down like dogs. They had been pushed to dark corners to lick their wounds in shame.

'I need to know where he is, Theresa.'

She nodded. 'I don't know where he is, Bobby. I can go to the site and check?'

He didn't want to take her help but he did.

'Yeah, check the site. Just look for him.'

But he knew his dad would not be there. He would be wandering, hopeless and hurt, drinking and sleeping somewhere. Bobby would need to find him once he could walk. He needed to lie down for a bit and get it together.

He went to turn back to his house in pain without saying anything else to Theresa.

It was not enough for her, the messenger. Watching him go, she shivered. It felt like the last time he would talk to her.

'Bobby.'

He sighed and turned. His belly twisting up inside from the way they kicked it.

'What the fuck now?'

'I saw something else too. I saw the girl you're with.'

'Chloe?'

Theresa bit her bottom lip. 'That her name?'

The mad in her coming out.

'Theresa, go home.'

Theresa's mouth thinned into a hard little line.

'No, hang on. I saw her in the pub with Connor. The one round the corner. Swear on my life, she was there and Connor was at the bar next to her drinking and buying her drinks.'

Bobby's head started to pound and a cold ache hit the back of his neck, a block of ice slipping down his backbone.

'You *what*?'

Theresa was full of shit.

'She was standing by the bar talking to him.'

'You're fucking lying.'

'I'm not fucking lying to you. She was there. She even asked me for a cigarette.'

Bobby couldn't think clearly. His head was full of pain and hurt and anger and he needed to lie down and sleep. He couldn't keep his eyes open. Connor and Chloe. Drinking in a pub. Why would she?

Theresa threw her cigarette to the ground.

'How was she talking to him?'

'Talking. With a drink. Like she knew him. That's why I noticed her.'

Bobby felt a dizziness come over him. Same way he felt after being punched. He couldn't hear properly. The air was heavy and grey.

'I just thought you should know.'

Tiredness crashed over Bobby. Sleep. He needed sleep and lots of it. He needed to not wake up for a few days. He couldn't see anything, everything was in shadow. And then the colour started to come back, and his breathing got quick again and Bobby didn't need sleep anymore. He needed to fight.

Like thunder, he stood over Theresa and moved towards her.

'You're lying.'

With the rage he had left, Bobby stretched his muscles to stand tall. But it hurt. It hurt to be angry and his hands began to shake.

But at least he was talking to her again. She looked at his face then down at his hands.

'You're falling apart, Bobby.'

She began to walk away.

'Theresa.'

She turned. Waiting to hear what he had to say.

But nothing. Bobby only stared at her. And then he shut the door.

30

Chloe was told Bobby had not left his room in two days.

'He's healing up very well.'

This was the first lie.

Bobby had been healing up quickly. He had good genes like that. But Bobby had also been drinking for the last two days and coming undone. There had been screaming and shouting and smashing. Cooped up for too long, Bobby had started making noise.

If she'd had the foresight, Maggie wouldn't have let Chloe in.

'Tea?'

'Yes please.'

Maggie bustled about in the kitchen while Chloe hung back in the doorway.

Always in doorways, that girl. Maggie looked over her shoulder and smiled.

'How is he?'

'He's doing better. Walking about. He had a bath last night; first one he's had since it happened. About time too.'

Maggie chuckled and took out two mugs.

'We've had a bit of drama. Nothing much, but Bobby got a bit of a headache from it. Had to have a nip of whisky to calm him down and help him sleep. Knock himself out.'

This was the second lie.

'Oh.'

It was best not to mention Theresa.

'What was the drama about?'

'Oh, this and that. Politics from round here. Goldfish bowl. The usual nonsense . . . Sugar?'

'No. No thanks.'

Chloe played with her mum's ring.

She did not know about the politics of this estate.

'Is he sleeping now?'

Maggie put the two mugs of tea on the table. Pristine and perfect as it had been last time, a vase of white daisy-looking flowers in the centre and the washing spinning round in the machine.

'He's up I think. I heard movements. But drink your tea first, love. Have a little breather.'

She didn't want Chloe going up there. All morning Bobby had been banging about. He'd calmed down now, but only because he was so tired. He'd nap, doze off for some part of an hour and then his eyes would blink wide open, coming back to life, and he'd gasp sharply. Like he'd been shocked back to life, some kind of pain had put a pulse back into his heart too quickly. He was a beast curled up sleeping until prodded by Maggie with a cup of tea, or a ham and mustard sandwich. When she left him alone to go to bed she'd hear him howl into the night, his sounds falling through the estate. Sobbing and sweating it out again until the temper left him and fizzled back into the air and he was just a boy, in a bed, covered in bruises.

That poor boy. Ever since Theresa had come round. That little tart, whipping up mayhem and mess wherever she went.

Chloe sipped the hot tea and looked around the room. Pictures on the fridge of Bobby as a boy, as a teenager, with his hair gelled and slicked back. Before he got his curly quiff.

'That your daddy?'

A big, dark man. Swarthy and heavyset with a big-boned face: big jaw, big neck, big black hair like a helmet around his head, Fifties side parting and hair much blacker than Bobby's. He was holding a little baby Maggie with huge ape-ish hands, hairy knuckles around her little dress.

Maggie turned and smiled. Smiled at how Chloe had used the word 'daddy'.

'That's him. Spit of Bobby, don't you think?'

Chloe didn't think they looked alike at all. Bobby looked only like Bobby. Nothing like Joe or his granddad. No chip off any old block.

'I was his special little girl, you know? He always wanted a boy and just got us girls and what could he do with that.'

Maggie took the picture from the fridge and looked at it closer. Like every day since he had died, Maggie missed him.

'Do you miss your mum?'

Chloe felt herself go pink. It was the first time anyone had asked her that directly. She didn't want to cry at Maggie's table. She put her tea on a coaster and played with the ends of the white tablecloth.

'Always.'

Maggie smiled.

'I remember the day my dad died, I didn't cry at all. I walked for hours. All night. It was dangerous really. But I just took myself off for a walk round here and sat on benches and walls. I wanted to spend the night with my dad. If that makes sense.'

Chloe nodded. It made perfect sense to her. Maggie carried on.

'He was a lovely man, my dad. Never liked Joe much.'

'Why?'

'Said he got into too many fights outside the ring to call himself a boxer.'

Chloe took her tea again.

'Bobby said your dad was a good boxer.'

Maggie smiled and looked at the photo.

'The best kind. He never brought it home. Never made my mum worry about the bruises.'

She put the photo on the table and took Chloe's hand. Warm from the mug of tea, Chloe felt calm being held this way.

'Chloe, if there's anything you need, come and find me.'

And she moved in closer, stepping from the chair and putting two hands on Chloe's shoulders. She leaned in and held Chloe to her, stroking the back of her neck. For a second, Chloe relaxed and heard her breathing, short and raspy, her face against Maggie's soft silk gown.

Chloe took her hand away and looked down. The tears nearly there. Somehow it always felt worse when people were kind.

'Thank you,' whispered Chloe.

They finished their tea.

'Can I see him now, please?'

Maggie put the photo on the table and nodded. "'Course.'

The two women went slowly up the stairs, one pensive and the other cautious. Maggie wished he was sleeping. It would be easier if he was; Chloe could come back another day.

They tiptoed in, Chloe peering from behind Maggie. Even though it had only been nearly a week since she'd last seen him, Chloe was full of nerves. More than nerves, Chloe felt she was being taken somewhere dark, somewhere where she couldn't come back from. Bobby felt like a stranger to her again, unfamiliar and wrong.

There was a smell. Chloe couldn't name it to herself. Different from when she'd last been there. It smelt like sex, but it wasn't. Stuffy, old and trapped, layers of skin worn off in sweat and in scabs. Old blood too, a smell like rot. And then the smell of some kind of aftershave. Bobby's smells as he tossed and turned in his bed getting better.

He groaned when they walked in. A half-sleep moan. Bobby rolled over into the patch of bed that was cold and opened his eyes, mumbling something through the haze of waking up.

'Who's there?'

'It's me and Chloe, love.'

He turned to look at them both. His face had healed. Where it had looked terrible a few days ago, it now looked a little cleaner, the skin a little less broken up by bruising spots and puffiness, his eyes starting to show through the swelling. Bobby was getting his stare back.

Maggie squeezed Chloe's arm.

'I'll leave you here.'

As she walked down the stairs, Maggie looked up at the doorway and saw Chloe standing in it, a small cut-out shape of a girl, waiting at the edge of the room. Maggie sighed. If she'd had a good, strong head on her, she'd have told Chloe to come back later. She could have lied; she'd lied about the other stuff. She could have told her that Bobby couldn't see anyone at the moment and was unwell. He needed some peace and quiet. She was his mum, she was allowed to do that, she was allowed to make up house rules.

But she didn't. Instead, Maggie looked away and went back down the stairs, thinking it wiser to not say a thing. Hoping Bobby would have a calm streak, that the rest would have done him good. Maggie walked back to her kitchen and left them to it.

The silence fell. Chloe felt on edge, treading on eggshells. Bobby's eyes hadn't left her and he said nothing. Even when she tried to smile, Bobby did not smile back, did not seem happy to see her, and did not ask her to come in. She moved closer to him, towards the bed, and perched beside him. Bobby did not move up to make room for her.

'Can I turn the lamp on?'

He mumbled something and Chloe stood up and switched the light on. She looked down at him in the soft lamp-glow, yellow and warm, at his body, still a little sticky as it healed, covered here and there in white gauze and tape. His face was recognisably Bobby's, the eyes shinier and blacker, his hair slept-on and curlier than usual.

Long, for Bobby. The cut above his mouth pulled Bobby's lip into a snarl, but his eyes looked tired. His hands were clasped at his stomach, sitting gently on a heart-shaped bruise. Chloe put one of her hands in both of his, then leaned over his body to kiss him lightly.

He smelt of sweat, metal and antiseptic. He didn't kiss her back and Chloe stood up again, backing into the doorway. His stillness frightened her and she didn't know him well enough yet to feel out these moods.

'Should I go? Are you tired?'

After several silent seconds that boomed around Bobby's low-lit box room, he spoke.

'Stay. Sit.'

Chloe did as she was told. Bobby moved over a little bit this time so she could sit at the edge of the bed next to him. Up close the smells from the sheets and from Bobby were furry, stronger. The evening was quiet outside. Saturday night hadn't begun and most were still indoors, doing their make-up, having tea and watching their televisions. Chloe could hear Maggie's radio downstairs, songs that were too faint to make out properly.

Bobby took his right hand and picked up Chloe's left. He held it softly in his damp palm and turned his body to her.

Chloe's heart beat hard inside her. She looked at his swollen, charred puffy lips. More silence. Bobby ran his tongue over his lips and edged his body forward a little more so it touched the side of hers. She could feel his groin on her hip and turned her body round so they were face to face.

254

With their hands together, fingers twisting into fingers, bodies breathing into each other. She couldn't stand the smell off his sick skin, but didn't want to hurt his feelings.

Bobby moved close to Chloe and held her hand tightly. Chloe was surprised by how strong he was, given the battering he'd had. His grip was firm.

Chloe's eyes wandered, not able to meet Bobby's stare, her voice lost somewhere at the back of her throat and her stomach sick. This didn't feel right.

'What have you been doing?'

She was watching his chapped lips move. Dry and sore from breathing out of his mouth.

'Not much.' She kept her voice calm. 'I took Devlin to the park earlier.'

He nodded.

Chloe kept talking. 'We put some of Mum's stuff in boxes. She had some lovely jewellery she never wore. We're working out who gets what.'

Bobby closed his eyes and his body went tense for a second. He opened his eyes. In pain, his voice was strained and quiet.

'Pass me those pills.'

She gave him two, placing each in his mouth and holding the glass of water from his bedside between his cracked, sore lips. He swallowed and lay there breathing heavily. She waited for him to open his eyes again.

'Why didn't you stay with me the other night?'

'Because you were sleeping. You needed to sleep.'

'Water.'

Chloe wet his lips again. She wasn't sure if it was the way his face was healing or the crackle of something unkind in his voice that was making her want to leave. She put the glass of water back down and inched her body slightly away from his. She could hear how hard it was for him to swallow.

'Chloe, were you in the pub with Connor?'

The way he asked her this, in his low whisper, made her feel like she had done something very, very wrong. She paused, taking her time to answer.

'Yes. But not with him. He was in the pub and I was there too.'

'Why did you stay if you knew he was in there?' He watched her face, reading her reaction; his eyes, so heavy with pain and swelling, blinked slowly.

'I just saw him and told him to leave me and you alone.'

'You told him to leave me alone?'

'For what he'd done to you.'

Bobby tried to sit up.

'So you had a good talk with him, then?'

Chloe craved to hear something or someone making some, any, kind of sound outside. But there was still nothing she could pay attention to. Just the muffled kitchen radio and Bobby's thick breathing between them. She should have felt safe, knowing Maggie was just downstairs, but she didn't. Despite their hug, Maggie was not her friend.

Chloe hadn't thought she had done anything wrong, but now she felt as if she had. Her mind raced and a flash of heat came over her. And though a voice in her head told her to say nothing, to keep herself safe for a little longer until she was out of this room, Chloe told the truth.

'It wasn't like that. I ran into him in the pub. I shouted at him when he tried to buy me a drink.'

Her voice was shaky. She kept talking.

'So he bought you a drink?'

As if the pills had suddenly kicked in, Bobby was able to sit up properly. From somewhere his strength came back.

'I just stood there and he came up to *me*. All I did was stand there.'

As her thin voice told the tiny tale, Bobby's eyes began to fill. The grip on her hand was so hard it began to hurt, his fingers digging into the soft skin of her palm, leaving nail marks. She tried to pull her hand away but Bobby did not let her.

'I want you to let go.'

Bobby shook his head.

'How did he even get close enough for you to shout? Why didn't you just walk away?'

Bobby squeezed Chloe's hand hard again and waited patiently for her to answer. And Chloe did, sweat creeping up her back like she'd been caught red-handed in bed with Connor. She stuttered it out again.

'I was in the pub. Alone. He was there. I'm sorry, but I don't understand what the matter is.'

Beneath the yellowing and browning of his bruises, Bobby began to turn pink, the hand that held hers shook, and his whole arm shook. He said nothing but stared at her. All this happened in slow motion. Chloe seemed to be looking into Bobby's eyes forever, and he seemed to hold onto her hand forever. Unable to move away, Chloe waited and then Bobby let go. He let go and moved away from her. He sat up on his knees and lifted his bedroom curtains a little to look out of the window.

Bobby got louder.

'You took a drink from him?'

He kept saying it.

'You took a drink from him?'

Chloe shook her head. Trapped in this mad moment of temper.

'No. No, I didn't, Bobby. What are you talking about? I didn't even smile at him.'

Chloe's voice was rising.

'You were meant to be in *my* corner.' Bobby was talking with so much venom that the spit fell from the corner of his mouth. 'You were meant to be on *my* side. In *my* world, not theirs.'

He was starting to breathe really fast, holding the back of his head and shaking.

'Why? Why you? Why you fucking me over? You like going where the thugs are?'

He looked up, rabid, sweating in one long stream, spit coming off his lower lip.

Chloe moved forward. Into his space. 'No, it's nothing like that. I just saw him . . . ' She tried to reach out to hold his body and keep him still.

'Stop it, Bobby.'

'He bought you a drink. You let him buy you a drink. He fucking tried to kill me and my dad, and you drink with him?'

Chloe started trying to move away. His body was building up power, she could feel it. In a count of maybe two, or three seconds, Bobby swivelled round and with a huge, wolfish snarl, he flung his right arm out. He made a fist. It connected.

At first, Chloe did not feel anything.

At first it was only shock.

Chloe did not know what had happened; she could not place herself, did not recognise this room or this man. She felt her head spin, giddy and light, tasting blood in her mouth, feeling it leak down the back of her throat.

With little breaths she lay on her back, trembling, looking up at the dark ceiling. The bent shape of Bobby's body hunched and sobbing into his hands. But it was all a mist; she couldn't make him out properly. The room was a cloud of quiet with slow moving shapes and sounds. Bobby's yells. Bobby's head tucked into his chest.

Tears ran down Chloe's face from the impact. She blinked them back and lay still, watching him. Bobby sat with his head in his hands, croaking out sorry. Sorry sorry sorry.

'Oh fuck, fuck, fuck, fuck. What I done, what I done, what I done . . .'

Chloe inched herself up on her elbows. Frowning, she tried to find his eyes and make him see what he'd done was wrong. He'd done something very wrong. She wanted him to know that. Chloe was silent for a second. And then Chloe screamed. Screamed as if she was being born, torn from her mother, torn from life.

Chloe's eyes, open and wild, looked at Bobby as if he'd tried to kill her. Her wails brought Maggie hurtling into the room.

'What's happened? What's going on?'

Maggie jolted when she saw Chloe's nose.

'Bobby, what you gone and done?'

She should have lied; just said Bobby wasn't well. Told her to come another day.

Before Maggie could stop her, Chloe barged past and flew down the stairs. They both heard the front door slam.

'Bobby, what have you done?'

But Bobby, like a little boy, had curled up in a ball. He would not look up. Maggie sat on the edge of the bed and put her hand on the back of his damp head for a moment. Bobby would not look up, his jaw clenched so tightly that the bones in his face stood hard against the skin and the veins in his neck pumped like they would burst. Maggie stopped shouting and kept the back of her hand pressed to his neck as if to lull his heartbeat.

'Bobby what have you done to her?'

He would not face his mum. Burying his ugliness in the pillow.

'Tell me what you did.' Gently she asked, coaxing it from him.

Nothing. Bobby panted. His body trembling.

She looked at the mess of his bedroom, too sad to shout. She kept her fingers on his neck.

Bobby turned his face and looked at Maggie. He spoke so quietly she could hardly hear him.

'I hit her.'

Maggie said nothing. She thought he had. Part

260

of her had always worried that side of him would come out. The worst part of Joe. She took her hand away and her lungs felt a thick pressure. Her breathing became heavy. She was suddenly very hot and went over to Bobby's window. She looked at some of the grubby curtains in the flats opposite. It was getting dark and a large group of Somalian women walked through the lamplight carrying huge bags of shopping.

'Do you understand what you've done?'

A muffled sound from her son.

'I didn't mean to.'

Maggie pulled Bobby's window shut so hard her hand began to tingle. She spat it out.

'But you did it anyway.'

She felt a rising guilt and misery. Of owning him. At failing him.

'Why do you think I threw your dad out?'

'Mum, I know. I fucking know.'

He said nothing and his silence made the disgust build and her voice got louder.

'What were you *thinking*? Answer me, Bobby! How could you do that?'

Bobby covered his face.

Maggie walked closer to him and yanked a hand away from his face. Bobby jerked his hand back to try and hide himself from his mum, but she gripped it until it hurt him. She stayed looming over his bed. She held him by his shoulders and shook him.

'No. Look at me. You will listen to me.'

She held onto him and bent her head to look into his eyes.

'You have a rage in you that I always thought

261

was a good thing. I thought you'd use it to do something. But you stayed too long. You're too big for this room. Too old for this.'

'Please, Mum.'

'Fight them out there. Not here. You *don't* hit her.'

Bobby looked down.

'Just like your dad. Playing silly bollocks until you're too old to change.'

He began shaking his head with his eyes shut, throwing her words away.

'I'm not my dad.' It was a whimper. He couldn't be cursed the same. He needed his mum's forgiveness to mend this.

He sat up, looking at Maggie, pulling his hand back again.

'I got nothing, Mum. It's all broken.'

She stepped back. She could smell the rot in him. His hands facing up, dead at his sides.

With his empty glass in her hand she left before he saw her cry.

31

Chloe was out of breath. She stopped running and started walking quickly down the canal path, looking for patches of light to lead her home.

At first she thought he was one of those drunks by the station. A real wino. The ones who'd had their noses broken three or four times and sat pissing onto their knees as commuters walked by. The scabby drunks. That's what Joe looked like now. Lying on a bench, at the bank of the canal, with his Special Brew, knocking it back to ease the pain at the back of his head and across his face. He'd landed face-down when he fell, splitting the bridge of his nose.

He looked bad, even in the dark. She turned the other way but that was the way she came and she could never go back there.

'Wait,' Joe called out. 'I know you.'

Chloe looked up.

'Here, come here. What happened to your face? Let's have a look, come on.' He stood and limped towards her.

She flinched, moving back sharply, keeping her face twisted away from him. Her breathing ragged and her throat so sore she could only whisper.

'Leave me alone.'

Joe went closer still, his shaky arms out in front of him, trying to speak in hushed tones. Chloe shifted from one foot to the other, her head still down. She didn't know what she should do, too stunned to move left or right. Joe's face made her feel sick. It was scabby where he'd fallen on his face. And it was dirty. His eyes flickering drunk. Drunk men were dangerous. Men like Bobby were dangerous. Just as her sister had said.

When Joe got too close, Chloe panicked and shoved him away as hard as she could and started in the other direction. Joe tumbled back a bit and caught his balance before he landed back on the bench.

'I don't want to hurt you. How could I, look at me! Come here. What's happened to you? You can't walk the streets with blood on you.'

'Keep away.' Chloe picked up a broken branch from the path and threw it in Joe's direction, sobbing.

'You need to have it looked at. Chloe. Chloe, is it? I know you. Come on. Come back here.'

'Your *boy*. Your *son*.' Chloe spat out the words. 'Look what he did.'

She took her hands away and showed Joe her face properly. A single punch to her small face.

It was bad, but it wasn't a break. Joe didn't think it was a break, he wasn't sure though. He'd seen and done worse. She was a tiny little thing. Her bones weren't made to take a whack from Bobby. All the times he'd done it to Maggie. He knew it was wrong then, and he knew it was wrong now. Joe scrunched his eyes up and felt a sting of pain. Chloe stood in front of him, her hands at her sides now, her face white. Whiter still with the moon and the street lamps behind her. The tears had run her mascara down her cheeks. She breathed out, trying to steady her sobs. Now she let herself cry properly.

'It looks worse than what it is. Trust me. That'll clean up just fine.'

Joe took her arm. She let him. He looked over her face.

Chloe swallowed and put her fingers to her nose again, tapping the top of the bridge, letting out a cry each time she did.

'Did he break it?'

Joe didn't know what to tell her. He couldn't tell, even close up, not when he was in the state he was in, drunk and dizzy.

'Nah, I don't think he went that far. You got a knock, that's all.'

Chloe nodded, calmer now. She had stopped crying and sniffed.

Joe suddenly bent down and clutched at his head.

'Fucking *animals*.'

Chloe blinked and looked around.

'Why are you doing that?'

He moved away from her.

'Fucking brick. Who throws a brick?'

'What happened?'

Joe cocked his head and smiled. 'I tried to do something good and foolish. For my boy.'

She went to move away, down the bank of the canal, to somewhere else damp and dark. Lost and shocked, she put her hands back to her face and walked on, stumbling. She was going to take a fall.

'I don't know where I am. I don't know where I am.'

Joe stood up, his face twisting in pain when he spoke.

'Wait, hang on,' he called out, rubbing the back of his head and wincing.

'I can't tell my dad. I can't tell anyone yet.'

Joe limped on. 'You don't have to do nothing.'

Breathless and giddy, Chloe began to walk off in the opposite direction. Joe moved after her as quickly as he could. One hand on his head.

'You're coming with me. Come here.'

Joe walked after her.

Chloe stopped and felt cold. She didn't know where she was going.

'Chloe.'

Joe made his way to her and put his arm around her shoulder this time, as tight as he could manage. Somewhere through his drink, he felt Chloe lean towards him, and he pulled her to him in a way that didn't make her feel frightened. Relieved to have someone look after her, Chloe did not mind the smells of stale sweat and sweet-bitter beer. She did not mind the smell of clothes that had soaked up Joe's drunk skin for days and days and days.

'You're coming with me. We're going to get you sorted. Can't have a girl walking about the canal looking like her old man's gone and belted her.'

She spoke into his smelly old coat. 'But where do I go? I don't know what to do.'

Joe held onto her and kept them walking.

'We're going to hospital. Come on, you help

me walk and I'll help you.'

Softly they stepped down the dark stretch of the canal and up onto the open road. From the safety of their cold, black, watery world they were hit by the brassy land above the bank. Blinking lights and streaming traffic and the stares of people wondering what an old man with a messed-up face was doing with a bashed-up girl. They were avoided. Passers-by looked at them as if they had emerged from the depths of the canal and had swum up from the swamp to walk among the others.

Chloe gripped Joe in shock. She couldn't smell the stench of unwash any more. His body was warm to her; warm and kind. She held on. All the way to the hospital reception, where she let Joe do all the talking.

Joe said they had been attacked at the canal. He said she was his niece. And they left it at that. Joe sat with her as they fixed her up.

'Do you want us to have a look at you too?'

Even though Joe's head pounded and the backs of his legs were shivering down the nerves, he said no.

'Nothing I can't clean up myself.'

'Please, we'd like to have a look.'

'Get your hands off me,' he shouted, like a proper old wino.

They let him go.

Joe took Chloe's arm and closed his eyes a little bit as they walked. His head thumped. He said he needed to lean on her this time. Whatever this was he was feeling, it was not drunk and it was not tired. Joe leaned on a wall. The colours turning black and white. He'd be alright after another drink. Maggie would give him another drink. He would go to Maggie's house and lie down.

He took Chloe to the bus stop and watched her get on a bus. She took her seat and fixed her eyes straight ahead. She didn't see him fall against the wall as the bus went round the corner.

Chloe took out a mirror from her bag. She put her fingers to her nose. The thumped nose had got wider as her eyes had got smaller. Nothing was as before. Her face was a stranger. Her black hair had long come out of its band and was matted and a mess, it framed her face in an electric shock. Her lips, bitten as she cried, were red. When she sniffed, it hurt. Inside, the dried-up blood made it hard to breathe, but her nose was too sore to blow, so she started breathing through her mouth, steaming the mirror up.

She wondered if Bobby had meant it. There had been a look in his eye. Where the black had filled out the colour of his pupils and stared into her, cold. But they weren't his eyes. It wasn't him looking at her. She hated him and she wanted to go home to see her sister.

'I fucking told you,' Polly would say.

Chloe didn't need telling. She needed a hot bath and she needed to hide. Her nose throbbed in pain and she had a splitting headache. She stood up at her stop, shock and rage making her hands shake as she tried to zip up her coat.

32

Bobby hit the wardrobe with his hand. He kept doing it until the whole thing was smashed and he'd cut open his knuckles again.

He punched himself too. Took shots at his own stomach, where the bruising was the worst. Trying to punch so hard he'd break into a kidney. He stared out of the window. Stone-faced. Drained and exhausted and glistening in a greasy cold sweat that left his bed sheets damp. His chest rose quickly, up and down, his breath sore. Everything he hadn't wanted to be. He'd never wanted to hurt her. He hadn't thought he would be able to. He'd just wanted her out of the room. And now he couldn't bear to be in the same room where he'd punched her.

His mum was in the kitchen letting him thrash it out. She said nothing.

Bobby threw on a hoodie and slammed the door on his shame. He kept his head down as he left the estate and he kept walking, listening to the change jangle in his pocket.

He moved clumsily on, swaying as his heavy body grew weaker. In car windows he saw his reflection and turned away, disgusted. He did not look tough, he did not look like a fighter; he looked ugly. He hung his head lower.

'You hit women now do you, Bobby?' he kept asking himself over and over again.

He stumbled around all night, following the

road that led down to the canal. He hadn't been down there since he'd cut Connor's face. The moon hung over the bank and the river. Quiet and cool. Dark and safe.

Bobby burned hot and cold. He sat on a bench, the ends of his fingers and toes tingling, the anger leaving a new bitter pain. The fresh air hurt against the cuts and grazes but it was clearing his head. He was back where he'd started, same place, same blood shining black on the same body. He'd won a fight and lost a fight. Won a girl and lost her. Not lost her, hit her. Thumped her like a beast that needed a bullet.

His gut turned and twisted and he vomited onto the grass, only just missing his trainer.

He thought about phoning her. He took his phone out and let it ring. No answer. It was 5 a.m. She could be asleep. He didn't leave a message because he felt ill and was sick again. Standing up to let it all out.

He sat back down, shivering. Wiping his mouth and feeling the roughness in his throat. The smell nasty and strong, mixing with the rest of his stale, scabbing body. Bobby breathed and then chewed on the knuckle of his thumb. His hands would not stop shaking. He remembered every moment in clear, cold flashback. When he thought of her, the pain of his cuts and twists and aches and thumps all came to the surface harder, her name searing through each one. The sound of her: Chloe. A cut, a stinging blade through the skin. Bobby imagined it had not been real. But it was and he shut his eyes and saw her scream again loud enough to give him a headache. He was tired and wrong and he wanted to say he was sorry.

Despite the cold, Bobby closed his eyes and stretched out on a bench. He would not win any fights now. The tournament would be over for him. Boxing, whatever was left of it, would have to start all over again.

He dreamed in dozes, replaying the moment that his hand lashed out. Seeing her face. The instant she felt the hit. Stunned before it started to hurt. A moment's flash, his body jumped on the bench, twitching and unsettled.

Then he woke freezing. And hungry.

Sitting up, he looked out at the canal water, flat and watchful. Grey in daylight. The ducks sitting on the bank and the morning coming through in shadow and sunlight.

Today was cold, but it was new. A man had arrived early for fishing and didn't take much notice of Bobby.

The cafe was around the corner and home not far beyond that. He walked up the steps, away from the caves of the canal and onto the quiet roads. It hurt to walk. Forgetting what he looked like, Bobby stopped at a car window. He stared. His body used to glow and pump full of good, red blood. Olive and burnished from jogging outside in summer. He used to be handsome. His face could take an odd black eye, a cut lip. But now it looked sloppy. He stank, he hunched and he stumbled.

At the cafe, Bobby crept to the counter to order coffee and eggs. He didn't want any conversation and kept his eyes to the floor when

271

the waitress asked how he was.

'You look a bit rough, how many fights you lost this week?'

Bobby said nothing.

He found a table by the window and sat down. The sun shone on Bobby and he took his hood down. On his split cheekbones, the sun picked out the black in the blood and the gold in his eyes. All wild and messy with fight.

The waitress put his eggs down. Two fried eggs and chips. The yolk already starting to run. Starving, he ate as if every bite was sewing him back together. He ate quickly, his mouth close to the plate, barely stopping to swallow one mouthful before loading another one in. He heard the radio playing something old and familiar, but he didn't know who sang it. A group his mum liked. He put three sugars in his coffee and, after tasting sick and iron, it was hot, sweet and healing.

He got up, leaving all his change on the table. It was about right. He might even have left a tip. He kept his head down as he felt the nervous looks his face was getting from people around him. They found the way he looked frightening. One man stared for too long, still dressed in his night-shift gear, the name of the cleaning firm on his T-shirt.

'You alright?'

Bobby put his hood up, opened the door and took a step back outside.

The air stung. Bobby started walking, his hands in fists, and his fists at his sides. Walking was real.

Not far to go, he only had muddy, bandaged thoughts going through his painful head as he walked on down the same roads.

Winding down roads. The looming blocks just like his. Grey on grey on grey, boxing in the chaos. From gym to estate: one ring traded for another. Back the way he came, Bobby could smell the different air as soon as he set foot in the bleak mouth of the block. Curries and laundry and blocked-up drains. The same old stink. The same old brick. Walking, walking, his heart beating and his breath sore and sharp in his throat, in his chest. Back to it all, all over again.

33

Maggie took one look at Joe on her doorstep and knew he wasn't right. She saw the blood on his shirt collar, rusting up. She saw the eyes heavy and swollen, the nose scabbed and bent and Joe's skin, pale and dry as dust. He had a smell about him as she let him pass, a quietness that was strange. He buckled at the door. She reached out and grabbed him, and he straightened up. Maggie walked him.

'He hit her, Joe. He hit her.'

'I know.'

It was warm inside. Joe could feel the heating curling up around his skin and he felt heavy, full of sleep.

'How could you know?'

'Saw her down the canal. She was running around lost, and I took her to the hospital.'

He made his way to the kitchen, looking for somewhere warm to sit. Somewhere to put his feet.

She knew he wasn't sure if he was welcome.

'It's alright. You can go and sit on the sofa.'

Joe did an odd stumble when he got to the doorway. A waltz that needed the support of the wall as he moved. Maggie watched him until he sat down. She didn't like seeing him like this. This was different to drunk; this was something she couldn't be angry about. Joe was not well. He leaned into the cushions.

'She was fine. Nothing broken.'

The kettle was on and the flat smelt like pine and linen and the pipes made a whirring noise as they heated up. He missed his home.

'Does that make it okay? That he didn't break something?'

The flat was warm and cosy but the air between Maggie and Joe was strained with the memories of what had passed between them years ago.

'No, but she's alright. She will be alright.'

Joe sat back.

'Where is he? I want to have a word with him.'

Maggie came out of the kitchen. A box of tea bags in her hand and a sad smile.

'Oh Joe. What good are you to him now?'

She couldn't help herself. He smiled sadly too.

'I'd tell him not to do it.'

She disappeared back to the kitchen.

'He left. Bolted right out of the door.'

Joe's voice was at its closing time. Hushed, rasping and hard to hear.

'But he isn't well.'

'Joe, he can lick his wounds alone. I almost can't stand to let him in after what he did.'

'For now?'

'For now. Though you should have seen the poor girl afterwards.'

'I did. Told you I did.'

Maggie came out with the teas. She put one on the table next to Joe and then sat on an armchair by the television. The dawn was an ugly light and made her look older than she was. They sat in silence and she looked on. The man on her

275

sofa was not the one she had married. His tea got cold and she took small sips of hers as the clock ticked on and the room they had once shared felt as safe and warm as spring. She remembered the glass bottles of proper French perfume she'd collected when Joe had money. The older she got the less they got used. It had been her dream to make perfume when Bobby grew up. Maggie had a good nose and she loved things smelling nice. There was a place in France. It was called Grasse; they made perfume there. Joe had made a joke.

'You going to grass? Who on? Not me I hope.'

Those things never happened. They were never meant to. She settled for making her home look nice. The yellow curtains, the soft beige sofas and the cushions with matching primrose print. She took one and held it on her lap. Joe had one eye open, looking at her.

'Where's my hat?'

'Your hat?'

'My black hat. The one those reggae boys gave me that summer.'

Maggie had all of Joe's things in her wardrobe. In a box buried at the back behind her dresses for weddings and funerals.

'It's upstairs. You want it?'

Joe shook his head. 'Just so I know it's somewhere.'

He tried to sit up. 'This head of mine, Maggie. It's killing me.'

'Too much drink?'

It hurt for Joe to shake his head and he put it between his hands and moaned.

'They threw a rock at the back of my head and I haven't felt right since. Really wobbly on my feet.'

Maggie could see the lump beneath Joe's greasy hair as he bent his neck. His hair thinning as he aged. As Joe got older it all fell out. His hair, teeth and nails.

'Well you wouldn't, would you? Having a big stone lobbed at your brain. You want to go to hospital?'

Joe mumbled with his face down. 'No, nothing that rest can't heal.'

'You need a good clean-up.'

She got up and went to the kitchen. She found the First-Aid kit under the sink and came back, then sat next to Joe. Her husband stank of old blood, old scabs, old stings that wouldn't heal properly and kept weeping. He bent his head and let her clean where he'd been hit. The ointment wet Joe's neck. She dabbed it on gently and heard him murmur with the sharp bite of alcohol hitting the open cut. She saw his body jerk and took care not to press too hard.

'Joe?'

He made a noise. He was trying to listen through the pain.

'How could you slip away so easily from what you were?'

Joe's hand held Maggie's leg for a moment. He sighed.

'I lost myself, Maggie.'

She stopped dabbing. The gash too big to treat with her gauze and antiseptic. Blood was all down the back of his shirt and the lump was big and tender. She didn't want to touch it. It wasn't doing anything anyway. She gently wound some gauze around his head.

'That's done.'

Joe grunted and sat up slowly. Leaning on the arm of the sofa, he coughed a little.

'Fucking mess of a man, aren't I? Look, can't even afford socks.'

He showed his bony ankles, grey and thin, as he crossed his legs. The black shoes looked sore on his cold feet, leaving red marks and dry spots. Joe could feel a sickness in his gut that he didn't recognise. He didn't know whether he would throw up or fall asleep. Maggie smelt of soap and tea roses. As he sat in the warm, her body and her skin became a cloud around him.

'I can't bear to look at him after what he done, Joe.'

'Don't you worry, Mags. He needed to run it off. He knows he's broken what he had. Let him go and be alone.'

'She just lost her mum. And he does that to her. Gorgeous, tiny thing.'

'She's no fool. She has a scream on her.'

Maggie got up and poured herself a small gin.

'I thought when I told you to go that he would know right from wrong. He could feel a life without the fear and the drink and me crying. I thought if it was just me and him he'd be a better man. Kinder. And he was. He is. But he has your heart, doesn't he, Joe? Every time you came out that ring, you were different.'

Joe asked for a gin. She put hers in his hands. He coughed and sipped some, wetting and warming his throat before he spoke.

'It wasn't the ring. I was happy in there. It was everything else. I was most myself in there, under those lights. There, it was just me, Maggie. I was alone. I liked it.'

He took another sip and closed his eyes. Then he opened them and spoke again, his voice harder to hear. Maggie had to come closer. Joe had never opened up so much about himself before.

'The grace and the feeling of being calm in my body before I heard the bell. Before I got a punch on the man in there with me. It was sweet and dark and even under those lights I was in the shadows, moving about like I wanted. But then you come out and it almost hurts your eyes. You're blinking around you and there's nothing. Just ordinary life and ordinary people talking about nothing. You can't connect.'

His voice running out of steam, puffing out his lines.

'Give us another, please?'

Maggie poured them both a glass.

'But life is ordinary, Maggie. We are ordinary.'

Joe sank the second. The sickness moving from his belly and hurting his head more. He went on. High on the pain.

'You spend your time away from the fights thinking about winning or losing them. Even when I wasn't in the ring, I was still in the fight. I saw everything in black and white: winning or losing. I got tired. I would drink so the world would get its grey back.'

'You wasted time.'

Joe shrugged.

'Maybe.'

He could hear his breathing, louder than usual.

'Where's Bobby?'

'He's out, Joe. You know that.'

'Oh. Yes.'

He put his hand out for another drink. The glass in the air, held by shaking fingers. Maggie took it from him before he dropped it.

'I want him home, Joe. I'd rather tell him off here than he get hurt out there. But I need to show him I'm angry with him.'

Joe nodded.

'One more.'

Maggie knew she would keep giving them as long as he wanted them. She felt Joe was living his last days in small luxuries. She filled it higher than before.

'When's he back?'

'I don't know, Joe.'

She put the glass back in his hand and watched him down the firewater.

'Well, when he comes through that door tell him I want a word with him.'

She took the glass from his hand. His voice was starting to gurgle. He was full of sound and sleep. His eyes closing. His breathing becoming slow.

Dizzy from gin, Maggie put her hand on the top of his cold head and smoothed down his hair.

'Goodnight, Joe.'

'Thank you, Maggie.' He squeezed her hand.

She left him flat on the sofa, his head on a primrose cushion. She could hear his breathing gentle and calm as the early morning, and she turned out the light.

34

Let me in, Mum.

Bobby was cold. Let me in, he said in his head. He begged it in his head.

Bobby's knuckles were too sore to knock and the bell was broken. He kicked his mum's door with his foot, as gently as possible so Maggie didn't think it was that lot coming to sort things out. He kicked a couple of times before bending down to call through the letterbox. He swallowed and spat and waited for the door to open.

Maggie's face was whiter than normal, her skin blotchy from neck to brow. He could see she had been crying. Wrapped tightly in her dressing gown. And the flat was in darkness. She looked up at him, saying nothing. For a long silence she stood, her chest moving up and down, her face sagging, a sadness pulling it down. Then Maggie started to cry again, her sobs so big they made her body tremble, and her hands reached out for Bobby to hold her.

Bobby took her to him and walked them slowly into the hallway.

'Mum, what's happened?'

Maggie stood shaking her head.

'What's happened?'

'It's your dad.' She sank to the floor, the effort of standing up was too much for her.

It took all of Bobby's strength to reach low and pick his mum up. To hold her steady and sit her at the kitchen table. Bobby could hear the metal echoes of the tap dripping. He could feel his guts turn and he needed the toilet. He sat at the table with her, his arms and legs too big for the chair. He put his hood down and ran his hands through his hair. Smelling chip fat on his palms.

She murmured on, her fingers worrying the silk of her dressing gown.

'He came to see you. To find out what you'd been doing. He thought you needed talking to because he saw the girl, took her to hospital. He knew what you'd done.'

Now the tick-tock of the kitchen clock.

'So sweet, Bobby. I've never seen him so small and sweet since we met. He turned up before dawn, white as a ghost, his hands shaking. He had money for you as well as a talking-to. He came to see you, Bobby.'

Bobby started to sweat. The flat was too warm.

'I turned up the heating for him before I went to sleep. I thought he looked so cold.'

Bobby went stiff. His mind blank.

'He on the sofa?'

Maggie nodded.

Bobby rose from the chair. The aching becoming dull and constant and regular as his breathing. He pushed open the door.

Thin, scrawny and white. His broken nose beak-like and shot with blue veins, his forehead creased with lines. Eyes open, his stare lost and gone.

His dad was dead and there was nothing violent about it. Bobby had never seen him so peaceful.

'One minute he was saying goodnight and I went to bed. Then the next thing, I come down and he's lying there.'

Bobby took his dad's hand. It was still warm.

'How long you been up?'

'Ten minutes. But I don't know how long he's been gone.'

Maggie's crying had turned to a rush of quick panting. She tried to calm herself down and took gulps of air. She whispered and wiped her eyes, walking to the tray of spirits she kept by the cabinet.

'He was moaning about his headache.'

'You what?'

Maggie came closer with a small gin in her hand, braver now her son was home. Brave enough to look at her husband.

'Had a brick thrown at him, he said. Said it wasn't something the drink was fixing. He fell over twice. But he wasn't drunk. I've seen your dad drunk and it wasn't that. I've never had to help him up before.'

Bobby nodded and with his sore fingers brushed Joe's hair from his face as softly as he could.

'Do his eyes, love. I can't do it.'

Bobby put a hand over his dad's face again and put him in a peaceful sleep, his fingers trailing his scar.

Maggie sank the gin. She walked over to get another.

'Want one?'

Bobby shook his head. 'No, I need to lie down for a second. Need to make some calls.'

Bobby hung onto the banisters. He limped his way up each step to his room, taking his phone out from his pocket.

Maggie had made his bed for him. Fresh sheets. Fresh flower smells. He lay down. Death clung to his home, a fire eating up the air. No anger now. There was no room for it. Bobby put his head on the pillow and looked at his ceiling. His blood cold and his body numb. He felt a quiet inside him. So silent he could hear the breeze lift his Tyson poster from its corner.

He turned his face to the side and rang Chloe again. She didn't answer.

35

At first she forgot. In that kind moment when sleep was still dream. Then, when she opened her eyes and saw the dark part of morning in her window, she felt the headache and the dull pain come back. Pulling up the covers to her chin, Chloe closed her eyes. She did not want the day to start yet.

Her breathing was bunged up too. Bashed up. She lay as still as she could until her head got too noisy. Awake. Up and out of bed, she felt her nose with the tops of her fingers.

Polly had put her to bed. Tea on the side, the heating on and a telling-off. Chloe had begun to shiver when she got home last night.

'If I see him, I swear . . . '

Chloe didn't care what Polly thought. Polly was one of those women who thought she was better than getting hit by a man. Or cheated on. Or dumped. Polly slept with a different man every Friday and cried about it every Sunday.

Polly stood over Chloe's bed, staring at the phone.

'That him ringing now?'

She picked up and shouted down the line.

Chloe cried, 'Just leave it. I'm tired.'

There was no sign of her sister now. The house was quiet.

Chloe moved carefully, first to the bathroom. On the toilet she touched her face again. At the mirror she stared. The blue tiles and the grey light made it look worse, but Chloe was shocked. Her face had become feline, her eyes swollen and small, and her nose large and flat. She put her hair up in a ponytail. It was knotted and greasy and needed washing, soft tears in her eyes the whole time.

She went back to her room and made her bed. A white pillow and a tiny mark of blood. Chloe turned it over.

Picking up her phone she could see the messages and missed calls. She held it in her hand down the stairs. The television was on and, feeling small and weak, Chloe hoped her dad would be sat on his chair when she opened the door. But he wasn't. He'd taken a job and all that was left behind was an empty mug and scribbled betting slips on the carpet.

The house felt big with no one in it. Chloe went to the kitchen and took a bar of chocolate from her mum's cupboard. She sat, with her back to the wall and the long-dead peonies in front of her. Petals on the table. Last night still coughing itself up in jagged pieces. She put her phone next to the peonies and opened the block of Dairy Milk. On the fridge a picture of her mum Lynn, with her hair up and cheeks flushed and shiny from the sun, smiled at her. White shell beads around her neck. A poppy-red dress.

Chloe remembered Fiona coming over and crying at this table. The marks on her arm and neck from Devlin's dad. Standing with Lynn at the door as she poured out the last few drops of heartbreak before going back home to be a mum.

Lynn would sigh. Shake her head. And back to the kitchen to finish her tea and paper.

It was hard, Lynn had said to both her girls, for Fiona to leave when she had a little boy. It was hard to tear your body away. Chloe didn't want to be that woman.

She looked around the kitchen. It needed a good clean. Polly had left her bowls piled up. Her dad had left his old tea bags in the sink, waiting for someone else to throw them away.

More chocolate and Chloe picked up the phone. One by one, she listened to her voicemail messages. In the last one, Bobby was crying. Chloe had never heard a man cry before and it was frightening. Her dad always kept that to himself, and she found the rough croak of a man's sobs grotesque. But she had to keep listening. Through the softer moments of crying, Chloe heard Bobby moan that Joe had died.

Chloe deleted that message too. She was shocked, remembering his kindness to her last night, but it was not a surprise. At the hospital, Joe had swayed as they walked, his white face sweating, his mouth frothing at the corners when he calmed her down.

For a moment, Chloe felt sorry for Bobby, more than she did for herself, and it felt good to pity him. She knew exactly how he felt. They had that in common now.

Bobby was a mess. Chloe touched her nose again.

The kitchen was a mess.

The bruises. Bobby had drawn a line between them. They were linked by the same kind of markings. He'd tarnished her with his brush, with his black and blue. Chloe felt a new intimacy between them. A naked hurt that embarrassed her. Now he also knew how she felt.

With her phone cleared of messages, Chloe had some more chocolate and walked to the sink. There were bowls that had been there for days. She picked up each dry tea bag and threw them all in the bin before running the hot tap and covering every plate with washing-up liquid.

More and more she squeezed, until the green liquid covered everything in the sink, until it had all run out. With a sponge she began to wipe the plates down. The tap running hot, the water bubbling foam. She couldn't rinse it off, so she picked them all up and smashed them on the floor.

36

The day they buried Joe marked the end of spring. It was May and the sun was bright. Summer was close and the air was warm, the sky a new blue.

Joe had left the world light and thin, carrying nothing. Maggie and Bobby dressed him all in black, with his porkpie hat and his favourite watch on his waif wrist. Joe might have died a drunk, but in his death, the small world felt the gap he left behind. The community took a blow. A big character had bowed out, and everyone turned up to wish him a safe journey.

It was open to all, and many came. Although Maggie had not wanted any of that lot there, a few did show up. As he carried Joe down, Bobby looked straight ahead. You couldn't stop people coming to funerals, but he knew Theresa had shown and he didn't like the space she was taking up. As with everything she did, Theresa showed off. She sat too close to the front. Too close to his mum. A black fur coat even though it would soon be summer. She acted like Joe had meant something and held Daphne's shoulder for comfort. Mother and daughter united. Daphne would not stop crying and this annoyed Bobby. He could hear her sniffing louder than Maggie.

The funeral was held in the gloomy church his

mum and dad had been married in. An organ shut out the noises of traffic and sirens off the Stoke Newington Road. As the priest gave a sermon on a life that men from all corners of East London had turned up to respect, Bobby looked down at his shoes and held onto his mum's elbow, trying to keep her steady. She had worn cream because she wore cream when they married.

'We are still married, you know.'

She shook and cried as much as Bobby stood still and dry-eyed, only looking up to see the sunlight stream through the stained glass.

The stuff about him being a dad. A husband. A boxer. Where he was born and where he grew up. Bobby had written it out for the priest, sitting with Maggie and Mikey at the kitchen table, making sure they didn't leave anything out.

They did leave some stuff out. They left out every time he got drunk. They left out the times he hit Maggie, and they left out how he died. They left it out to make him a hero, because in his death, Joe had become one.

Boxing stories raised laughter and some tears. Trainers from Clapton, old boxers and a few old boys from the pub, including Frank and Freddy, were at the back. With flat caps and fat guts they kept their faces down, ashamed they could not cry properly.

Walking to the front, Bobby straightened his tie and kept his head down. He had put together a few words so the service had a heartbeat.

For the first time in his life, Bobby had a

beard. Partly to cover the scabs and cuts, and partly because he had tried to shave with a tender hand, too scared to go over the wounds and swellings. It was painful and he left it, clipping his beard as neatly as he could. It upset him that he turned up to his dad's funeral scruffy. Bobby was a clean-cut boy and he made sure his suit was sharp. It still hurt to blink in bright light and he looked to the floor, eyes still shot with blood.

'He shared his name with Joe Louis. He loved that.'

Ashamed of his beard, the fight and his face. He spoke to the floor and only looked up at the end of his piece.

They were two shadows at the back. Bobby felt them grow in size. Someone started clapping. Denny stood, as alive and big as Joe was small and dead. Bobby walked back to the pew and held his mum's hand tight.

'Don't think about them,' Maggie whispered.

Connor stood up too. A white shirt, a dark suit and a drunken grin. A cheap purple tie loose at his neck. He had a freshly shaved head.

'None of them matter.'

But Bobby boiled inside as his mum went white and frowned, and he was startled to see them both at the back. Maggie held her son's hand, her long nails leaving marks when she let go.

'They aren't here to say their goodbyes. They're here for trouble.'

Bobby had not said goodbye to Joe so did it now, walking up to the coffin for one last look.

They'd side-parted his hair and given him a blush. He would have looked asleep, but the cheeks were sunk and hollow, a face Bobby didn't want to remember him by. They'd chosen a nice picture for the front of the programme. A soft-focused, caramel-coloured shot of him grinning ear to ear at the races, his hair blown about in the wind. That scar pulling his eyelid down at the corner like his signature. Joe the boxer.

The organ played them out. Bobby held Maggie's hand as they walked down and the trainers carried Joe out. A couple of old boxers from Joe's day at Clapton took the back.

'You think people will come to the club for a drink and a sausage roll?' his mum asked him. 'Amazing Grace' led them away in moaning organ chords.

''Course. It's Joe.'

Outside in the afternoon, the rabble stood waiting for cars and rides to the cemetery, where Joe would be buried. The sun beat down on them. Warm but not too hot.

Bobby watched his mum be hugged and held by the women who lived above and below her in the flats. Hands lighting up cigarettes and blowing smoke around her head.

'The sun shines on the righteous, Maggie.'

Bobby saw his mum try to find a bit of space and move to the left of the circle.

'He must have done something right.'

Maggie tried to laugh. Her laughter turned to crying, and the women pulled her back to the middle of the circle.

Bobby turned for a moment to be alone and let the day sink in. He moved into the shade, by the side of the church and kept his eyes down. He was trying to remember the last things he'd said to his dad. It was in his hospital bed. Bobby was glad they'd had that. It wasn't enough, but they'd talked.

When he looked up again he saw them. The two of them, stood together. Bobby put his hands in his pockets, legs apart, his head tired. He wanted them to leave him alone.

Denny moved to him, one hand held out in peace. He was not steady on his feet.

'Bobby boy, do you know where there's a toilet round here?'

His face was red and big as ever. His eyes too. Tinted and whirling, so drunk he smelt of spirits and rust; so hot his sideburns were sweating. His St Christopher caught on a lapel. Connor turned his back on them both and unzipped his suit trousers. He left a wet piss print on the grey stone of the church wall.

'There it is.'

Denny walked over to join Connor. He unzipped his trousers clumsily with one hand and pissed too.

Bobby looked quickly to his right to see if his mum had seen. She hadn't, and the ladies were keeping her busy. He waited until Denny and Connor had finished using the church as a toilet. He waited to see them turn round again. They took their time and Bobby watched them stuff their cocks back into their pants, laughing and wheezing.

When they turned, both had leaked through their suit trousers.

'Lovely service. Your dad would be proud.'

Bobby felt a rage, but he did not see red. Instead, he turned his back on them and walked away, back into the sunshine. The cars were lining up and in traffic jams heading to the cemetery. Maggie was looking for him. He raised his hand to tell her to hold on but first he ran over to the crow-black shape of Theresa, feathers in her hair and a veil across her face, a cheap lace that caught her fake lashes.

She lifted the veil when she saw him.

'Bobby, I'm sorry.' She meant it. Joe had always been kind to her.

He nodded, not interested. 'Yeah, listen. Do me a favour?'

Her eyes wide as she waited to hear. Glad to be part of Bobby's life in any way.

'I want a straightener with Connor. Sort it for me.'

She nodded and put her hand on Bobby's waist, excited too that the story was still going, that she was still part of it. That she might be part of the happy ending with Bobby. Her nails were painted black. It sent shivers through him. Wide-eyed and in his glare, she nodded.

'I will. I'll do it. I promise.'

'Just tell Connor. Tomorrow, or the next day, or the one after that. When he's sobered up, I want this sorted and I want this done. Soon as possible. Tell him that.'

She moved closer. Fag-ash breathing in his ear, she pulled herself closer.

'I will, Bobby.' She nodded, serious. 'I am sorry about Joe.'

He took her hand away from his waist.

'Just do it.'

He left Theresa nodding and jogged to where his mum was, waiting in the car. The big lilies on the coffin were Maggie's choice. She wanted something with perfume and she wanted something pretty.

'It's all been ugly enough while he was alive,' Maggie had said.

Joe was buried and Bobby threw soil on top of his grave. He waited until everyone walked a few yards away. Out of his pocket he threw in a medal. The first one his dad had ever won at Clapton Bow when he was eleven. No trumpets, no flags. Just tumbled soil and sun on Joe's coffin. A buried treasure of this area. The world Joe left behind was cold. The one he joined, colder. Bobby thought of Joe's bones lost in the heavy earth.

He walked on after the crowds, to have drinks and sausage rolls at the Mildmay Club, to hear the sound system play some swing and some reggae that Bobby had asked for and knew his dad would've liked.

People danced but Bobby sat still. He undid the buttons of his jacket and tried to let his body ease up. His shoulders were tight. He watched his mum's handbag while she got drunk and danced with her friends. This would not end until he ended it. Without a straightener, they could go on fighting him forever.

His mum laughed as she was twirled around by Big Frank.

Joe was deep in the ground and Bobby needed to bury the rest with him.

'This was his favourite song.'

Bobby smiled at her and nodded. His right leg nervous and shaking.

'I know.'

37

Two days after Joe's funeral and the flat was full of flowers and cards.

The wedding picture of Maggie and Joe now stood in the middle of the kitchen table, next to the fruit bowl. There were others too. Photographs of Joe as a young boxer, pictures of him holding Bobby, and more framed cinnamon-tinted shots of Joe and Maggie when they were young and lovely.

He'd tried to call Chloe and left voicemails. Once, Polly answered and told him to fuck off. On the messages he repeated himself, said he didn't know where to begin, saying sorry was nothing. He told her about Joe. Then felt shit because he'd used his dad's death to make her feel pity. But he hadn't meant that at all. He just wanted to tell someone. He just needed to tell her.

After the funeral Bobby was stunned and spinning in a world that left him without a witness. Bobby was just a boy.

A boy who had not been hurt this much before. There were parts of him still shaded in a sickly sheen of yellow. His face, especially, had had a grey-tinged deadness about it but now he had started to get his colour back. Almost clear of the puffy swelling and the fat lip. The whites of his eyes less spotted with blood.

Bobby had his first shave and filled the sink up

with the black metal filings of his beard. He took baths, not showers, so hot they nearly peeled the skin. It hurt his ribs to stand in the shower. Bobby studied his body in the bath and in his bedroom mirror every morning, watching it come back. Each scab slipping away like an old leaf until the gold flesh underneath started to fill out slowly.

But it was Bobby's head that had taken the worst of it. Denny's punch had knocked him out and turned off a light Bobby couldn't switch back on. He knew his fight was not the same.

Bobby moved without being sure. He walked to the shops and looked behind him more than he used to. He stayed in after dark. There were the nightmares too. The fear at dawn when his eyes were wide open, his body cold in the blankets. The room white and blank. The seconds ticking as Chloe screamed and he fell back. They stopped him sleeping. Nothing to cling to that helped the terror fade. When she wasn't screaming, his dad was rotting. Layer after layer of skin peeling off Joe's thin and toxic body. Chloe and Joe. Both dead and gone. Just Bobby left on his own.

His dad was dead and that should have finished things. But it hadn't.

'Where you off to?'

Bobby didn't want to tell his mum. Since the death Maggie had drifted back and forth between sleep and wake, trying to finally understand that she was not married. Her dressing table was piled with sleepers and gin, and her sheets needed changing because she sweated so much in them.

'Going for a run.'

'There's no fight now. You can't train for anything. Why not give your body a rest?'

Bobby was dressed head to toe in black. His hood up, he could smile again without it hurting.

'I need to run.'

Maggie was cooking. In the two days since burying Joe she had planned meals for morning, afternoon and night, making sure the fridge was full and there was always something in the oven. She'd got home, tipsy after Joe's send-off at the club, and the next day put on her weekend trousers and walked straight to the butchers to get good cuts.

They all knew Joe well and sneaked a pound of liver in with her shopping. She didn't see it until she got home and cried at the kindness.

She was nervous. She didn't want Bobby to go far.

'You going to come back?'

Bobby nodded. ''Course.'

He went to the door.

'That girl, by the way. Have you heard from her yet?'

'Chloe?'

'Yeah, she ever talk to you again?'

The guilt and dirt of what he'd done rose up like bile.

'She won't take my calls.'

Maggie touched her hair and looked in the hallway mirror. She thought she had aged.

'Perhaps you need to try harder.'

Bobby was too ashamed. 'I don't know how.'

She stared at herself in the mirror for longer. Patting the dark roots of her hair. Then her shoulders dropped and Maggie began to cry.

Maggie had not missed Joe when he was alive. Now he was dead, she felt the pain of her broken marriage with more hurt than ever before. Still crying, Maggie began opening oven doors and sliding a tray of potatoes onto the top shelf to go with her dad's special chicken recipe. The smell of oranges and onions thick and cloudy in the radiator-warmth of the flat.

Bobby came to the doorway. 'Mum.'

He brought his mum close and gave her a hug. She turned her head to his chest and closed her eyes, enjoying the feeling, the moment's peace. She blinked in the tears and her tired face was drawn and lined in a way it hadn't been before. He squeezed her tightly before he let her go. Bobby could see that his mum was getting older, thinner, more bent. The blonde hair more grey at the roots.

She wiped her eyes and pulled away. Her voice colder. 'I just can't bear to see you make a mess of things as well, Bobby.'

Maggie went back to her hot kitchen, distracting herself with the roast. She cooked as if she were expecting guests. She wanted company. She wanted Joe's friends to come knocking like they used to and sit round her table as she watched them eat and talk over her with their mouths full.

Bobby stood at the kitchen doorway. 'Mum.'

Her face hot and flustered. Blotchy in heat

and tears. He put his hand out and she put a pan down to hold it. He kissed her on the top of her head and put his hand on her shoulder.

'It's not like I haven't tried. I will try.'

Maggie tried not to crumple. She went back to her pan, filling it with cold water for the vegetables.

Out into the open and the sun was bright. Bobby's nerves crept along jagged and wiry, catching him in the throat and making him thirsty. But his taste for drink and cigarettes had vanished. Bobby walked as tall as he could, trying to find the fire in his belly to fight. Summer and bloom in the air, the birds and cherry blossoms made this Friday afternoon sweet. In the playgrounds of the estate, white flowers grew by the concrete and buds brightened the trees. He looked at Theresa's flat. The curtains were drawn and the lights were off. Nobody home. She'd be waiting. She'd set the date, done her duty.

Down by the cafe, he could see the pub in the distance and thought about going in. But without Joe, Bobby couldn't face that bar or the landlord. Couldn't look at the jukebox or the pool table he'd seen his dad clean up on time after time.

Here, watch this. And Joe would pop the balls in neat and clean, as if they already knew where they were supposed to go.

Nearer to the canal, Bobby stopped and looked at the sky. He moved his fists about, clenching and spreading them, jabbing at the air. A few half-hearted jabs. He thought about his dad. Elbows in, head down, quick feet, and top off. Keep quick and get in first.

'Watch out for these boys, Bobby. They know how to win by losing.'

Down the steps, Bobby found himself by the tunnel of the canal where he'd first fucked Theresa. Where he'd slept and cried. Different now in sunlight. Different now he was calm.

They were grouped together, a lot of them. In blue and black tracksuits and vests, glistening gel in their hair. Gathering and laughing, more and more of them joining the pack, circling around Connor's red head. He was pacing up and down and laughing. His top already off. His hands in bandages. He was grinning, ducking and diving, and looked a lot more sober than when Bobby had last seen him. Denny was there too, with a few other faces that had taken potshots in the changing room. He didn't know their names and he didn't want to.

Denny saw him and laughed, excited to be there. To him, this was history.

'You didn't come with your friend? No Mikey?'

Bobby had told no one about this. He didn't look right and he didn't feel right. He didn't want anyone to see today.

'Just me. This isn't a show.' And with a nod to Connor's pack, 'You brought a lot of people.'

Denny smiled.

'We were very sorry to hear about your pa.'

Bobby said nothing and remembered their pissing up against the church wall. There were things you didn't do over a dead man's body.

303

An old boy who took on all the straighteners walked towards Bobby. The referee, Tony. Bobby had made sure he was there to see this. Overweight and in his sixties, he was there to keep the fight going as best it could.

'No biting. No cutting. Keep it about the fists boys, and keep this clean.'

Connor smiled. Bobby could see the scar, still pink, and the smile too big, on his meaty face. They were both nervous. Each met the other's stare.

'Come on then, Bobby, you called this one.'

Bobby unzipped his top. No one on his side, he had no one to hand it to. He left it on the bank and stood sadly, trying to make the most of himself. He had not trained, run or fought since the day at York Hall and he was soft. His whole body was struggling as he stepped forward. He had taken off the bandages. He followed his long black shadow and walked towards the group, leaving space for Connor to come forward too.

Connor looked him up and down, he was ready. The others crowded just behind him, acting as an army in a battle scene. A couple skipped out to the side and started doing a strange dance as if Connor had already won, their skinny legs jumping about, imps in blue tracksuits.

Even so, Bobby moved forward again, but he stood with his arms at his side, his back straight, his eyes fixed on Connor. In all the years they'd known each other, Bobby had never waited. Connor knew the way Bobby fought. He expected Bobby to come at him hard and fast, like he always did. They were the same kind of fighter.

'Come on, let's kick this off.'

The crowd began to shout, clustering around. Their faces full of menace and pain.

Bobby stood still. He looked at them all. He looked at Connor.

Connor spat at the floor near Bobby's trainers. He began to shift side to side with his hands in big stone fists and the thought of pain scared Bobby. He did not feel strong anymore. He felt tired. He heard Denny cough in the background and crack a joke with another man. The canal lay flat and deep. It kept Bobby's secrets. The sky was clear and the sun warm on their bodies.

Bobby knew he would lose. That he had to lose this one.

Connor's fists were up. Bobby put his fists up too.

But the sun made him squint and, keeping his head down, Bobby felt the ache in the back of his neck. He could see Denny. The Big Man in a cream shirt, laughing from his big belly. The man who'd thrown a brick at his dad. The man who got him beaten black and blue.

The sun burned. Connor's face was already reddening. Bobby felt so tired.

He would lose this fight.

Connor spat again.

'You here to fight or daydream, Bobby?'

The others were getting restless too. They wanted to see these two go at it again, and they wanted to join in. One of them picked up a stone and threw it at Bobby's leg. He felt it sting his shin. The pack began to howl and laugh.

'If you don't move, Bobby, we'll stone you to death like your dad.'

'Make this fair, boys.' The referee edged in closer.

Bobby's fists were up, just below his jaw. His elbows in. His eyes straight at Connor.

And he waited. And he waited some more.

'Just go and wake him up for fuck's sake!' Denny boomed and it began.

Connor threw a right hand and caught Bobby in the face. It suddenly went very quiet. The crowd held their breath.

Bobby stumbled back straight away, his fingers feeling the blood pouring fresh. He'd been caught at the corner of his eye and would need stitches quickly, before the scar tissue gave him a lopsided stare. They called them pirate scars. With his heart pumping so hard and frightened, the blood came out fast. He couldn't see and squinted.

Bobby didn't come to win this fight; instead of trying to hit back, he just let it happen.

The ones that just want to fight aren't worth fighting, his granddad had always said.

He still had his hand over his mouth when the second one came. His other arm held out, trying to keep Connor back. He heard the crack. Something made a noise. Maybe his jaw. As Connor went to hit him again, Bobby raised his arms and pulled Connor to him. He held his body to his in a tight hold, as tight as he could, and put his head on his shoulder, bleeding onto Connor's bare skin. He whispered through the pain.

'No more.'

Connor pushed him off so hard Bobby nearly fell. The blood made him feel dirty.

The push kept Bobby moving backwards.

'Hit him proper, Connor. Hit him again and finish it,' a voice crowed from the crowd.

Bobby's legs felt too tired to stand. Weak, he sat on the ground with his legs up. He rested his arms on his knees. His head between them.

Connor turned.

'Get up. You can get up.'

Bobby looked up and shook his head. He would not get up.

Connor turned to the rest of them. 'He won't fight.'

He said it again, louder. 'He won't fucking fight.'

Tony ran over to Bobby and looked into his face.

'You done, boy?'

Bobby nodded.

Denny marched over, smoothing down the sides of his hair.

'What do you mean he's done?'

Bobby twisted slowly and reached out for his top. He gently put his arms in the sleeves. His lips had melted with the punch. He tried to talk.

'I'm done. No more.' His tongue didn't fit his mouth.

Denny bent down and talked at his ear.

'Get up and don't shame yourself.'

Bobby tried to stand. A body of jelly. He stood.

'I can't. I can't fight you no more. I'm done.'

Denny pushed Connor forward. This wasn't how it got sorted. This wasn't a fight, Denny wanted a proper brawl. He smoked his cigarette quickly, hungry for more hurt.

'Make the bastard fight you. Make him fucking fight you.'

Tony jittered between them. He wanted to stop things before this pack started baying for blood.

Connor stumbled into Bobby. He looked at the blood running down Bobby's face, into his mouth. Bobby stood and waited for it.

'You won, Connor.'

Connor didn't want to knock Bobby out. They'd already done that. He wanted him to fight. He wanted him to be a better fighter than this. He dug into his ribs with body shots, trying to get him to defend himself. But Bobby took it. He kept taking it. Connor put another right in Bobby's guts to bring him down. Bobby fell on his knees and stayed there on the bank of the canal watching the little ripples in the water as the wind moved plastic bags along.

Bobby's weakness made the men angry, but instead of the thudding herd coming at him, they hung back. Twitchy and skittish by the sides, they didn't know why Bobby had given up. They didn't know how to fight him with his fists down. Men had wanted to pick fights with Bobby his whole life and a few of this crowd had thrown punches at him in the changing room. Now, when he didn't want to fight back, they put their fists down too. Bobby had gone from muscle to meat. They waited to see how their man Connor would finish this for them.

'Enough. I told you he's out. This is not how it's done,' Tony moved in and shouted, and the pack started to jeer. One after the other, one man copying another man's battle cry until they were all the same noise.

Bobby could see sky from a flickering part of his left eye and the sun still hot and gold. The shouts and the heat around him roared.

'Get out the fucking way.'

Bobby could see the blade. Could taste the blood from the blade. A neat, sweet cut from eye to mouth, neater than the jagged mark Bobby had left on Connor. And he could hear them all. The crowd of cowards, all screeching and swearing, thrilled to see him cut up. To see Bobby being sliced up under the sun.

When it was done, Connor stumbled back dizzy, dropped the blade into the canal and looked at his hands.

There was a cheer, like a packed pub clearing after a football match. Men jostling each other and yapping, holding onto each other in dizzy hysteria.

Denny laughed with the rest of the men.

'Connor, you got away with yourself there.'

Connor was shaking. He went to Bobby and held his hand out.

'Get up.'

But Bobby wouldn't take it.

'Bobby, come on now, I give you my hand.'

Bobby turned away. Connor began to mutter.

'It's just a cut.' Connor spat on the ground. He whispered over and over to himself, 'It's just a cut, it's just a cut.' Denny put his big arm round him and led him away. Some followers lingered over Bobby's body, too excited to go just yet. They leered at him, kicked dirt in his face, into the wet and open wound. As Denny yelled for them, they began to leave, one by one, heading towards the pub. The skinny men who'd danced around Connor began recording Bobby's body on their phones, getting close-ups of the cut.

'Stop fucking filming him!' Theresa screamed as she ran from the top of the steps where she'd watched it all. She pushed between her dad and Connor, whose head was still hung so low he hardly felt her pass. Only Denny kept his eye on her as he let her say her goodbye. She let out a small gasp when she saw what was left of Bobby.

'Fucking leave him now. Go on, fuck off.' She grabbed one of the phones from the ones still filming and threw it into the canal.

They sloped off and called her a slag, safely out of Denny's earshot. But she didn't care.

She knelt down and checked Bobby's eyes were open. His grimace through the blood looked like a smile. His teeth blossom-pink with spit and blood, his left cheek carved out.

He had lost. Finally.

She touched his shoulder, her eyes running over the punches and cuts.

'Bobby, your face.'

'Theresa, get on!' Denny barked down to her. She looked up at them and Bobby saw the tears.

'Why didn't you fight back, Bobby? Why? Why did you let them do this?'

He smiled. Tired, he let her pull him up and

smiled punch-drunk. Bobby took his shaking, blood-tipped fingers and touched her hair.

She held him upright, trying not to hurt him. She moved his hand to her shoulder.

'You would have won if you'd given him a fight.'

Denny shouted for her again.

She turned Bobby towards a bench a few yards away.

'Bobby, sit down for a second, please, and let me see how bad this is. You need a hospital.'

She went to lead him with her but he moved back and shook his head again. Sighing, she took a tissue from her bag and softly dabbed the blood from his nose, chin and lips. It was sore, but he let her.

'It looks nasty.'

As she cleaned him, Bobby took a hand away and rested it on her waist, pulling her body in as he held himself up. She wobbled in her heels. They stood there together in a strange hug, waiting to get steady.

'God, it looks so bad, Bobby.'

Worse than when she'd seen him at his door. He had fight in him then. Now, he had given up. There was fear in the way she spoke.

Theresa put some tissues in his hand and Bobby held three on his face. The blood soaked through them all.

Theresa put the rest of the packet in her handbag and breathed hard before any tears could fall. But they did. Bobby could see them and he could hear them in her voice.

Theresa knew. She had always known how it would end up.

They were concrete and chaos and rage and skin bashing skin and fire and hurt. Now silent and at rest, they would always have each other splintered somewhere in each other's body. He felt a shudder of pain up his back. Even now he could feel her. They came from the same brick and dust.

'Theresa!'

'Please.' She spoke in a whisper.

'Go, Theresa,' he whispered back. It was sore to say. He was bleeding fast now, from somewhere in his insides too, and had started to go into shock. His pulse fast and his skin pale. He mumbled.

'You have to leave me alone.'

He was going to fall.

She looked to the ground, a frown that held back the sobs she wanted to let go.

'Please don't make me go with them.'

She tried one last time to make him keep her.

Bobby held his cheek and dribbled pink blood. He said nothing.

Theresa took a step back. She put on her sunglasses, took a cigarette from her bag and lit it. She went back up to meet her dad. The long skinny legs in golden leather heels looked as if they'd snap every time she put a foot down. At the top she pulled at her dress. Denny pulled her by the ponytail. A few steps in, she turned and pretended to look in her bag for a lighter as she searched one more time for Bobby's cold white face.

It was over.

38

For the best part of the summer, Bobby hid.

Then slowly he came back. Out from under his rock, into the light. He looked down from his balcony and could feel the shade on the estate and the boys leaning on their bikes. He looked across at the hanging baskets filled with red flowers in the flats opposite and raised a hand to a neighbour.

He'd been told to take time off, not just for him, but for the club and the boys too. Derek said that while things were cooling between him and Connor, it was safer for Clapton if Bobby stayed away.

'You also need to have a long rest, son. You and your body have taken some knocks.'

Bobby was happy with the ban, but he was hurt too. That was his home. For weeks he slept, ate and pissed a painful, smoky urine until he was ready to show his face again. A different face. Maggie wouldn't look at him at first. He got his pirate's scar. He'd had stitches, but the skin tissue had twisted the corner of the lid down and his eye drooped. The scar from the knife wound was violent and ugly on his face. And with it, Bobby went from handsome to thug. Every day he stared in the mirror to try and understand it, every day he moved his fingers up and down it to try and get used to it. It did not suit him the way some scars suited tough men.

Bobby's face and the scar did not go together.

Everything healed slowly. The pain of Joe and Chloe had knotted together like a tumour, getting into his blood and his bones. Some things you live with night and day. They made him so tired; he lay in his bed and waited for sleep. Staring at walls and ceilings and television before dropping off some time before dawn. He couldn't even call Chloe anymore. She'd changed her number before the funeral. He missed the sound of her voice on the voicemail.

He wasn't the only one. One day, while Maggie was unpacking Joe's suitcases that had been put away for years, she burst into tears. Maggie still cried most days.

And she cried harder as she took out Joe's old boxing gloves. The laces thin, the leather grey with dust.

There were his posters. His dad had loved the Sugar Rays, Robinson and Leonard, and there were pictures, posters and records of fights. Bobby stuck them on his bare walls, next to Tyson. They made him get closer to the best of Joe.

When the bruises were not as bad, Bobby started to walk outside. He walked with care, as if he'd had both legs broken and was scared they'd be taken away again. He had to go out to sign on. They made him feel like shit and he didn't know if they'd treat him better if he was still good looking. They told him to apply for security night shifts that took an hour and a half to get to each way. Bobby nodded, taking the printout and putting it in his pocket. When he rang the number, the jobs had gone.

But the chaos of his world had grown calmer. Theresa had moved out and Denny's name was talked about in the distance. Daphne got her flat back and Bobby made sure to always smile when he saw her. He felt sorry for her. Even Maggie smiled at her if they met. The way she shook, they both knew she wouldn't be too far behind Joe. Daphne had told Maggie that Theresa was now engaged to Connor and was going to move onto the site. A few weeks later, he saw them together. Connor limped alongside her with a stick and she waited for him to catch up before she went into a shop and came out carrying the bags. Bobby stared at them, his body tense. He'd heard stories about what had happened to Connor's legs to make him lame that way, but didn't know the truth. He didn't want to listen to the rumours.

Bobby was a different boy. His was a different body. He looked left and right a lot more before he went straight. He made his own bed, helped with dinner and made his mum tea. They sat together, watching television in a quiet they both needed.

He finished the cup of tea in his hand and went back inside.

Derek had rung.

'I was thinking it would be nice to have you around again. You don't have to train for a fight, just show up and have a walk about. We miss having you here.'

Bobby missed his club. He missed Derek. He

needed a job. He said he'd come down that morning.

Out of the block and into the ring he'd grown up in. Sun hitting stone and the boys still on their bikes.

He wore a green sweatshirt that was too heavy, jeans and a new pair of trainers. White and box-fresh, the only thing Bobby could afford to buy with the money Joe left. After the cost of the funeral there was just enough for a pair of trainers and a new sofa for Maggie. She didn't want to keep the one he died on; she said it was a horrible memory to keep in the house.

Too long away from the boxing ring and Bobby forgot how to walk back into it. At the doors of the gym, Bobby felt like a stranger. He felt shy. His face made him feel a new loneliness. No longer tough, not a boxer. That wasn't a bruise, it wasn't from bone and muscle, it was deeper and darker. It was a scar from a blade. It would always be seen first and it would shame him.

He ran a hand through his hair and pushed the doors. The same smells and noises. The same heat and echoes in an old building with rusty pipes and new paint. He wondered if anyone would want him there. He'd messed up the lot. There was nothing that wasn't broken. He had not been the fighter he was supposed to be.

He could hear the bags being hit. Hear the stern, gravel-throated barks of the old trainers. The hum of high-pitched children talking at each other. The speakers blaring their favourite music.

He saw Derek first. You couldn't miss him. He stalked around the room, the biggest of all, his large body taking its time.

Seeing Bobby, his face broke into a grin and he began to laugh.

'There he is.'

He took Bobby into his arms and held him there in a warm, bear hug. The hug was strong and Bobby let it wrap him up. For once, safe. Bobby closed his eyes. He fought hard not to cry. Not now and not here. He held Derek and felt his body soften for the first time since spring.

Derek pulled away and looked. He blamed himself for what had happened, and kept a strong hold on Bobby. He didn't want to let him go. He'd known him since he was seven.

'You got fat. Like me.'

He laughed and pinched Bobby's waist. Bobby smiled. He had gone soft. He was carrying a little belt of fat round his middle that was never there before. He was carrying a summer of shame and loss.

'But you got your looks back, at least. Still handsome.'

Bobby touched it.

'Derek, you don't have to.'

Derek stopped and looked serious. The scar was ugly and he didn't like seeing it on the best face in his club. Bobby was their poster boy.

'You should have told me what you were doing. I would have gone with you.'

'It's not your world, not your problem.'

'I'd have kept you from getting a knife down

your face. That how you draw a line beneath things?'

Bobby felt the words sting, the way the scar on his face did. Still tender and boiling beneath his skin.

'It will fade, Bobby. You're still handsome.'

Derek put a hand on the back of Bobby's neck. He knew Bobby looked like just another thug.

'It all fades.'

It was hot in the gym and the slapping sound of bags being punched began to calm Bobby's nerves. For the first time in a long time, Bobby felt okay. The tiles and the chalky paint on the walls, the curling posters and the songs blasting from the sound system brought him to life.

'How you been, Derek, how's it been here?'

Derek led him down the side of the gym.

'It's been quiet, Bobby.'

A couple of trainers saw them and shouted over. They looked at the scar they'd heard about and said nothing. It had happened and there was nothing that could be undone. Business as usual, they would let Bobby live his life.

'Get back in that ring, boy.'

Bobby laughed. 'Soon as I lose this belly.'

They laughed back.

Business as usual. Everyone moved on. No jokes about the scar. It was too ugly, too real. Scars like that weren't in the rulebook.

Derek brought it up.

'Connor hasn't been here since. He's lame, you didn't hear? He got a cut nerve from a bad fight. He won't be coming back.'

Derek sniffed, loyal to Bobby.

'He knows he's not welcome.'

Bobby nodded and said nothing. He didn't want to think about Connor. He listened to the punching on pads, the orders being given in the ring, watched the trainers walking around belly-first. He was home.

'You going to fight again then or what?'

Bobby didn't know. 'Maybe.'

Bobby had liked the white lights showing him off in the ring. With his face a mess, he didn't feel as brave. He knew he would become a different kind of fighter because of it, and that scared him.

Derek understood.

'When you're ready, you'll be back.'

Bobby looked at his hands. He put them into fists and stayed quiet. He took the sweatshirt off and hung it on the back of a chair. Underneath he wore his club's black T-shirt. The red letters big across his chest.

Derek put a hand on his shoulder.

'Get back to work first and see how you feel.'

Bobby looked around. He knew most of the faces. Some had grown taller in the last few months: focused, tougher and harder. They kept their eyes down. Some were shy of Bobby. A lot were frightened of his scar. He was a hero, and heroes weren't meant to get hurt. They'd heard what had happened. A couple of kids ran over to him and said they wanted Bobby to watch them spar.

'Come on then. Show me what you got.'

He smiled down at their faces, freckled noses

peeking out under head guards.

And then he saw another boy he knew. All by himself.

'Hang on a sec.'

The boys watched Bobby walk to the corner of the gym where a tall, skinny boy was jabbing and hissing at the air.

'Do you want to try that on a bag?'

The boy turned round. He grinned when he saw Bobby.

Devlin had changed a lot in a few months, the way young boys do. A growth spurt in his legs and the long, blond hair cut short, shaved close at the neck. He had a small bruise. A tiny little shadow under his left eye.

'Got your first shiner then?'

Devlin wore it proudly.

'One of the best fighters here gave me it.'

'Who?'

Devlin pointed at a black-haired boy doing ropes. He was well built, his shoulders wider than the other boys'.

'What you fighting a heavyweight for?' Bobby smiled and his eyes were kind. He put his hand on Devlin's chin and looked at the bruise closer.

'It suits you.'

Devlin curled his lips into a small snarl and smiled. He wore a club vest and Puma shorts, his arms still thin, his legs skinny and wiry.

'Will you hold the bag still for me?'

Bobby did. He wondered.

Devlin began to punch. Bobby let him go for a bit before he started talking.

'You come alone?'

The blur of punches packing the air full of heat, bringing the blood back to his body.

'Chloe takes me still.'

Bobby looked at the clock. Her name hung in the air.

He spoke above the thumps and chatter.

'She picking you up?'

Devlin nodded and hit harder.

Bobby breathed it all out.

'Don't tear into it. Keep those jabs soft.'

He looked at the clock again.

Acknowledgments

I am grateful to Chatto & Windus for publishing this book. Thank you to Parisa Ebrahimi for acquiring *Boxer Handsome* and getting it into shape. I couldn't have wished for a better editor. You understood everything about this book from the beginning.

Thank you to my agent, Simon Trewin, for believing in the book so early on and taking such good care of it.

Huge thanks to my teacher of many years, Andrew Motion, for guiding my writing with such support and kindness.

Jo Shapcott, Susanna Jones, Glenn Patterson, Robert Hampson and Mona Simpson: I've been lucky to have your supervision, thank you. Thanks also to my teachers at Pimlico School.

A very special thank you to Crown & Manor Club, especially Maureen Walker and Frank Shillingford. It has been wonderful getting to know the club that changed my granddad's life. Thanks also to Ryan Pickard and the trainers at Repton Boxing Club for all the help and information.

Ramona Stout, Declan Ryan and Iphgenia Baal — I am grateful for your thoughts on the book as it went along.

Mary and Charlie, and the Adams family across the pond, thanks for the other room to write in. Most importantly, thank you to my dear mum and dad, who read me lots of stories and always listened to mine. You make everything possible. To my brilliant sister, Alice, for shining a light on everything. And to T, for supporting always.

And thank you, Grace Paley. Your books have mattered so much.

We do hope that you have enjoyed reading
this large print book.

Did you know that all of our titles
are available for purchase?

We publish a wide range of high quality
large print books including:
Romances, Mysteries, Classics
General Fiction
Non Fiction and Westerns

Special interest titles available in
large print are:
The Little Oxford Dictionary
Music Book
Song Book
Hymn Book
Service Book

Also available from us courtesy of Oxford
University Press:
Young Readers' Dictionary
(large print edition)
Young Readers' Thesaurus
(large print edition)

For further information or a free
brochure, please contact us at:
Ulverscroft Large Print Books Ltd.,
The Green, Bradgate Road, Anstey,
Leicester, LE7 7FU, England.
Tel: (00 44) 0116 236 4325
Fax: (00 44) 0116 234 0205

THE WOMAN WHO DIVED INTO THE HEART OF THE WORLD

Sabina Berman

Following the tragedy of her sister's death, Isabelle moves from her home in California to her birthplace in Mexico to take over the running of the family business. There, in her sister's dilapidated house, she is woken in the night by a wild child — a thing with no name, who could just be the niece she never knew she had. So she sets herself the task of turning it into a human being, named Karen. To start, she must teach Karen her first word: Me. And then begins the greatest journey of all, as Karen learns how to become 'Me'. It will take Isabelle to the bottom of the ocean, to the farthest reaches of the planet . . . and into the heart of the world.

THE FOLLOWING GIRLS

Louise Levene

When Amanda Baker was fourteen, she found a letter written by her runaway mother to her unborn child: 'Dear Jeremy (or Amanda)', it began. Now, in the 1970s, she is in the hands of disaffected parents seeking to find a new school for their disappointing daughter. The happiest days of your life? Not for Baker, sixteen and sick of it as she moves miserably between lessons packed with palm fibre and the use of the dative. Baker's only solace is her fifth-form gang, The Four Mandies, and a low-calorie diet of king-sized cigarettes — until she teams up with Julia Smith, games captain and consummate game-player. So begins a passionate friendship that will threaten Baker's future, menace her sanity, and risk the betrayal of everything and everyone she holds dear . . .

HOMECOMING

Susie Steineer

Up on the North Yorkshire moors, the Hartle family is about to have a life-changing year. Ann and Joe, with more than thirty years of marriage between them, are torn between giving up and pressing on with their struggling farm. Max, their elder son, is set to inherit the farm, and his wife Primrose has news to share, but is he ready for these new responsibilities? The younger son, Bartholomew, escaped to the south as soon as he could, building a new life for himself with his girlfriend Ruby. But when tragedy strikes, he is forced to return home — and come to terms with his past, in order to create a future.

THE TILTED WORLD

Tom Franklin with Beth Ann Fennelly

April, 1927: After months of rain, the Mississippi River has reached dangerous levels and the little town of Hobnob is under threat. Residents fear the levee will either explode under the pressure of the water or be blown by saboteurs from New Orleans, who wish to save their own city. But when an orphaned baby is found the lives of Ingersoll, a blues-playing prohibition agent, and Dixie Clay, a bootlegger who is guarding a terrible secret, collide. Little can they imagine how events are about to change them — and the great South — forever. For in the dead of night, after thick, illusory fog, the levee will break . . .